A Taste of Forbidden Fruit

The First Taste

A Taste of Forbidden Fruit

The First Taste

by NIKITA C. HUGHES I

Chief Editor
Gail Miles

Senior Publisher
Steven Lawrence Hill Sr

ASA Publishing Corporation

ASA Publishing Corporation
An Accredited Publishing House with the BBB
www.asapublishingcorporation.com

The Landmark Building
23 E. Front St., Suite 103, Monroe, Michigan 48161

Book Title: A Taste of Forbidden Fruit *The First Taste*
Date Published: 09.15.2018 / Edition 1 *Trade Paperback*
Book ID: ASAPCID2380714
ISBN: 978-1-946746-32-0
Library of Congress Cataloging-in-Publication Data

This book was published in the United States of America.
Great State of Michigan

Table of Contents

A Taste of Forbidden Fruit

The First Taste

by NIKITA C. HUGHES I

This novel is dedicated to the loving
memory of my Grandparents:
"John William Sr. and Fannie Mae Baker"

Thank you GOD, for without your love, guidance and inspiration, this could never have been possible.

Even though our family heritage on 162 South East 3rd Court, the land I so fondly remember,
has long since vanished,
I pray that the memory of our home will live on,
both through this book and in all our hearts.

John and Fannie Mae, may you now, and always, rest peacefully.

In Remembrance of you,

Nikita Cetewago Hughes 1st

To my Mother, Doris Shirley Baker-Simmons:

Where would I be without my Mother? Your love and compassion has guided me through life. I could feel your warm embrace, protecting me, every step of the way.

The Lord says to honor thy Mother and thy Father so that your days may be long upon the Earth. Therefore, I humbly honor she who has given birth to me and sacrificed so much, so that I may have all that I needed to progress in this life.

Through thick and thin, you nurtured me. Through good and bad, you were there to guide me.

Yes, GOD created me, but he left me in your loving care to shape and mold me into the man I am today.

To My Father, Rufus James Hughes, Sr.
Father, though you were not there in the beginning, I have felt your love.
Spiritually, you have helped to keep me on the path of righteousness.
Today and Every day, I Honor You, my Mother and my Father.

Lisa Ann Hughes

My life was once empty, deprived of the love I so longed for. Just as I had all but given up, the Lord spoke unto me and you were mine. What I thought I would never know, became a twinkle in my eye and a song in my heart. You are my life, my heart, my love . . .
You Are My Wife!
Love Always!

Nikita 2nd, LeQuicha, Lisha, Andre and William

To my children, I simply say this: Always keep GOD first in your life, for nothing or no one matters more than 'From HE whom all blessing flow.'

It took many years for me to understand this simple phrase, but I am thankful for the opportunity to finally get the message.
Always keep love in your heart, not just for those you choose, but for all of GOD's creations. For without love, all shall perish.

Daddy Loves You!

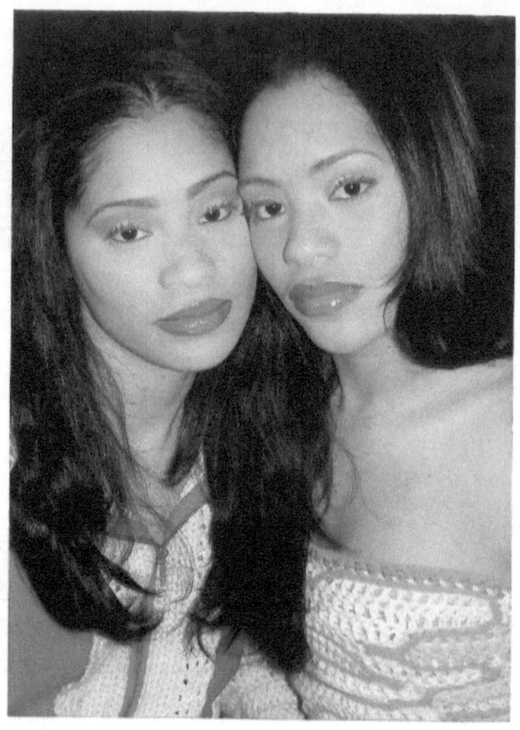

"A Special Message for My Daughters"

God is Good! For He saw fit to bless me with not one, but two incredible women! I am so very proud of you both for your strength, and faith, in Our Lord and Savior, Jesus Christ.

Even though Satan has tried to discourage you, and sway your faith, you continue to persevere, you continue to fight the good fight! Though he has tried to affect your lives in different ways, you continue to rise above his negativity.

Because of your unwavering faith, I too, have been touched. You help me to find the courage I need to keep on living. I want to thank you for taking the time to assist me with my works, and always showing your support in my efforts.

I love you both so very much! For you are, and always will be, "Daddy's Babies!" May God continue to bless you both, with the courage and strength to keep on fighting, until the day He blesses you with all you deserve!

"And the Holy Spirit Said Unto Thee . . ."

"Within the pages that follow, you will find gross conduct, explicit language, murder, mayhem and lude sexual behavior. In other words, these pages are filled with the sins of the world in which you live today."

"However, I say unto you: Do not shy away or be grossed out or misled by what you read, for these are the times in which you live. Instead, I say to you simply this . . . Close thine eyes and open thine heart so that you may see. Let the Holy Spirit guide you. Do not be offended or insulted, for these are but mere words used by Satan to corrupt your thoughts."

"The flesh has put perverted meaning to the words used within, but if you let Me guide you, you will find that there is nothing to be disgusted by or afraid of! You must walk by Faith! If you are truly a child of God, this should be but a simple task. "Trust in Me sayeth the Lord and all things are possible! And yea though I walk through the valley of the shadow of death, I shall fear no evil, for Thine art with me!"

"Pray unto Me before you begin, and I will bless you with sight beyond sight. You, as My Child, will be able to read between the lines and accept the message meant only for those whom I deem worthy. Pray for those who still have not accepted Me so that they may also come to understand. My children must always pass on what he or she has learned, even to thine enemies, if they are truly willing to accept and become enlightened by the word of God. Even if you can enlighten but one, you have done well."

"I have charged My Servant to write the story only as he could. Within the contents you will find the truth, cleverly hidden amongst the twisted lies and perverted languages used by the devil.

Mr. Hughes has been blessed with the gift of using Satan's

very own tricks against him to deliver My Message. And what message is that you ask? Simply this: The time is near, and I will return like a thief in the night! You are living in the last days, so you had better get your house in order! **You have been warned!"**

Tasting the Forbidden Fruit

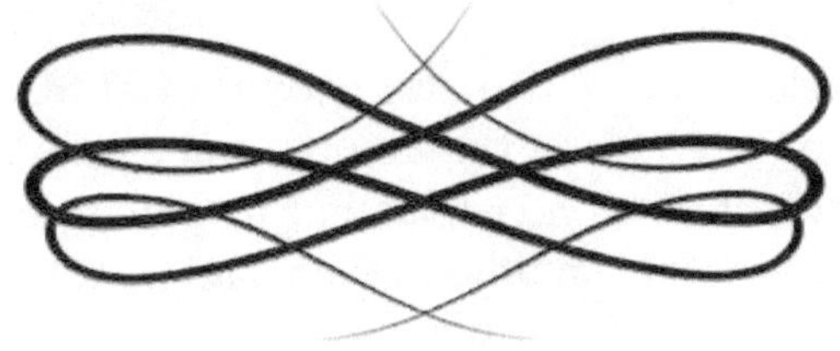

How it All Began.

She lay motionless across the bed, her legs still spread apart and hanging off, with her feet upon the floor. Her body was bruised, bleeding and racked with pain. She slowly managed to push herself off the bed and onto the floor. Down on her knees, she struggled to gather a few items scattered about, placing them in a small plastic bag. She struggles to get to her feet, her body trembling from the brutal attack. "How could you do this to me?!" she groaned in the direction of a woman standing near the corner of the room. As the injured young woman struggled to stand, she made her way towards the nervous woman. Anticipating what was about to happen, the woman shouted, "Don't you understand? Don't you get it? I did this for us! This is all for you!" As she nervously backed away, she raised the piece of paper she was clutching in her hand.

The pain turned into rage as the battered woman took one mighty swing! Both women collapsed to the floor, one from the pain of a brutal rape, the other from a right hook to the jaw. "Give me that, you bitch!" she exclaimed, snatching the paper from the now semi-conscious woman's hand. After reading the contents, she ripped it up, and then tossed it in her face. "**That** is what this was all about?" sobbed the woman as she slid along the wall in an attempt to get back on her feet. "Don't you ever come near me again!" She cried as she wrapped a sweater around her waist, while trying desperately to make her way out of the room. She made her way down the stairs as quietly as she could, so as not to alert her attackers. Eventually, she slipped out the front door unnoticed.

She welcomed the late afternoon shower from Mother Nature as she staggered along the empty rural road. With no food, drink, or money, she had no choice but to walk as best she could, while stopping to rest from time to time. She wanted nothing more than to get as far away from that place as possible. Dizzy from the heat, loss of blood and pain of the attack, she didn't even hear the truck as it slowly approached her from behind. "Excuse me Miss, but could you use a ride?" inquired an elderly man in an even older, beat up and rusted out pick-up truck, as he pulled up alongside of her.

Frightened and a bit hesitant, she finally whispered, "Thank you," as she struggled to get in. The young woman had slowly walked for hours until her body had become numb.

"This is no place for a lovely young lady, such as you, to be walking alone in the dark," he concluded.

"The dark?" she mumbled, as she paused to look about the sky.

Disorientated, she had not realized the sun was setting. Huh, the sun was setting, but all she could remember was the comforting afternoon rain, the shower that briefly seemed to wash away the memory and stink of her attackers earlier in the day.

After about a mile or so, the old man attempted to break the silence.

"What's a pretty young thing like yourself doing out here all alone anyway?" However, there was no response. She just sat there with a blank look on her tired face. "You hungry? I have a couple of turkey sandwiches, and some coffee, left over in my lunch box there," offered the old man. Once again, he was met by the cold, blank stare of the injured woman.

"Stop here!" she said abruptly, while glaring out of the window. "Thank you for the ride. I'll just get out here."

"Ah, the old Brande Plantation. What a beautiful place it is now," he said.

"Yes, it is," she thought, as she attempted to climb out of the truck.

She didn't understand why, but that is exactly why she wanted to stop. She needed a place like this to clear her mind. It seemed so peaceful. She was drawn to its serene energy. It gave her a warm feeling of security. In her heart, she knew this was where she needed to be at that particular moment. She groaned in agonizing pain, clutching her abdominal area as she hung onto the door of the truck.

"Miss, are you alright?" asked the old man concernedly. Again, not a word, but she did manage a half smile as she closed the door.

She fought back the pain, unaware that her sweater had just fallen from her waist as she walked gingerly towards the main entrance. "The old man was right. This place **is** beautiful," she thought as she watched him drive away. Carefully, she crept into the yard. She walked along what seemed to be an endless row of tropical flowers. They grew along the inside of the six-foot wall of shrubs, which appeared to encase the entire main house. "Wow! Now **that's** incredible!" she whispered aloud. Something she found amazing had caught her eye as she slowly approached a secluded area in the center of the huge front lawn.

"A ten-foot-wide, heart-shaped arrangement of red rose bushes!" She stood there staring in amazement! Inside of the shrine, on either side, was a dark green granite bench, trimmed in gold. At the top center was a matching granite tablet with gold lettering, resting upon a golden stand. The rose bushes were grown, and skillfully maintained, to give a raised appearance. The base bushes were about two feet tall. The size was gradually increased to around five feet at the top of the heart. This was a remarkable sight indeed. “I was right about this place. I can feel the love just emanating from it. I think it's safe for me to rest here.”

There was about a two-foot opening at the base, which served as an entry point. Granite stones were embedded into the ground from the entrance to the tablet. “I wonder what's inscribed on it?” she thought as she entered the shrine. “We Walk by Faith . . .” I wonder what **that** means?” she pondered. The scent was breathtaking. If not for the tropical climate, the smell of all those roses would have really been overbearing. Suddenly, she felt weak and became dizzy. The pain had returned to her stomach, as she began to feel a warm wetness between her thighs. “What happened to my sweater?” she thought as she felt between her legs. “Oh my GOD!” she cried out, looking at the blood on her hands. Sobbing, she fell to her knees thinking, “Maybe someone in the house will help me.” However, she never got the chance to find out, because she couldn't get back to her feet. She slumped over, onto the ground, then fell into unconsciousness.

“It's Karma! . . . You reap what you sew! . . . You got what you deserved! . . . What goes around, comes around!” Now we have all heard phrases like these all throughout our lives. We place them in the “that’s what happens to people who do bad things” category. But what of those who have done nothing to deserve what they have encountered, the few who strive to do what is right? Hum-m-m . . .

“The Devil watches over all. He punishes those who do good things and rewards those who are bad. Now GOD is all seeing. The devil will always cause pain and suffering to weaken the righteous, but GOD will uphold those who fight to remain loyal. He will reward

you, not just financially, but with an overall wealth beyond your comprehension. Remember, you must remain strong and hold on to your faith. And you must also have patience for GOD is watching. He has a multitude of blessings for each and every one of his followers, when ***He*** *feels you're ready to receive them. In the meantime, remember . . . you must strive to "fight the good fight!"*

Chapter 1
Introductions: Meet the Family

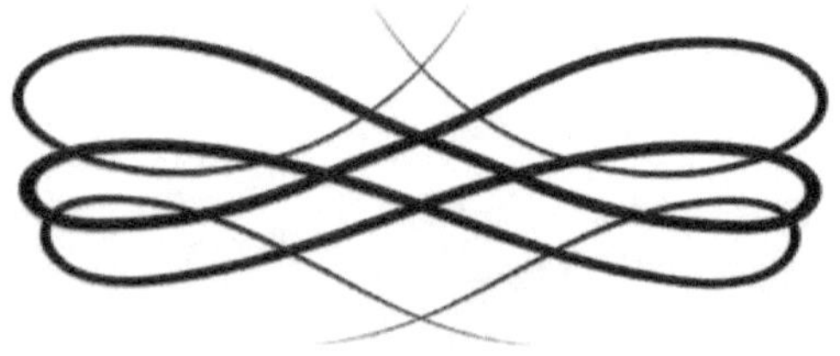

My name is Nathan Brande. I am the proud owner of "Passion Fruits," a family owned and operated mango plantation in South Florida. My brother James, and my sister Monica, joined the struggling business five years later. Monica, who was fresh out of law school, took charge of the company's finances. To save the potentially doomed business, she was able to obtain several government grants and loans. She did this by declaring the estate "historical" due to its original use during slavery in the late 1800s. We went from nearly being foreclosed to being very well off in just over five years. James, who had recently retired from football, was placed in charge of the plantation's security, while I handled sales and distribution of the fruit.

Fifteen years ago, I persuaded my mother, Sheryl and her four sisters (Loraine, Betty, Jean and Jeri) into keeping their late parent's rundown estate so that I could attempt to rebuild our family's heritage. It was a difficult task in its own right and being black made it nearly an impossible feat. To make matters even more complicated, the state was offering a hefty sum to the sisters for the "prime location" real estate. I was eventually able to convince them that we could earn a lot more by keeping the land for farming. Several miles away, lived Richard Sullivan, a long-time farmer. He was the main supplier of lemons, limes, oranges and mangoes for the state. Let's just say he was less than pleased with the competition.

In order to repay my mother and aunts for their trust, they received a new home and the first twenty acres of trees. Whatever was grown and sold there, was divided equally among them. Try as we may, Mom flat out refused to move into the main house with us. She was happy just being back on the land she once called home. There were five other homes established on the land up to date, each with ten acres of trees and run by relatives. An eighth home was under construction while the rest of the land was being cleared. The process was slow, as it takes several years for the trees to mature and begin bearing fruit.

Chapter 2
Rebuilding the Past

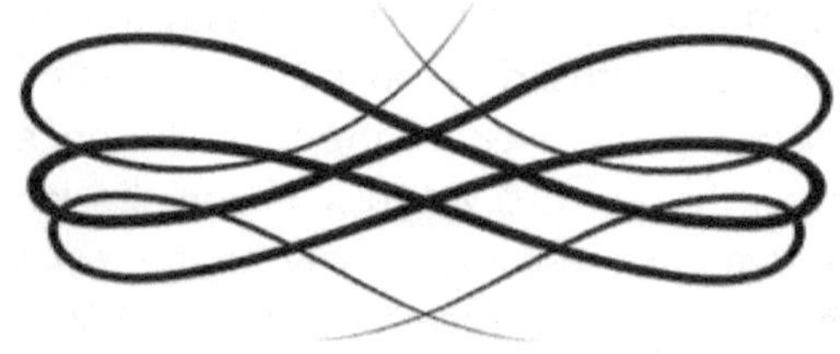

"When I was young, about twelve or thirteen, I made a promise to my grandmother. I swore to, one day, return to the home of my childhood upbringing and help repair the dilapidated, but once proud southern home. But unfortunately, that day never came . . ."

While I was In the Air Force, she passed away just prior to her eighty-third birthday. I was devastated by the loss. I turned to drugs and alcohol for a short time, which led to my early dismissal. *"As children we sometimes blindly make promises, unaware of the pain of unfulfillment. As young adults, our decisions are often spontaneous and wrong at best. In other words, poor judgment can make an ass of us all."*

Determined to make good on my word, I mortgaged the property, rebuilt the old mansion and began clearing the acres and acres of fields, which were once rich with cotton during the days of slavery. *My grandfather had been given this old slave plantation by his father. According to my mother, John Baker, a wealthy plantation owner and member of the KKK in Georgia, gave the land to his only Jewish son, then disinherited him for going against his families wishes by marrying my biracial grandmother. No longer the heir to the multimillion dollar family fortune, my grandfather was left to fend for himself and had only this piece of land to live off. Without the financial backing from his father, the fields died out.*

Not quite the heritage I was proud of, I was determined to turn this clouded past into something the family could look up to. I began farming the fields by using the seeds from the oldest and only remaining tree on the plantation, my late grandmother's favorite mango tree. This tree gave birth to a new beginning and a new legacy for the Brande family.

During her time here, my grandmother had grown several varieties of mango trees, one of which I had spent many hours in, practically every morning, eating mangoes and daydreaming. (Chuckle) I can remember many a day when my grandmother playfully prodded me down from her favorite tree with a long bamboo pole she used to retrieve the ripened fruit. She would say to me, "Boy, get down from there! You're gonna get sick from eating all of those mangoes!"

Remembering that still brings a smile to my face. I miss her so much! Sadly, my grandfather died when I was only seven and the memories of him are vague at best. However, I do remember the rides on the back of his Ford Pick-up truck to the store though. He would buy my brother and me a treat every time he went, so we made it a point to go whenever we could. I can recall him as a quiet, kind and hardworking man.

Never once did I get sick from eating the mangoes though. How I really loved that fruit! When there were no longer any ripe ones left, I would start eating the green ones. I could never get enough! I guess it's ironic that my sister, who also enjoyed them, developed a severe allergic reaction to mangoes and was restricted to just one a day. Well, that left more for me I guess!" ("Sorry, that was so wrong of me to say.")

However, my brother was our complete opposite. He had no real desire for the fruit at all. All he cared about was football, partying, and women. He had a talent for the game but was too much like our father. He had an extremely bad temper, loved to party and loved to sleep around. After walk-on tryouts, he made the team and played a couple seasons in Pittsburgh. He was later forced to retire under, let's just call it, a cloud of controversy. Still, he is my brother, so I welcomed him aboard with open arms.

Eleven years later, with a lot of prayer, and help from my siblings, we had established a thriving business. We had restored our family's pride and my grandparent's great name. I could feel them smiling down upon me from heaven. I am thankful to GOD and proud of our accomplishments. I felt so blessed! But regrettably, I was so busy rebuilding my heritage, I was neglecting to rebuild my own life. I needed someone to share it all with, that special someone who could help to ensure that the Brande Legacy lived on. My last relationship had ended over five years ago. Even though I was now happily surrounded by my family, I still felt somewhat alone. *"Irony can really be a bitch sometimes!"*

Chapter 3
To Catch a Fallen Angel

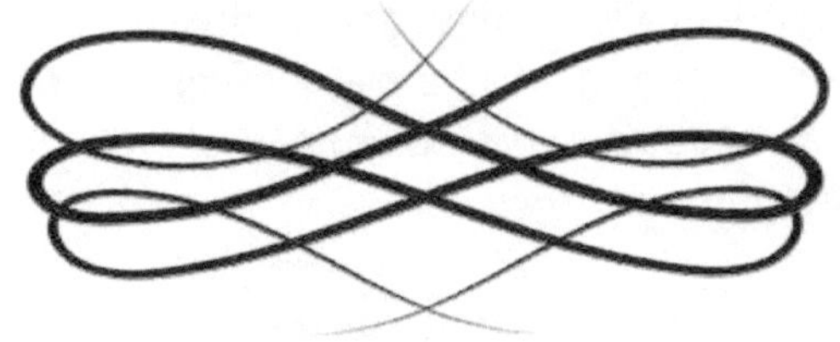

It was sunrise, approximately 05:53, when I awakened to start my day. I sat up on the edge of the huge oval bed and groggily looked around the room before heading into the bathroom. After a long and refreshing morning pee, I stepped out onto the balcony which overlooked the far side of the front lawn. My so called "room" actually consisted of the entire fourth floor of the five-story mansion, which resembled a small hotel. It had several enclosed balconies on each floor. My sister lived on the third floor and my brother, the second. The fifth floor was vacant and rarely used for anything other than occasional storage. I sometimes went up there to just sit and think. The fifth floor also had access to an atrium, which was ideal for star gazing, something I had enjoyed since my childhood.

This particular balcony in my room happened to be my favorite because the sun rose onto this side of the house, breathing life into the memorial rose garden. My mother, Sheryl, and her sisters, designed it. We all had a part in planting it as a dedication to the memory of our family members who have long since passed on.

My mother and aunts took great pride in, and insisted on, maintaining the shrine. They refused to let anyone, outside of the immediate family, onto what they felt was "sacred ground."

My naked body embraced the warmth of the sun. *For some reason, I was unable to sleep in clothing. I felt trapped beneath the sheets. It was as if I was bound and couldn't move.* It felt kind of naughty standing outside naked, but without any neighbors for miles, I could relax and bask in the southern warmth. This was my most favorite time of the day. I smiled as I looked across the horizon, giving thanks to GOD for blessing me with yet another day, and all that I survey. Without His strength and guidance, none of this would have been possible. *I may not be overly religious, (if there even* ***is*** *such a thing), but I do recognize, and I give thanks to . . . "He, from whom all blessing flow." Amen.*

I took one last stretch, to relax the tense muscles of my 6'4" 250 lb. frame, before returning inside for a shower. Just as I turned to walk inside, something caught my attention. "What the hell?" I slipped on my silk pajama shorts and matching robe, then quickly headed for the stairs. The elevator was on the first floor and just took too long reaching me. The steps were much faster. I moved so rapidly through the first floor and out of the front door, I didn't even notice that my brother and sister were already up and having coffee out on the front porch. "Morning Nate," rang out both voices, as I passed swiftly by. I was so preoccupied with where I was going, I didn't hear them, nor did I respond to their early morning greeting. "I wonder where **he's** rushing off to?" questioned James, who was busy checking his cell phone messages, as he glanced over at Monica.

As I sprinted across the lawn towards the family memorial, I began to wonder if what I had seen was just my imagination. But as I approached the area however, I realized that I wasn't seeing things. As I got closer, I could see a foot, and then a leg, in the grassy area between the marble path and the marble seating. My pace slowed as I was not sure of what I was going to find. My mind began to race. Is it possible that someone dumped a body in the yard? I then thought of James, who had often pleaded with me to fence in the main house. I refused because I felt it would take away from the natural warmth you get as you approached the main entrance. Was he right? I was not mentally prepared for what I was about to find.

I was now standing over a woman, lying almost face-down and motionless, on her right side. Her right arm was stretched out with her head resting on the bicep, while the left one was at her side with her forearm resting across her hip. Her right leg was straight while the left one was slightly bent over onto the grass. At first glance, I thought she was dead, but then I could see she that was breathing ever so slightly. The obvious question was, who is this? and why is she in my family's shrine?

The stranger moved slightly, moaning as though she was in pain. Slowly, she slid her left knee upward along the grass. Now overcoming my initial shock, I realized I was staring down at what appeared to be a young Hispanic female, asleep in our shrine. As she moved her leg, I noticed some dry blood on her inner thigh. Her white linen dress resembled a type of uniform, something a housekeeper or a hospital employee might wear. It was stained in the lower back area with a small amount of blood and soil. That was when I noticed where the blood on her dress and thighs had come from. It was still hemorrhaging slightly, from her vagina. What happened to this woman, and how did she end up here?"

"Are you alright?" I finally whispered softly, in an attempt not to startle her. "Hello?" She moaned, then slowly and slightly opened her eyes. They were green! She had Emerald Green eyes! How awesome is that?! Suddenly her eyes opened widely, as she became frightened by my sudden appearance. She began shouting, "Get away from me and leave me alone!" as she utilized her left leg to push away, while attempting to cover up the best she could.

"I swear, I won't hurt you," I said, in an attempt to gain her trust. I then slowly inched forward kneeling down beside her, while covering her upper body with my robe. I gently slid my arms beneath and around her shoulders, lifting her trembling, chilled body against my chest. I looked deeply into her eyes, hoping to give her reassurance. "Don't worry, you're safe here with me," I whispered. Her eye lids began to flutter, then her eyes rolled back into her head, as she once again slipped into unconsciousness.

"Nate, are you okay? I heard someone shouting!" called Monica, as she and James came running across the lawn. "Call 911! There's someone badly injured out here!" James, who had forgotten and left his phone on the table, turned and ran back toward the house to make the call.

As my sister approached, she asked, "Who's that?"

"I don't know." I replied. "I saw her from the balcony. She began yelling at me, telling me to get away and to leave her alone. Then she passed out."

"You really shouldn't be touching her Nate. Please put her down!" complained Monica, observing the woman's tattered, bruised and bloody condition.

I gently laid her back down onto the lawn. As I slowly stood up, I observed blood on the lower front area of the dress, with a stained piece of cloth hanging out from under it. It appeared that her panties had been torn. Damn, she had been raped!

"Who could have done such a vile thing to this poor young woman? No one deserves to be violated in such a violent and brutal manner!"

My brother, James, just stood there gawking.

"Why don't you head out front and point the ambulance and Sheriff in the right direction."

It seemed like an eternity had passed while waiting for help to arrive.

I just couldn't keep my eyes off this strange woman who had suddenly come into my life. With my robe draped across her, it appeared as though she was sleeping peacefully. "Maybe you should go inside and put something on before the Sheriff and Paramedics get here!" I was so deeply concerned for her well-being, Monica had to repeat herself in order to break me out of my trance. "You would be hard pressed to explain why you were standing over her, in just your boxers, with her being in that condition."

Chapter 4
I Hate Cops

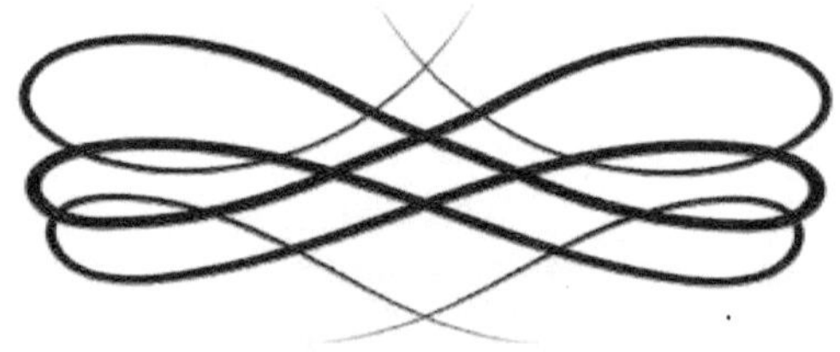

Man, she really looks to be in bad shape," said one paramedic to the other, as he tossed the robe aside. They quickly began attaching the heart monitor leads while taking her vitals.

"Does anyone know who she is or how she got here?" questioned the Sheriff.

"We have no idea, but maybe together, we can get some answers," replied Monica.

"She's in pretty bad shape. Looks like a rape case, Sheriff," replied one of the paramedics, as he motioned for the Sheriff to come over. "Make sure they use the kit!" he reminded.

"What ever happened to her didn't happen here," claimed the paramedic. "This area is way too clean and everything looks undisturbed."

"Just handle **your** job and leave the investigating to me!" complained the Sheriff.

"Yeah alright, see ya at the hospital."

"Damn, this place is really amazing!"

"Yeah, I wonder how they could afford to live in a place like this?" discussed the paramedics. "They're probably some of the servants!" they joked.

"Rednecks . . . Will we ever overcome the racism?" pondered Monica, who was just close enough to overhear the snide remark.

I came across the lawn just in time to see her being placed into the ambulance. "How is she, will she be alright?" I stammered.

"Mr. Brande, I presume. I don't suppose you can shed any light on what happened out here?"

"I have no idea Sheriff."

"Of course you don't." replied Sheriff Clinton Melbourne, sarcastically. "I was out on the balcony there when I saw her lying on the lawn. I rushed down to check on her, then covered her with my robe."

"This robe here?"

"Yes, that's it."

"Good, I'll be keeping **this** as evidence."

"What the hell do you mean by that Sheriff?" exclaimed James.

"It's fine. I'm sure the good Sheriff wasn't implying anything." However, it was clear that the Sheriff was already drawing his own conclusions as to what had transpired. To ease the tension, I invited Sheriff Melbourne up to the house. The paramedics had stabilized and secured the unknown female and were now preparing to leave.

"I'll bet you throw one hell of a party in here," suggested the Sheriff, as he glanced around upon entering the house. The three of us looked at one another but did not respond to the Sheriff's accusation.

"This way Sheriff," directed James, while fighting to maintain his composure. This guy was a real asshole! As we walked into the conference room, the Sheriff replied, "I didn't ask for a tour. I can get a search warrant for that."

"Before you jump to any more conclusions, I thought we might possibly attempt to find some answers **together**," Nate answered annoyingly. "Our **surveillance room** is this way."

"James handles all of the camera work."

"Would you like some coffee Sheriff?" asked Monica.

"Na, no thanks," he replied.

"I imagine a couple shots of Moon Shine would be more to his liking!" whispered James, causing Monica to snicker.

"You okay with this Nate, or should I call our attorney?" inquired Monica.

"Maybe later, just to fill him in."

"Then I'll go and get myself together before starting breakfast." The Sheriff tilted his head to the side with a puzzled look on his face.

"No Sheriff, we aren't into slavery here," replied Monica. "We don't have any servants. This is a family owned and operated business. We **all** do our part."

"And we are proud of it," added James.

A few minutes later, we had some clues as to how the injured woman ended up on our property. The camera coverage throughout the grounds was very efficient. Video footage revealed the unknown woman getting out of a truck, while staggering as she walked along the west end of the property. She appeared to be clutching her abdominal area as she approached the main entrance. Motion detectors picked her up as she entered the yard, enabling the cameras to track her movements.

"As you can see, Sheriff, there was no wild party here, and she appears to be already injured."

"Maybe you should be looking for the driver of that truck," James stated, as he pointed out the stains on her dress.

"This is quite a system you folks have here, better'n the one we have back at the station."

"Yeah, it has to be. You never can tell when some redneck

son-of-a-bitch might try to pin a crime on you," replied James. The Sheriff just ignored the comment as he watched things unfold on the monitor.

"Say now, what's that you're doing there?" questioned the Sheriff, watching as I knelt down, still not quite convinced of my innocence. "She was trying to say something, but I didn't really understand her at first."

"Looks more to me like she's trying to get away from you," he stated, as the video continued.

"She came to for a couple of seconds and was frightened. Then she passed out again, that's all."

"Here's your copy," interrupted James, as he removed the disk from the dubbing unit.

"Hold on now, you just put the rest of that footage on there, right up until the time the ambulance left! I want it all, ya hear?!"

"Someone might be interested in why you picked her up," added the Sheriff.

"Don't worry, it's all there," replied James.

"I just wanted to let her know that she was safe. It was just a reflex."

"A reflex huh? You didn't happen to come across anything, did you?" asked the Sheriff.

"You saw what she was wearing. There was no room for any type of identification in that dress. And as you can see on the video, she wasn't carrying anything when she got out of the truck. I didn't remove anything from your alleged 'crime scene,' Sheriff."

"Dark Passions calling for Mr. Nathan Brande. Please pick up on line two," announced a voice over the automated answering system. "If you don't require anything else Sheriff, we do actually have a business to run," stated James.

"No, I don't need anything else, not right at this moment anyway. But I'm sure you've all heard the phrase, 'Don't leave town'," he concluded, as he walked out the door.

"Just look at what he's doing to the lawn!" exclaimed Monica. We watched angrily as the Sheriff "fish-tailed" across the yard, towards the driveway.

"Son of a Bitch!" shouted James.

"I'll give the lawn service a call," sighed Monica. Damn, I hate cops!

Chapter 5
Back to Business

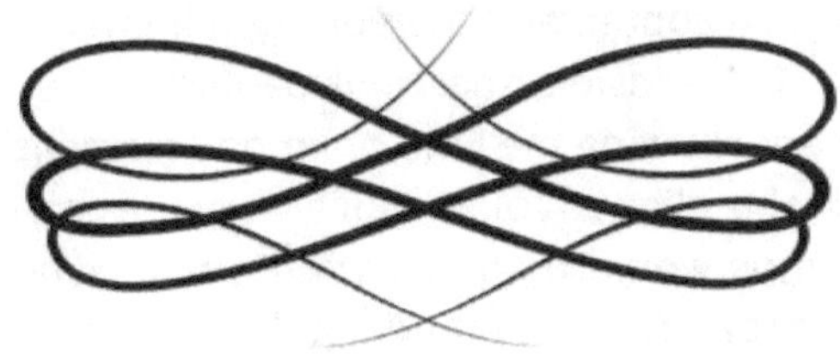

"Good morning, Mr. B."

"Oh, hello Tony. I'm sorry about the delay, but there was an incident at the house this morning. Will six cases be enough?

Ten? Okay, I'll be there in a couple of hours." Dark Passions was my baby and Tony Clemons was my right-hand man. It was a huge success and the only source of income needed outside of the family business.

I acquired the once popular strip club from an owner who had run his business into the ground. On the verge of losing everything, he sold the club to me for a modest six-hundred-fifty-thousand dollars. Given its location, minutes away from all the action, just outside of South Beach, the place was a gold mind waiting to be discovered. Three months and a small fortune later, Dark Passions was ready for the grand opening, but not to the public. No, I wanted something different; something no other club could ever pull off.

I opened the first and only "Celebrities Only"

establishment. The outskirts of Miami were the perfect location for a club like this. No advertising, no parking lot and no valet. Just a large three story, black glass encased, building, with platinum lettering. It was protected and surrounded by an eight foot, wrought iron, upper-bladed security fence. This place was just far enough away from the action to go unnoticed, but close enough to be where the action was, within minutes. For the most part, the place looked deserted. Perfect.

Any client, and his or her entourage, would be escorted here via limo or helicopter, and then brought immediately inside the security gates. Once inside, the front panels of the establishment would slide open, allowing the limo or limos access inside. Once the panels closed, the clients could move about freely without ever being seen. Limos would then exit via the rear panel doors. Tony would then escort all persons immediately to their reserved suite.

Inside were six huge bi-level suites. Each was equipped with private rooms, DJ booths, dance floors, pools, Jacuzzis, bars and dining rooms. The decor for each suite was exquisite. I sank nearly my entire fortune into starting this business. Monica and I spent another two months hiring the proper staff. Each suite would require chefs, servers and butlers, all of whom would be required to clean and prep at the end of each event. This was nonnegotiable. The salary was one-thousand dollars apiece per shift, with chefs making fifteen-hundred. Any tips were shared equally, collected by the Maitre 'D at the end of the night. Not bad for one night's work, huh?

The employee contract was brief and to the point. "Any persons hired by this establishment are sworn to secrecy." "The privacy of each client, and their guests, is of the utmost priority." "Any employee divulging information pertaining to any client, and/or the goings-on in this establishment will be terminated and sued for the sum of one-hundred-thousand dollars for violating the "Client

Confidentiality Act." For the kind of money the employees were being paid, everyone signed off without question. You get to meet lots of celebrities, cater to their clientele and have plenty of fun. Just keep your mouth shut and make a lot of money! Now that is one heck of a job description!

Each half-million-dollar suite could be rented for six to ten hours. My asking price was fifty- to seventy-thousand dollars. It may seem a bit extreme but when you consider the fact that some of the world's most famous celebrities could do what he or she wanted without observation or consequence, the price was very reasonable. For insurance purposes, however, all six suites had to be equipped with surveillance, which was installed by James. To ensure client privacy, anyone securing a suite would be allowed to enter the surveillance room to observe the disposal of their suite's footage at the end of their visit, as long as there was no damage to the property. If there was an incident, restitution had to be made prior to the disposal of the footage.

We've been in business two-and-a-half years now without incident, and the suites have been booked for the next four years. Not bad, not bad at all. As an added bonus, twenty percent of the proceeds went to the church building and maintenance fund. Some might ask, just where is the bonus in **that**? Well, any time you can take dirty money and use it for the good of the Lord, I'd call it a blessing! If that's not a bonus, then what is?!

Chapter 6
My Hospital Visit

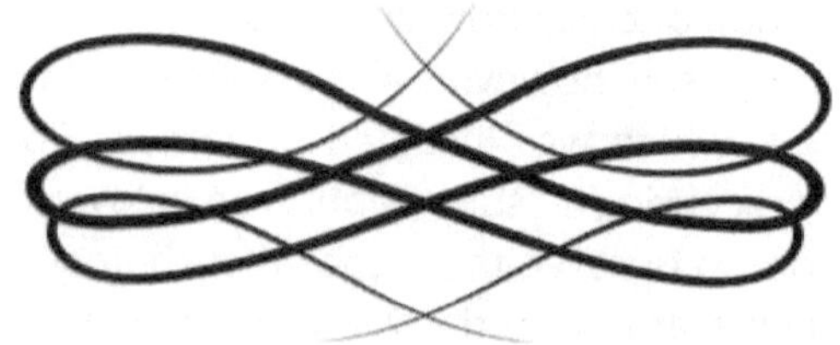

This is just what I needed: a relaxing drive. Now that I've finished my delivery, I'm ahead of schedule. A trip to the beach sounded nice. I hadn't taken the "Vet" out in quite a while. She really felt nice and handled well. Besides, I had not heard from the Sheriff since the mystery woman appeared on my lawn two days ago. "I wonder how she's doing? I just can't get her off of my mind! Maybe a little music might help to ease the tension . . ." The system was bumping! *"We're stretchin out and hangin loose in a rubber band; we're stretchin out spreadin funk all across the land!"* ***Bootsy Collins*** *is still my favorite artist, even after all these years. And his latest dedication was nothing short of sheer brilliance!*

A phone call interrupted the music. "Hello, this is Sheriff Melbourne." (Damn, speak of the devil himself!)

"Well-well, what can I do for you Sheriff?"

"You can come down to the hospital **if** you don't mind," he replied. (Did I mention that I hate cops?!) So much for my trip to South Beach, I had better phone home.

"Hello?"

"Monica, the Sheriff requested I come to the hospital. Will you handle the meeting today?"

"No problem, big brother. You watch yourself."

"Love ya Sis. Talk to you in a few." Now back to the music . . . *"I'd rather be with you-ou, yeah!" "Girl I'd rather be with you-ou-ou-ou!" I just love me some **Bootsy**!*

"How is she, Sheriff?"

"She's stable, but she's still in and out of consciousness."

"Okay, so what do you want with me?"

"Are you sure you've never seen her before? It seems strange that she would just stroll into your place after never having been there."

"Sheriff, stop wasting my time! Maybe this will help your case. The gardeners found this sweater in the street, outside of the entrance. It has blood on it. I think it may be hers. I really suggest that you do your job and stop harassing me! Oh, and by the way, I have a lawn care bill for you as well."

"Yeah right! Look don't go getting all snippy with me! I just thought you might have some additional information, that's all."

"I don't have time for this."

"She's awake, Sheriff," interrupted a sexy looking nurse, while sticking her head out of the patient's room.

"I don't suppose you would care to come in, being how busy you are and all?"

"After you, Sheriff." Damn, I hate cops! sighed Nathan.

"Hello Miss, my name is Sheriff Clinton Melbourne. Do you feel up to answering a few questions?"

"Si, um-m yes, I guess so," she whispered softly.

"What's your name Miss?"

"Melina, Melina Delgado."

"Well, Ms. Delgado, can you tell me what happened to you?" She paused for several seconds.

"Some men, some men hurt me!" she stammered as she

began to cry. "What do you mean, they "hurt" you?" inquired the Sheriff.

"They raped me, and they hurt me. They hurt me bad!"

"Why don't you step a little closer to the bed so she can get a good look at you."

"Sure, anything you say, Sheriff." "What a dick!" mumbled Nate. "Is this your sweater?"

"Yes, I believe so. I think I lost it when I got of the truck."

"What truck?" inquired the Sheriff.

"An old man stopped and offered me a ride while I was walking down the road."

"Do you know **this** man?" inquired the Sheriff. "Was he one of the men who attacked you?"

"No, it was two white men," replied Melina. "I do not know him, but I think he tried to help me."

"Now Sheriff, can I respectfully tell you to go f--k yourself?!" whispered Nate, into the sheriff's ear. "By the way, you can keep the robe. Consider it a gift." With that, Nate exited the room. "Excuse me nurse, may I speak with her doctor?"

"Are you a relative of the patient?"

"No, I found her unconscious on my property. I just want to discuss the billing arrangements."

"I'll see if the doctor is available, but we can't discuss the patient's condition with you."

"I'm aware of that nurse. Thank you very much."

"Hello doctor, my name is Nathan Brande."

"Hello Mr. Brande, what can I do for you?"

"Look doc, I know you can't discuss her condition with me. I just wanted to discuss her medical expenses. I want you to give her the very best treatment available, do you understand? Here's my card. You can charge all of her expenses to me." Once the doctor looked at the card, he realized who I was.

"Oh, **that** Nathan Brande."

"Yes, that's me, and you can call me Nate. **Now** can you give me a little insight as to what is going on here?"

"Take a walk with me to my office, would you?"

"Sure, doc, no problem. Lead the way."

"Look, if the Sheriff finds out . . ."

"Don't worry. The patient already cleared me as a suspect. You were saying . . ."

"Ms. Delgado has massive internal hemorrhaging as a result of repeated and forced trauma to her vagina and uterus," explained the doctor.

"Exactly what does that mean?"

"It appears Ms. Delgado was a virgin before she was attacked. Her assailants brutally raped her. Being a virgin, the vagina and the surrounding organs are constricted. Never having been penetrated, the vagina is small and tight. The sudden and repeatedly forced thrusts to that area basically ripped her apart inside. There **is** one other thing that I am not quite sure of though. She is also blistering and infected inside. I believe she had a severe allergic reaction to something."

"It **is** possible her assailants used condoms."

"Obviously, that's good news, but the bad news is she could have been allergic to the latex. We will have to wait on the rape kit and blood test results to confirm my diagnosis though." Damn, hearing that nearly made me sick to my stomach! "It was a miracle she survived the night," he concluded.

"What are you trying to say doc?"

"What I mean is, as a result of all these things, she has been severely damaged inside. For her safety, and in her best interest, she needs a hysterectomy?"

"You mean she will never have the opportunity to bear children?!"

"Mr. Brande, I mean she may never even be able to have enjoyable sex. She has been physically and emotionally torn apart. The pain may never go away!"

"Look doc, you do whatever it takes to keep her whole, do

you hear me?! Fix her up as good as new! She deserves to have something to look forward to in her life after all those bastards have taken from her!"

"Mr. Brande, what you are asking is nearly impossible. Not that it's any of my business, but why should **you** care? You don't even know the young lady?"

"Listen doc, I believe she ended up on my property for a reason. Call it fate if you will. I intend to do all I can to help her. She can't be any more than nineteen or twenty. Her life is just beginning, and she deserves better than this! Having money means nothing if you can't help someone. So, you keep her together, keep me posted and bill me. One other thing, when she's ready to leave, and has no one else to turn to, or she needs a place to stay, call me. I mean it doc. You keep her here until she's a hundred percent, understood?"

"Yes sir, Mr. Brande. I'll do the best I can."

"If you can't, then get someone who can. I'll be back to see her tomorrow. I'm just going to look in on her before I leave, okay?"
"That's fine."

"Thanks doc. Look, if there is anything I can ever do for you, don't hesitate to ask."

"Well, since you're offering, how about a couple of Dolphins Playoff Tickets," chuckled the doctor.

"I'll tell you what, if you keep Ms. Delgado here, and in one piece, you can join me in the Sky Box throughout the playoffs, Super Bowl and all of next season!"

"Holy Shit! Are you kidding me!" laughed the Doctor.

"You hold up your end, and I'll hold up mine." After a healthy hand shake, with mutual admiration and respect, we parted company. *"It doesn't hurt to give a little when you stand to gain so much!"*

"She slipped under again, just as the Sheriff was leaving," whispered the nurse, as I entered the room. "By the way, my name is Ashley, Ashley Simmons."

"Nice to meet you. I won't stay but a minute. Hi, Melina, can you hear me?" I whispered, while taking her gently by the hand. "I have to go now but my prayers are with you always. Stay strong and get well. I'm here for you, do you understand? Hang on. I'm here for you." My eyes lit up when a partial smile came across her lips.

"I guess she heard you," stated the nurse quietly, with a smile, as she placed her hand gently upon my shoulder. I can't explain it, but I had the feeling Melina and I were destined to be together. Even though we didn't know one another, our lives would forever be intertwined. "Mom-mee, did you do this? Did you send this angel to fill that empty void in my heart? I love you too!"

Chapter 7
A Meeting of the Minds

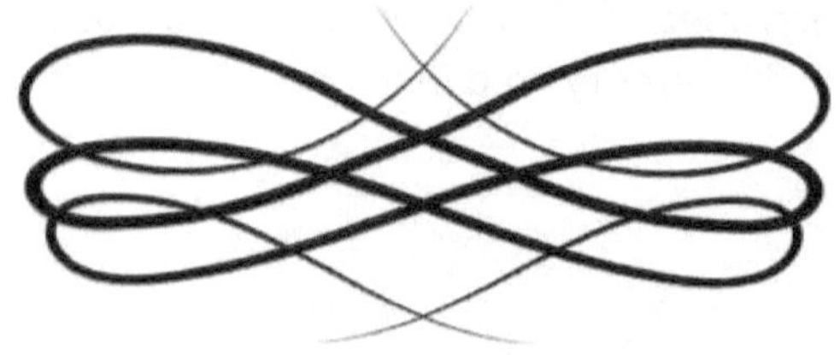

As I began my drive home, Monica phoned. "Hey sis. Yeah, everything's okay. That asshole of a Sheriff shouldn't be bothering us anymore. Melina, yes, that's her name. Melina woke up long enough to tell us she was raped by two white guys. I'm on my way home now. Is James around?"

"Yeah, he's out cruising the fields, making sure everyone's doing what they're supposed to be doing." answered Monica.

"That's cool. Look, I want to sit down with the two of you when I get there, so have him cut his rounds a little short. See you in about an hour."

"Nate, are you sure you're okay?"

"Yes, I'm fine."

"Well, alrighty then. See ya!"

My mind began to wander as I maneuvered the long, abandoned road. Even though I was able to afford more expensive sports cars, I only owned Corvettes. *I've had a thing for them since I was a kid.*

"Where did she come from? There's no one else living near us for miles. The closest neighbor was the local competition. So young and so beautiful. Where's her family, and why aren't they with her?!" It took everything in me not to turn around and go back, just to be by her side, to be there when she opened her eyes, to be there for support. And then just like that, I was home. "Damn."

"What was so important, I had to stop my rounds?" complained James, playfully.

"They are our family, and they'll do everything they must, in order to maintain their share," reassured Nate.

"You never can tell when someone might get a little ambitious and try making a little side money," complained James.

"Everyone doesn't think like you," disputed Nate.

"Will you two stop it?! Can't we ever have a meeting without the two of you going at it?! You're both right. You should trust in your family, but unfortunately, you must keep them honest. After all, you're talking serious money. At three dollars apiece, our mangoes are worth a small fortune per tree each season."

"Mom-mee's tree, the only one that had survived all these years, has given us so much to be grateful for, but that is not why I wanted to speak with the two of you. Melina is in very bad shape," stated Nate.

"Who the heck is Melina?" James asked.

"I'm sorry, the "Jane Doe" from the shrine a couple of days ago? After speaking with the doctor, it seems that there is no next of kin, either that or no one knows she's there. Whatever the case may be, right now, she's all alone. I have spoken with the doctor and suggested he bill me if no one shows up by the time she is ready to be released. Right now, she is still slipping in and out of consciousness. Maybe they can get more info out of her in a few days."

"What's the extent of her injuries?" inquired James.

"Apparently, she was a virgin before she was brutally raped.

The doctor said she was completely screwed up inside. He actually wanted to remove her entire reproductive system."

"Damn, that's messed up," replied James.

"After a long discussion, I decided that he would do everything possible to save whatever he could."

"Nate, those hospital bills could cost us in the hundreds of thousands of dollars," complained Monica.

"Look, I know we always talk things over and then vote, but I'm sorry. I **want** to do this. It's a minor financial setback at best. Just cover it with the revenue from Dark Passions. This should not affect the family business."

"I had only seen that look in my brother's eyes but one other time," thought Monica. "Katrina, his high school sweetheart, had that same effect on him. *He was so in love with her! Their relationship seemed to be the real thing. Strangely though, it ended abruptly. When* Nathan *asked her to marry him, she just ended it, just like that!* Nate *was so devastated! He cried for months! He wouldn't go out, and rarely ate a thing. He lost so much weight from alcohol and drugs,* he ended up in the hospital for a month! I really thought I was going to lose my big brother, and I don't think I could handle going through that again," thought Monica.

"Look Nate, please be careful, I can't . . ."

"Don't worry, sis," he interrupted. "I know where you're going with this, but I have a good feeling about her."

"Shit! Nate is going to be the death of me yet!"

"Not to change the subject, but how was our revenue last month?" "As much as I hate to admit it Nate, your idea for adding the solar powered lamps throughout the fields, was pure genius. Production is up thirty-five percent from last season. Not only that, the fruit increased in size and flavor."

"Damn I'm good!" bragged Nate.

"I must admit," continued Monica, "I thought an investment

of that magnitude would surely wipe us out."

"Come on, sis. Even though the other place is separate revenue, you know that was my back-up plan if things got a little tight. Besides, the government paid for over half of it."

"I don't want to sound like a broken record, but how about that security fence?" demanded James, just as he does each month.

"You win," decided Nate. "Keep it simple and decorative. I don't want to lose the warmth of our home. And while you're at it, price enough cameras to be mounted on each of the solar panel posts. It will make your job easier when it comes to monitoring the collection process."

"It's about time," mumbled James as he got up from the table.

"Before we go, I would like to suggest something," motioned Monica. "Putting up cameras around the fields is not going to go over well with the rest of the family. They're going to feel as if they can't be trusted. Besides, something the Sheriff said made a lot of sense."

"What's that?" inquired James.

"Why **don't** we have one hell of a party? Invite the entire family into the main house, then inform them of the upcoming changes. Make it seem as if they are a part of things. We could say that the cameras are for their safety or something."

"That may work," added Nate. "To ease the tension, maybe we can announce an increase in each of the family's shares . . . say by three percent? After all, the price of each mango will be going up and the trees **are** producing a lot more fruit. The increase will help to keep everyone honest."

"Damn, can't you ever keep money and not give it away?" Monica complained playfully. "You really do make me earn my pay. I want an increase too! Meeting adjourned."

We have really become tight over the years, my siblings and me, I pondered, as I watched Monica and James leave the

Conference Room. We had all gone our separate ways and were in different parts of the country. It was this bit of land, our grandparent's legacy, that intervened. Our family was meant to stay together, to stay strong and to make a difference. We showed others that, through hard work and perseverance, anything was possible, even for a black family in a country primarily run by whites. *All you need is faith*. "Thank you, Jesus!"

Chapter 8
Flashbacks

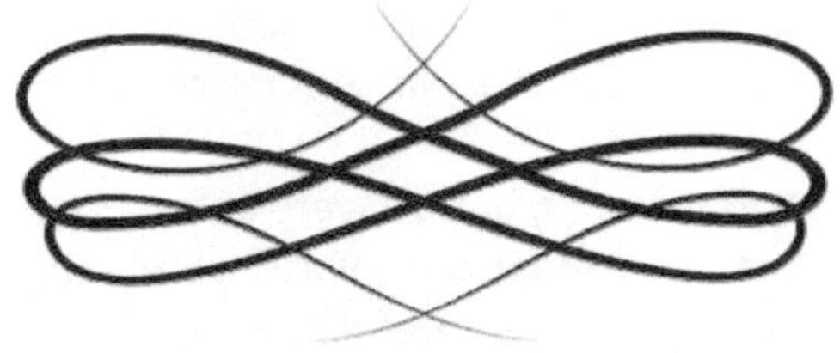

"Mommy, why?!" Melina pleaded. She watched in disbelief, as her very own mother held her arms down while she struggled to get free of her attackers. Try as she may, Melina could not overpower the two men as they took turns violating her. Her mother shouted, "Hang in there, baby. It'll all be over soon!" Stretched out across the side of the bed, her screams fell upon deaf ears as the two men took her repeatedly, until finally, their perverted needs were fulfilled.

A loud scream pierced the serenity of the hospital room as Melina suddenly sat up in the bed. After nearly two weeks, the Sleeping Beauty was finally fully conscious. The horrifying event that placed her in the subdued state had visited her in her dreams. It was all coming back to her. What she had hoped was a bad dream, or horrible nightmare, had become a painful reality. "O-w-w-o-u-c-h!" groaned Melina, while clutching her lower abdominal area, as the pain of surgical repair became obvious. Gently, she laid back down. The medical staff rushed in, as some of the monitors she was hooked up to, alerted them of her sudden movements when they became disconnected.

"Welcome back. My name is Dr. Marshall. How are you feeling young lady?"

"Weak, dizzy, and there is a lot of pain inside my private area," she sighed.

"That's normal," reassured the doctor. "You had to be heavily sedated for a few days in order to increase your chances of healing properly."

"What do you mean?" she asked. Melina began to cry uncontrollably, as the doctor explained her condition as a result of the attack.

"It took a lot of work, but we were able to save both ovaries," continued Dr. Marshall. "Your uterus was severely shifted but is back in place now. I want you to be careful moving around. There is a lot of healing going on inside of you. There was also severe trauma and lacerations to your vaginal and the uterine wall. Your allergic reaction to the latex condoms your attackers used is also much better. Normally, after such extensive damage to this area, a hysterectomy would have been performed, but it was requested that I do everything I could to avoid it."

"Requested . . . by who?" she interrupted.

"We will talk more about that later, but for now you need to rest."

"Her pressure is high doctor, but overall, her vitals are strong and stable," stated the nurse.

"Okay, let's get her on her feet in a couple of hours. She needs to start walking."

"Yes doctor."

"Hello, this is Dr. Marshall calling for Sheriff Melbourne."

"Hold on please for a transfer."

"You have some news for me doc?"

"Your victim is awake Sheriff. I'm going to keep her here a few more days until she's strong enough to leave."

"Well, I have a few more questions for her, **if** she's up to it."

"I believe she's strong enough to handle your full interrogation." "Good, I'll be right down."

"Take your time Sheriff. She's going to sleep for a couple more hours before we get her up and walking around."

"Oh, one other thing doc. Has anyone been there to see her?"

"No, there hasn't been any visitors, other than Mr. Brande. He's been stopping in just about every day."

"Now why do you suppose he's doing that?"

"Well, that's not the half of it. He's even picking up the hospital bills."

"Now **that's** very interesting. Okay, bye doc." Two and a half hours later, Melina awakened to a sight of sheer disbelief. Her room had been engulfed in flowers! She slowly turned onto her side in an attempt to ease the pain, as she tried to sit up on the edge of the bed. "I'm glad to see you're finally awake," stated the nurse as she walked into the room to check on her favorite patient.

"What **is** all of this?" Melina questioned.

"Apparently, there has been someone watching over you. He has been here practically every day, sitting and talking to you for hours on end. He even picked up the bill for everything."

"What do you mean?"

"I mean, Mr. Brande paid for your stay, your surgery, your medications, everything!"

"He doesn't even know me. Why would he even do a thing like that?" inquired Melina.

"I really can't say, but the way he looks at you, so deeply and caring, I'd say he has a thing for you," concluded Nurse Ashley.

"After all that has happened, the **last** thing I need is another man trying to have his way with me!" stated Melina in disgust.

"I think you're wrong about him. If he hadn't found you and called for help, you would have bled to death. All men aren't bad people Ms. Delgado," said the nurse, as she ran some warm water in a basin.

"How would I know? The only other men I have ever known raped me!" There was nothing more to be said as Nurse Ashley left the room while Melina washed up.

(The cell phone on the table rings, but there is no answer.)

"Good Morning Mr. Brande. Dr. Marshall here. I just wanted to let you know that Ms. Delgado is out of her induced state. Her condition has stabilized, and she should be up and walking in a few hours." (End of message.)

"Damn, how did I miss **that** call?!" complained Nathan, while drying himself off, after a few laps in the pool. He quickly went up to his room, showered, then dressed. The elevator stopped, unexpectedly, on the third floor.

"I know where you're going. Mind if I tag along?" asked Monica. "You want to ride with **me**?"

"Sure, as long as you don't take that Corvette," she said, jokingly. "Well, the ride to the hospital won't be as much fun," teased Nate. "I'll just be glad to get there in one piece!" sassed Monica as they entered the garage.

Nate didn't believe in buying overpriced vehicles. His taste was modest when it came to his cars. His most elegant car was the Mercedes CLS500. I liked it okay, but I felt the Lexus was much nicer. He also had a BMW and a couple of Cadillacs, but none put a smile on his face like his dream cars, the Corvettes he owned: a completely restored 1978 Stingray, a 1990 convertible, his actual first vet, and a brand new ZR edition, barely a week old. "Okay, sis, your choice, you drive."

"The Lexus it is then," she said. "I wish you wouldn't leave the remotes and keys in each of the cars," complained Monica.

"Who's going to steal them? Unless you have the key card, you can only enter the garage from the inside."

"You never know what may happen."

"Sis, if you don't mind, please shut up and drive!" teased Nate, as he pressed the garage door opener.

Chapter 9
The Story of Melina

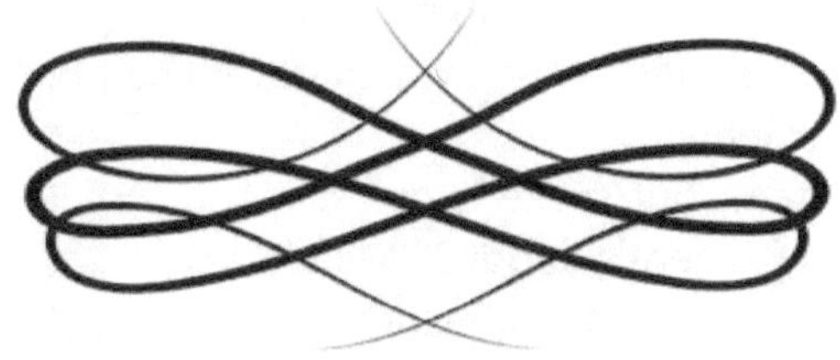

Ten years ago: Melina's mother returns home from work:

"Hi, Momma!"

"Hi sweetie! Were you a good girl today?"

"Yes, momma." An eleven-year-old Melina runs and then jumps into the weary arms of her mother.

"How were your studies today?"

"She's doing very good, Miss Delgado," said the tutor seated at the dining room table. "She is still having a little trouble with Spanish though."

"But mommy, I don't like Spanish," complained Melina.

"Now Mel, we have been over this. It is important that you hold on to your heritage."

"But why mommy, why is it so important to you?"

"I promise you will understand when you are older sweetheart. Now say goodnight to Mrs. Johnson."

"Bye, Mrs. Johnson!"

"I'll see you tomorrow Melina! Bye ma'am." Hiring Mrs. Johnson was the best thing Mrs. Sullivan could have done for me.

She would teach Melina more than she could ever learn in **any** public school.

Melina was growing up so fast! I hated being away from her for so long every day, but I had to provide for my daughter. Her so called father was a low-life piece of crap! Melina was the only ray of sunshine to come out of this dark period of my life. I hated the way he refused to acknowledge her as his own! One day, I'll make him pay for this, I swear!" thought Valencia.

"Okay, playtime is over Melina, time for dinner."

"Aw mommy, can I finish this level?"

Valencia smiled, as she watched Melina play her Wii Super Mario Brothers Game.

"Sure baby, but make it quick." And just like that: "Game Over." "Mommy, where's daddy?" Melina asked.

"Damn, I knew that question was coming," I thought, as I went over her studies on American Family Structure. "Even though he is not here, he still manages to take care of you sweetheart. He didn't love your mommy, so he went away. One day, when you're older, you will meet him, I promise. Now let's finish eating so we can have our bath."

"Always when I'm older," pouted Melina, under her breath, as she got up from the table.

By the time she was sixteen, Melina had her high school diploma. She had become an intelligent and extremely beautiful young woman. I was so proud of her and all of her achievements! One thing's for certain. I sure was glad she didn't attend any of the public schools. The boys would have been such a distraction.

"Just look at her!" admired Valencia, as Melina stood in the bathroom mirror fixing her hair.

"Mom, stop staring at me!" scolded Melina, who was wearing just a bra and panties. She playfully grabbed her robe to cover up.

"You remind me of myself at that age, that's all. Oh, to be

that young and beautiful again!"

"Will you stop it and turn around, so I can get dressed. We're going to be late!" giggled Melina. My little girl was practically all grown up, and now she's going to work with me in the main house.

"Damn, just five more years to go. I can't believe I'm going to do this to my own daughter. May God forgive me!"

As they walked the path to the main house, Melina sighed. "One day, mother, we'll live in a big house just like that one and we will only be cleaning after ourselves."

"What's wrong with **our** home Melina?"

"Nothing mom, but after working so hard to raise me, you deserve a lot more than a two-bedroom house right behind your employer's mansion."

"Good morning Mrs. Sullivan."

"Hello Melina, Valencia." Mrs. Sullivan was a quiet, stern southern woman. You heard very little out of her, except what she expected from day to day. She was also very sneaky. You never saw her unless she made a point of it. She would occasionally pop up to critique your work, or to give out another list of chores. The Sullivan's had but one child, Richard, Jr., who was just a year older than Melina. "Looking good Mel!" he whispered into her ear as he passed by. Melina blushed, and then looked down at the floor. "Good morning Richard," she mumbled.

"Melina, you can start with the bathrooms and I'll take the bedrooms today."

"Okay mom. I'll be in to help you when I'm done."

"Your daughter is getting to be quite the looker," sounded a raspy voice, as he quietly entered the bedroom.

"Good morning, Richard."

"That's Mr. Sullivan to you."

"I take it you're here for your daily screw," barked Valencia.

"I was thinking more along the line of tasting that tender piece of young ass on your daughter."

"You stay away from her, you hear me?! I mean it! You wouldn't want your wife to find out about anything would you?!"

"Take it easy and keep your voice down. I'm only teasing. That would be a sick thing to do. Besides, I'm saving **her** for Junior."

"You are such a bastard! It's still wrong and you know it."

"Enough with the pleasantries. Turn around and bend over!" Valencia buried her screams in the pillow as Richard entered her firm, ready behind. This went on practically every morning. Valencia didn't mind it much. It was part of their pact, something they had agreed upon years ago when she thought they were in love.

"Mom, are you in here?" whispered Melina as she approached the master bedroom. As she slowly opened the door to enter, Melina stopped suddenly, as she observed Mr. Sullivan mounting her mother. Shocked, sheltered, and never having had sex, she was curious. And even though she tried, she just couldn't look away.

She had learned a few things by secretly watching porn on the internet, but she had never experienced sex, up close and personal, like this. Her eyes widened as she watched Mr. Sullivan begin to spasm. Valencia quickly maneuvered around and got down to her knees, as he finished in her mouth. "E-e-e-w-w-w! Now that's disgusting!" she said under her breath, while covering her mouth as if she would gag. Melina quietly closed the door and returned to her chores, in an attempt to forget what she had just witnessed.

She had always wondered about the two of them though. She thought back to her childhood days, remembering the countless times he would come into their home. Even though her mother would always send her to bed, she could hear their strange sounds coming from down the hall. "How could she do something like that?! He was married, and we worked for him! Not to mention the fact that his wife was usually home!" she pondered.

"What's wrong?" Melina flinched. Surprised, she dropped

her cleaning sponge into the bath tub. “I'm sorry, I really didn't mean to startle you,” stated Mrs. Sullivan.

“Oh. Oh, I'm fine. I was just daydreaming, that's all.”

“Are you sure. You look flushed. You look as if you had seen something disturbing.”

“No ma'am,” Melina answered.

“Did my husband come in here?”

“What a choice of words!” thought Melina. Oh yeah, he came all right, just not in here! Feeling guilty, Melina looked away, then mumbled “no ma'am.” She knows what they did! thought Melina.

Mrs. Sullivan walked briskly away as she called out to her son. “Junior, tell your father I'll be back shortly.”

“Do you know where he might be mom?”

“Oh, I'm sure he's around here somewhere. Why don't you check with Valencia?” she answered, as she removed the cell phone from her purse. “Hello, this is Patricia Sullivan calling for Mr. Peter Crawford. Please let him know that I will be in his office within the hour. I trust he will have everything in order upon my arrival. That will be fine. See you then. I think it's about time I took care of business.” As she opened the car door, she smiled, glancing up at the place she has called home for over thirty-five years.

With the vision of what she had seen replaying itself over and over in her mind, Melina had a hard time concentrating on her work. “Oh, excuse me, but have you seen my dad?” asked Junior.

“I believe he's in the master bedroom.” As he turned to walk away, Junior took a nice long glance at Melina's body while she stretched to clean the shower. “Damn!” he whispered, tilting his head, in an attempt to get a peek under her short skirt. Feeling overexposed, she stopped cleaning after realizing Richard had not yet left the area.

Valencia had been so careful over the years, trying to hide

her daughter from the truth. Not just about her and Richard, but about sex. She knew that it was only a matter of time before Melina would become sexually active. "I'll be glad when this is all over with," whispered Valencia, as she wiped her mouth with the bed sheet. "You know you love this dick!" boasted Richard. "Maybe you're tired of me."

"No Richard, I'm just tired of this whole situation."

"I control this 'situation' and don't you ever forget it. You know what, maybe you need to be reminded of who's in charge here," said Richard, as he left the room.

"I can't believe I once cared for that arrogant bastard!" whispered Valencia, as she eased up off the floor. I was only eighteen when Mrs. Sullivan hired me. Pregnant at the time, she required live-in assistance at the mansion. My mother was more than happy to see me leave home. I was the oldest of five sisters, and at eighteen, I was becoming more of a financial burden than anything else. Unable to find work, this was thought to be what was best for us all.

"I think it's time you became a man, son," spouted Richard, as he ushered his son into the bedroom.

"Richard please. Don't do this!" begged Valencia.

"Shut up! Now, who would you say was in control of this situation?"

"Mr. Sullivan, I'm so sorry, please . . ."

"Just shut your mouth and spread those legs, or the deal is off! Here son, put this on," he whispered, slipping his son a condom. The proud father looked on as his son lost his virginity to the humbled woman. "That's right son, 'Bang her! Bang her!'" Richard cheered and laughed as Valencia squirmed beneath his son.

"You are such a low-life bastard!" Valencia cried, as she pleaded for Junior to stop.

She cried as he groaned in ecstasy. "Go get yourself cleaned up son."

"Thanks dad, you're the best!" sighed Junior, as he gave his father a "High-five."

"**Now**, you can get your ass back to work! Remember, I'm in charge here!" boasted Richard.

"I hope you drop dead! Bastard! I hope you die!" cried Valencia. "Such gratitude! You should feel honored to have had sex with such a fine young man! Now open up a couple of windows. It smells in here. I trust you've learned your lesson."

"Yes sir," conceded Valencia. It was a painful struggle getting up, but Valencia managed to get back to work as ordered. What a messed-up way to make a living!

Chapter 10
Sucker Punched

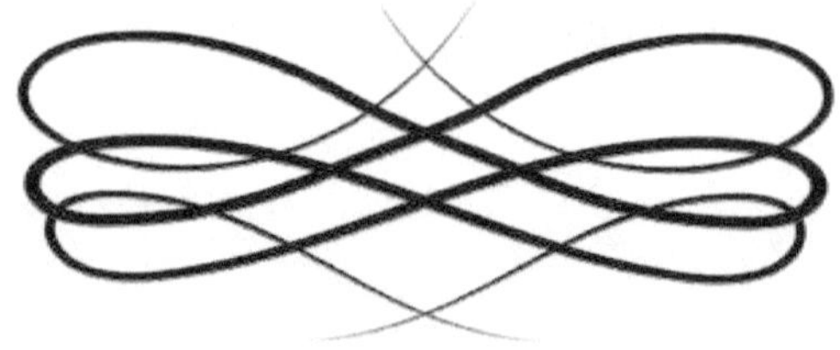

"You just missed the Sheriff," joked Dr. Marshall, as he walked up behind us in the hall.

"Yeah, that's real funny doc," replied Monica.

"Dr. Marshall, this is my sister, Monica. So, how's she doing?" inquired Nate.

"Take a look for yourself." Melina had just rounded the corner. I could see her determination as she slowly made her way back towards her room. "She's a strong young woman with a lot of will," explained Dr. Marshall. "Once she had gotten over the initial shock of what happened, she was determined to get back on her feet. At this rate, she'll be ready to leave in a few days."

"Her strength is her anger," observed Monica. "I could sense it as she walked down the hall."

"That's very observant of you. The Sheriff felt that she was purposely holding back the true identity of her attackers."

"Has anyone else been here?" Nate inquired.

"Not at all. In fact, she claims to be an only child with no parents. The Sheriff and I both find that hard to believe. There has to be more to it than that."

"There's a **lot** more to it than that," replied Monica, as she watched Melina enter her private room.

"Monica, why don't you and the doctor discuss all of the billing arrangements, while I speak with Melina."

"Your brother seems to care a great deal about her," remarked Dr. Marshall, as he and Monica walked towards his office.

"You're looking at a man with everything, and no one to share it with. You wouldn't know it to look at him, but he's very sad inside." "If I'm not being too forward, may I ask what happened to him?" "His fiancé suddenly left him, years ago." "Before he came into all of the money, *he wanted to get engaged to his long-time, high school sweet heart. They were happy together for quite some time, but when he decided to propose, she gave him back the ring without any type of an explanation. He hasn't seen her since."*

"Now that's enough to mess with anyone's head," Dr. Marshall concluded. "Here we are. After you, Ms. Brande," offered the doctor, who was checking out her rear view as she entered his office. She grinned knowingly.

Melina was sitting in the chair next to her bed, staring out of the window, as I entered the room. She turned and glared at me with a blank expression on her face. "I remember you. Thank you for all of your help. Dr. Marshall told me about all of the wonderful things you did for me." (Damn, those eyes! They could melt the iciest heart or brighten the cloudiest day!) "My room is so beautiful!" she exclaimed. "The flowers really helped to lift my spirits. I could never thank you enough," she whispered.

"Ms. Delgado, just seeing you sitting here is thanks enough."

"Please, will you call me Melina?"

"I'm not sure if you remember, but my name is Nathan."

"Listen Melina, I know you've gone through a great deal, but if you will let me, I would really like to continue to help in your recovery. If you need anything, anything at all, please let me know. I have plenty of room at the mansion. It wouldn't be any trouble. You could have your own floor, complete privacy."

"I appreciate the offer. I really do, but no thank you. When I leave here, I'm getting as far away as I possibly can." Stunned by her rejection, and without even attempting to reason with her, Nathan slowly turned, then walked out of the room. He felt as though he had taken a punch to his gut from Mike Tyson! He was dazed and completely numb.

"Nate? Nate?! Where are you going?!" called Monica, from down the hall.

"She said thanks for everything, but when she gets released, she's going away," he sadly admitted.

"Wait! She doesn't even know you Nate!" reminded Monica. "Shit, Nate, will you please wait a minute!" begged Monica, as she tried to catch up.

"Come on, what did you expect?" she asked, placing her arm around his waist. "Did you think she was just going to fall into your arms? Those men repeatedly raped her! The last thing she probably wants is to be near another man right now. She's been through a lot." My brother was crushed, and I hated to see him this way. "Have a seat. Better yet, why don't you wait for me in the car."

"Where are you going?"

"I need to speak with the doctor about one other thing. I'll be right back." Besides, she thought, as she re-entered the hospital, it wouldn't hurt to run into that Dr. Marshall again. He's kind of cute!

"Look," said Monica as she entered the room, "My brother has spent nearly a million dollars on your hospital bills. I know you didn't ask for it, but all he wanted to do was help you get back on your feet. He doesn't expect **anything** from you. He just wants you to be okay. Listen, my brother sees something good in you. He just wants to get to know you better, that's all. I don't know if you have any family, or a boyfriend, or maybe even a girlfriend, but what I do know is that my brother was the only one who spent hours, day and night, holding your hand, and praying for you to get better. No one else bothered to even check on you. He's a good man."

"I know that the last thing you want right now is to be around another man, but my brother means well. How about this. Come stay with us for a week or two. If you still want to leave, you can. I'll even make sure you have whatever you need to start your life over again. Think about it." With that being said, Monica walked out as Melina continued to glare out of the window.

"How about dinner sometime?" rang out a deep voice.

"Do you sneak up on everyone that way?" giggled Monica. "Sure, why not? Call me!" she agreed. *"No good deed goes unrewarded,"* she thought as she handed him a business card before walking out towards the car.

The ride home was frustratingly quiet. Nate didn't even turn "Bootsy" on. "Stop worrying about it Nate, she'll come around," said Monica reassuringly. "Think about it. She has nowhere to go, and it seems she has no money to get there anyway. I think she'll reconsider your offer over the next few days. I suggest you don't go back to the hospital. Give her some time to think everything through, and to get over what has happened."

"I know you're right," Nate stated, finally breaking his silence. "But there's just something about her. And those eyes . . . when I looked into them, they seemed to reach into my very soul. For a moment, just being with her took away all my pain and sadness!"

"Men!" exclaimed Monica. "You see an attractive woman and you go all to pieces!"

"Ha-ha, very funny," teased Nate. The truth is, I had never seen my brother react like this over any woman. Even Katrina didn't make him talk or react in such a sickening manner. I was beginning to believe that this might be the woman my brother was destined to be with. Call it a woman's intuition if you like. I just hope Melina understands, and learns to use it before it's too late.

(A siren sounds and flashing lights become visible in the rear-view mirror . . .) "I can see how this day is going to be," grumbled Nate, as he pulled onto the shoulder of the road. "Well I'll be damned. Its Sheriff Melbourne," he continued, as he watched the officer get out of the car.

"Afternoon Mr. Brande."

"I'm really not in the mood for you Sheriff."

"Why'd you stop us?" Monica inquired, clearly frustrated.

"Take it easy you two. I know I haven't been your best friend, but I thought we could start over. Maybe together, we can figure this thing out."

"Oh, you mean since you can't pin it on my brothers?!" snapped Monica.

"Okay, listen, there's something strange about that young woman. I really believe that she knows who raped her, but for some reason, she's refusing to say. The rape kit, uniform and sweater all came back clean, so without her complete cooperation, we may **never** know what really happened."

"She's not talking to us either, but if we hear anything, you'll be the first to know." The Sheriff nodded then returned to his vehicle.

Chapter 11
Meanwhile, back on the Sullivan Farm

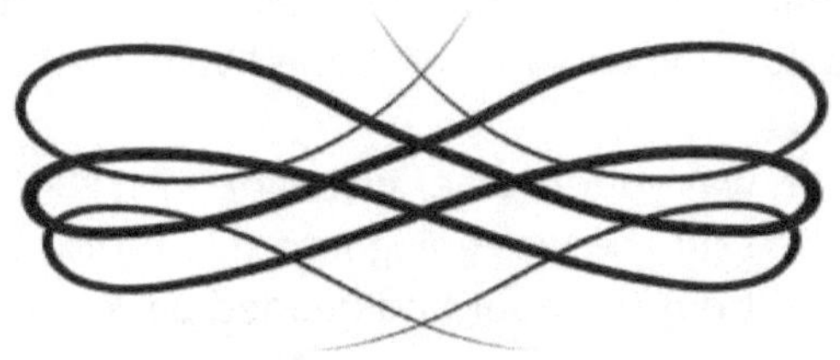

"Richard, it wasn't my fault!" cried Valencia.

"Do you know what will happen to us if she tells anyone about what went on here?! Well do you?!" scolded Richard. "We would all be locked away for life, that's what! We'll **both** lose everything we worked so hard to get!"

"Look Richard, just calm down. She'll turn up! She has no money, family, or friends to turn to, so she'll be back."

"Stupid Bitch! It's been weeks since she knocked your dumb ass out! She's **not** coming back!"

"Dad! Dad! Turn on the TV, hurry!" shouted Junior, as he ran into Valencia's newly acquired home. "If anyone has any information pertaining to this woman, contact Sheriff Clinton Melbourne at the County Office."

A number flashed across the screen beneath a photo of Melina Delgado. "Oh man, we're so screwed!" shouted Junior.

"Let's not get ahead of ourselves." stated Valencia. "She obviously hasn't told them anything or they would have been here by now."

"So why wouldn't she talk?!That just doesn't make any sense!" said Richard. He flipped through the channels in hopes of catching the broadcast in its entirety.

"Breaking news: a woman, identified as twenty-one-year-old Melina Delgado was found unconscious on a local plantation."

The three perpetrators watched nervously as the story unfolded. "Well, at least we know where she is, and according to the news, they don't know very much," sighed Valencia.

"Oh shit, was your mother watching this?!"

"No, she said she was going into town for a while," replied Junior, as he went out the door and headed back towards the main house. "We need to come up with an excuse for her disappearance," stated Valencia.

"She's **your** daughter. Y**ou** fix it!"

"Are you for real Richard? You're joking, right? You've kept me prisoner on this plantation for most of my life! Hell, I don't even have a credit card or a driver's license! I've never even been more than five miles away from this place since I was eighteen years old!" recalled Valencia.

"Haven't I always taken care of your every need?!"

"Sure you have Richard, and I've got the stretch marks across my ass to prove it!"

"Very funny. Look, can you at least call the hospital and speak with her?"

"Sure, and say what, I'm sorry?! After what I helped you and Junior do to her?! We may as well turn ourselves in right now!" Valencia pointed out.

"Maybe if we knew when she was being discharged, we

could follow her and then pick her up."

"Richard, are you saying you finally want to be seen with me in public?"

"Don't get smart. Our asses are on the line here!"

"Richard, all I know is you had better come up with one hell of a story to tell your wife. She's a lot smarter than you give her credit for."

We had one thing going in our favor: Melina had been so restricted to the plantation, hardly anyone even knew of her. Only the family and her tutor had ever really seen her. There were but a few of the farm hands that were even lucky enough to catch a glimpse of Melina, who had been raised just as I, her mother, had been raised . . . all alone. Why have I done this horrific thing to my daughter, my only child! I had raised her so innocently. She loved and trusted me wholeheartedly, and all I did was betray her! And for what? She had been defiled and humiliated for this stupid piece of paper!" Valencia stared at the taped-up document with disgust.

"I had been blinded by my own selfish greed. I've lost my child, for what amounted to nothing more than a few dishonest dollars. Fine time for me to be getting a conscience!" thought Valencia.

"Wait a minute!" she shouted. "The news said she was found on a local plantation! There's only one place close enough for her to reach without transportation, and that's the Brande Estate!" she said. "I'll see you later," grumbled Richard, as he hurried out of the door.

"Richard, have you seen the news?" asked Patricia Sullivan, as she walked in the door. "I thought you said Melina was sick?!"

"Slow down, one thing at a time," stalled Richard. "Melina **was** sick, but during that time, she and her mother were said to have gotten into a bad fight. After that, according to her mother, Melina stormed off."

"You couldn't tell **me** about this?"

"I just found out about it myself!"

"We'll need to contact the Sheriff's office," responded Mrs. Sullivan as she picked up the phone.

There was nothing Richard could do. If he attempted to stop her from calling, there would be too many questions. Junior sat in the chair staring nervously at the TV. Richard placed a finger up to his lips motioning for him to remain quiet. "A call went out to the Sheriff. He should be stopping by soon," stated Patricia. "Junior, will you call Ms. Delgado and have her come up here. I'm sure the Sheriff will want to speak with her as well. I'm going to freshen up before he arrives."

"Yes mother," he replied, as she left the room.

"What are we going to do dad?!" he whispered.

"We'll just stick to the story and see how it plays out. Just tell Ms. Delgado to get here as quickly as she can." As Valencia entered the house, Richard explained everything. "Stick to the story and everything will be just fine. Understand?" Valencia stood in the middle of the room, in a panic, as Mrs. Sullivan walked in. "I'm sorry for lying to you ma'am," stated Valencia. "I just didn't want to involve your family in my personal business. I had no idea she would run off and stay away like that."

"Well, just how bad **was** this so-called fight?" inquired Richard.

"It became a little physical, but not bad enough to put her in the hospital! She said some inappropriate things and I slapped her, that's all. I swear!"

"It just seems so strange. The two of you have always gotten along so well," pointed out Mrs. Sullivan.

"She's all grown up now and has a mind of her own. In fact, that's what the fight was mainly about. She had been rambling on about wanting to leave for several months now. I guess she just finally got up the courage to do it."

"But she's an employee of ours and there was an obligation

to notify me that she was gone," stated Patricia.

"But I thought that after a day or two, she would calm down and return home. After all, this isn't the first time she has run off you know."

"Yes, but in the past, it had only been for a few hours at most, and she would always stay on, or close to, the plantation."

Richard interrupted, sensing Valencia was running out of answers. "Honey, who knows what could have happened once she ventured off the property. That will be for the Sheriff to figure out." He placed his arm around his wife's waist in an attempt to show genuine concern. A cold chill went up and down her spine when Richard touched her. Patricia fought back the urge to vomit, as she struggled to maintain her composure.

"I guess you're right. I'm just upset, that's all. She's not just my employee. She's always been like a daughter to me." Valencia scoffed at the comment. She did not care for Patricia's motherly feelings towards her daughter one bit.

The Sheriff arrived shortly thereafter and questioned everyone. Afterward, Valencia was made aware of her daughter's condition and what had happened to her. She managed to fake a few tears as she listened.

"Okay, I'm just about finished here," said the Sheriff.

"So, Ms. Delgado, she just up and left and never came back, you say?"

"I wasn't too concerned about it. As I said sheriff, she had done this before, but had always come back. I feel so bad about the whole thing! If we hadn't fought, none of this would have ever happened!"

"I'm curious about something though. Why didn't you report your daughter missing?"

"I really expected her to come waltzing in the door at any time,

Sheriff. Will she be discharged soon?"

"The doc said she would be leaving in a few days."

"Can I see her?"

"I don't see why not. She **is** your daughter, isn't she?" "That was really a stupid thing to say," thought Richard, while cutting his eyes in Valencia's direction.

"Do you have any leads or suspects?" asked Valencia, trying to sound a bit more concerned for her daughter's well-being.

"I have a few leads, but don't you worry. I'll get the bastards that did this to your daughter, ma'am. I promise you that! Though I must say, you don't seem to be all that upset about it."

"We hardly ever fight. I guess I'm still shook up about everything that's happened."

"Well I suppose so. Anyway, I'll be in touch. You folks have a good day now," he concluded, as he walked to his car. "Now that's damn peculiar!" thought the Sheriff. "I have a strange woman, who nobody seems to know, with the exception of this family. Then she ends up face down on the lawn of the Brande family. Shit, I'm no closer to solving this case now, than I was a few weeks ago!" exclaimed the Sheriff, as he sat in his car going over his notes, while contemplating what his next move should be.

Chapter 12
Starting Over: A New Outlook on Life

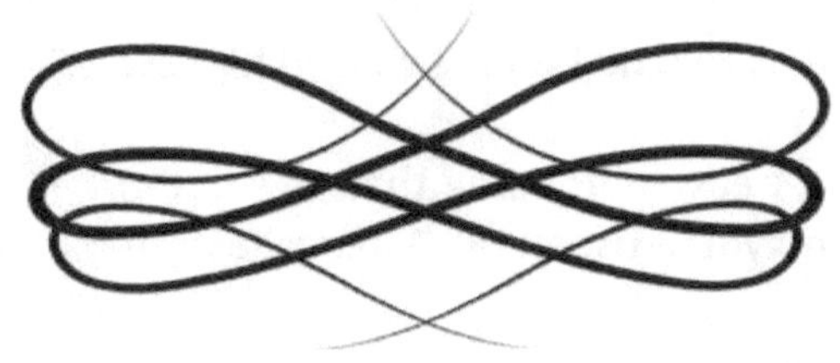

"Melina . . ."

"Yes Ashley?"

"I've been your nurse for nearly three weeks now. For two of those weeks, I've watched Mr. Brande come here, just about every day, to be by your side. For an absolute stranger, he sure does show a lot of interest in you."

"Yeah, I guess . . . Though I must admit, I do kind of miss seeing him," sighed Melina.

"I don't mean to interfere with your personal business . . ."

"It's okay," interrupted Melina. "You've become like the sister I never had."

"Well, in that case, I'll just come right out and say it. If I had a man that showed me half the attention he's given you, I would be ecstatic!

"Have you forgotten that it was a man who put me in here in the first place!" whined Melina.

"No Melina, I haven't forgotten. Was **he** one of the men that did this to you?"

"No."

"Then don't punish him for something someone else did. You're only cheating yourself out of much deserved happiness. All I sense is love whenever he enters the room. You can see it in his eyes every time he looks at you. Look at me, I'm attractive."

"Don't you mean conceited." mumbled Melina.

"Whatever. Guys ask me out all the time, yet he has never even so much as given me a second glance. On one hand, I'm insulted, but on the other, I'm extremely envious!"

"I don't think you should be. It's been nearly a week, and he hasn't so much as called. I think I chased him away."

"I wasn't eaves-dropping that day, but girl, he extended his heart to you and you crushed it!" Ashley illustrated it by twisting her palms together.

"Tell me something, how am I supposed to trust **any** man after what I've been through?"

"By trusting you heart! Are you afraid of him, or do you feel safe when he's around? Does he make you feel special, or does he creep you out? Think about it. I know **I** would feel special if someone did all those things for me! The man spent a fortune putting your entire damaged reproductive system back together! If that doesn't tell you all you need to know, then nothing ever will!"

"Are you supposed to be my nurse or my shrink?"

"I'm sorry Melina, but if I were in your shoes, I'd hold onto him for dear life! After all you've been through, don't you think you deserve someone good in your life? You're about to be discharged from the hospital. Where do you go from here? At least take him up on his offer for a place to stay. You can always leave whenever you want." Ashley paused and playfully knocked herself upside her head. "Hey, what am I, nuts? He's sensitive, he's single, he's hot, **and** he's also rich! I should just watch you let him walk away, then latch onto him for myself!" she said, jokingly. "Well, I have to finish my rounds. Think about what I said."

"Thanks for talking and being so honest with me. Hey, Ashley, you want to hang out sometime? I really could use a friend."

"Sure, anytime. And by the way, find out if he has a brother!" Melina blushed at her friend's obvious assumption.

Melina paced back and forth in her room, for what seemed like hours, glancing at the business card she was holding in her hand. Finally, she sat in the chair and picked up the phone.

"Hello?"

"H-hello, is this Monica Brande?"

"Yes, it is. Who's calling?"

"It's me, Melina."

"Oh hi. How are you?!"

"Doing much better, thanks. I just wanted to thank you and your brother for all you have done for me. I didn't mean to seem ungrateful, but I had been through so much, you know, with the questioning and all that happened?"

"It's okay. I can't even pretend to know what you're going through. Would you like to speak with Nate?"

"Actually, I'm about to be discharged and I had hoped to thank him in person."

"Are you saying you want to visit us, here at the house?" Melina paused briefly as she became nervous.

"Actually, yes, yes, I would, that is, if the invitation still stands." "Don't be silly, of course it does! It just so happens we're having a party for the family tonight, and it would be nice to have you here."

"I don't mean to impose, but could I bring Ashley, my nurse?"

"Not a problem, I'll send a car to pick you both up around six, and don't worry, I'll take care of everything." Relieved, Melina walked out into the hall giggling.

"Hey, Ash, wanna go to a party?! Hey, where did she go?"

wondered Melina, as she looked down both ends of the hall, while awaiting a response.

"Hey, you take it easy there young lady. No wild parties for at least six weeks!" Melina turned to see Doctor Marshall, as he walked down the hall. "What's this nonsense about a party?"

"It's not really a party Dr. Marshall," lied Melina, as she tried to keep a straight face. "Guess what, I've been invited to stay at the Brande Estate until I can get back on my feet. The party thing, well that was just a joke!"

"I should hope so. However, I **am** glad to hear that you're taking Mr. Brande up on his offer. I hear nothing but good things about him. You will be taken very good care of there. Here you go. These are your various discharge instructions, and these are your prescriptions. I will need to see you once a week for the next eight weeks, as long as there are no complications."

"Melina, it's very important that you follow these instructions to the letter and take all of your medications without fail."

"Yes sir."

"How are you getting to the estate?"

"Can you believe, they're sending a car for me?"

"Of course, I can believe it. I'll see you next week, okay."

"Thank you for everything," said Melina, as she shook the doctor's hand.

"You are so welcome. Listen, be safe and don't overdo it."

"Trust me doctor, I won't. I promise!"

Melina was so excited, she had totally forgotten about the work clothes she had arrived in, as she slipped out of the hospital gown. Hanging in the closet, or so she thought, was the very symbol of the attack, a bitter and painful reminder of being violated as her very womanhood was forcefully taken and not willfully given, the way she had dreamed it would be. Terrified, she just stood there naked.

She dreaded seeing that dress, the one she was raped in.

Unaware it had been confiscated by the Sheriff's Department as evidence, she trembled, as she slowly opened the closet door. "Oh my GOD!" she sighed into her hands. Slowly, a smile appeared on her face as Melina reached in and removed the card attached to one of the gift-wrapped boxes in her closet. The card simply read, "Just a little something to get you started. I did promise to take care of you, after all. I hope it fits! signed Nate." Inside the boxes was a designer dress with matching shoes, purse, and an assortment of personal effects.

Her hands trembled as she reached for the diamond studded designer clutch bag. Inside was a cellphone, five thousand dollars in cash and a note which read: "If this isn't enough to get what you need, just give me a call." After carefully placing everything out on the bed, Melina laid out a towel, then sat in the chair to take it all in. It was all just so overwhelming! She felt as if she were in some sort of a dream and could not wake up. She was both happy and sad at the same time. She cried.

"What's wrong?" asked Ashley, returning from her rounds.

"I just don't know what to think of all of this! Why was I raped?! Why is this man being so nice to me?! Look at these clothes! And that purse! This stuff had to cost him a fortune! And just look at all of that money! Can you believe he said I could just call him if it wasn't enough?!" Realizing she was still naked, she grabbed a pillow to cover her exposed body parts.

"Ashley, please say something. I don't think I can handle this!" She pulled over a chair, sat in front of Melina, and then took her by the hands.

"Believe it or not, all people aren't bad. I think you ended up at Mr. Brande's mansion for a reason. Call it destiny, or you can even call it fate. Who are we to question why things happen the way that they do. Sometimes you just have to accept the blessings as they come. Something very vile and nasty was done to you, but somehow you survived. I truly believe that this man was brought into your life to help you get through it all." After a long pause in the conversation, Ashley stood up, took a few steps toward the door, looked back then said, "So Ms. Delgado, what's it going to be?" Melina paused, looked down at the gifts, then looked back at Ashley.

"Ms. Simmons, would you like to go shopping? A car will be here at six to pick us up. We've been invited to the Brande's Mansion for a party."

"Now that's my girl," said Ashley softly, as she smiled. "Thanks, but that money is for you."

"And I want my 'sister' to help me go shopping."

"Oh, what the hell," sighed Ashley. "It's time to punch out anyway. And after all, what are sisters for?! It's been a long time since I've been to a party!" They embraced with a sigh. Once again, someone had been placed in Melina's life to guide her, and to help her to understand the many things she had been sheltered from for most of her life.

The clothes fit Melina perfectly. She felt uncomfortable wearing the dress, but she knew that pants were still out of the question, due to the recent surgery. "How did he know my size?" she whispered, admiring herself in the mirror. The panties pressed painfully against her vagina. Melina winced. Her surgically repaired injuries still needed a little more time to heal. "There is no way I can wear these. I can't believe I'm doing this," thought Melina as she carefully slipped the panties off and put them into her hospital bag.

"Holy Shit!" exclaimed Ashley as she walked back into the room.

"You look fine as hell!"

"Thanks." she blushed. "But I can't wear the panties," she whispered.

"Don't worry, we'll get everything you need. But for now, just wear some extra sterile padding inside the medi-briefs you have. We don't want you getting an infection. That new coochie of yours cost someone a lot of money. Can't go letting anything happen to it just yet!"

"Ha-ha, you are so very funny!" responded Melina.

"I think I know someone who's looking forward to having a good time with that perfect, pretty little snatch of yours . . . some-day!" hinted Ashley.

"Shut up!" blushed Melina, as she playfully pushed Ashley's shoulder. For the first time in weeks, Melina began to feel good about herself. She smiled as the orderly entered with the wheelchair and whistled.

"Your chariot awaits."

"You're kidding right?"

"Sorry, hospital rules. Everyone leaves in the chair." Melina felt awkward sitting in the wheelchair. She tugged at the dress, which barely covered thighs.

"Here," said Ashley, as she placed a sheet across Melina's lap. "Damn!" thought the orderly, as he knelt down to unfold the foot rests. The new-found friends smiled as they set out to embark on their new adventure.

Chapter 13
A Fresh Start with a New Friend

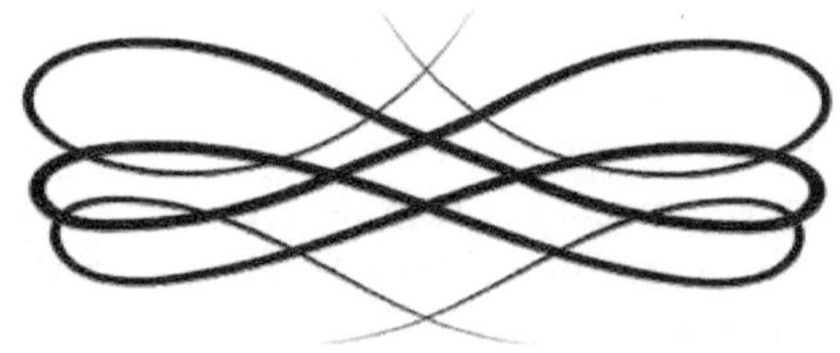

Melina's pulse raced, and she began to breathe heavily, as she neared the lobby doors. Seeing the panicked expression on her friend's face, Ashley took her by the hand. "It's okay," she whispered. "I'm with you." Melina smiled, took a deep breath, then raised up out of the chair.

"Take good care of yourself!" said the orderly.

"Melina Delgado?" asked the chauffeur as he opened the door to the Mercedes Limo. "Nate said look for the most beautiful woman I had ever seen, but d-a-a-m-n!" thought Brian, as he held the door.

"Y-yes, that's me," she stammered, as she and Ashley slowly walked over to get in. They both giggled like little school girls. "Can you believe this?!" Melina whispered, as she looked around at the interior.

"And to think, you were going to walk away from it all!" remarked Ashley. "I really have a good feeling about tonight," she continued. "Maybe this is the start of a new life for the both of us," replied Melina.

"What do you mean the both of us?"

"I mean, I want you to be a part of this Ash."

"I don't think he intended for both of us to be moving in Melina." "Well, if he can do all of this for me, the least he can do is take in my nurse as well."

"Hey, you might want to slow your roll a little! Let's just enjoy the night. We'll talk about everything else tomorrow." A voice over the intercom interrupted their conversation. "Good evening. My name is Brian. If you ladies need anything, just ask. For now, just sit back, relax and enjoy the ride." Ashley thought about what Melina had said, as the two enjoyed the soft music while they admired the lights of downtown Miami. She had just ended yet another bad relationship and was considering moving back to New Jersey. She and Melina could be good for one another. One, to protect the others naive innocence, while the other regains some of what she lost, some years ago.

"My instructions are to take you shopping and fill all of your prescriptions," announced the driver, as he reached his first destination.

"Thank you, Brian. We'll be ready in a couple of hours," stated Ashley as she took the scripts and placed them into the slot below the glass divider. The women walked hand in hand as they ventured from shop to shop. They talked about their lives in general, as Ashley reminisced about her past love affairs, admitting to having had nine boyfriends by the time she was twenty-four years old. Now this interested Melina a lot, since she had never experienced a real relationship of her own. She blushed as Ashley spoke of the different places and ways she had sex. "Oh, don't be such a child!" They laughed themselves silly, as they arrived back at the limousine.

"Ashley, is sex supposed to hurt?" The laughter quickly turned to silence.

"Oh baby, no." Ashley explained as they climbed in, "Really?

You have never done it before, have you? I mean besides what happened, and **that** was not sex!" Melina's head slowly dropped.

"I really was a virgin before all of that happened. I was waiting, saving myself for my Prince Charming," she admitted.

"Aw, come here," whispered Ashley. She held Melina close as she tried to explain.

"When the right guy does finally come along, you will know it. A feeling will come over you like no other. It will reach deep down into your very soul. You will begin to feel both apprehensive and anxious, all at the same time. But it'll be a good feeling. You'll welcome and eventually, even embrace it." Ashley had a way of helping Melina deal with her bad emotional scars. By manipulating the conversation, she was actually helping her to learn how to cope. "Anyway, trust me, it will be a magical experience for you, I promise. You just need to heal inside, both physically and emotionally. I promise you that one day soon, you will be happy again."

"We will be reaching the Brande Estate in about thirty minutes," announced Brian, over the intercom. Ashley began to undress. "What the heck are you doing?!" gasped Melina.

"You don't expect me to arrive at the party in my uniform, do you?"

"But what about the driver?"

"Don't worry, he can't see anything through the glass. But if he can, I hope he likes what he sees!"

Melina couldn't help but admire Ashley's body. Her wavy dark red hair was neatly cut just below the shoulders. She was tall for a woman, about five-feet-eleven-inches of thick, killer body! Ashley was an Amazon! She seemed to tower over Melina's five-foot seven, Latin frame. Her Hazel eyes accented her soft white, and slightly tanned, skin. "Oh. . . My . . . God!" Melina blushed and looked away as Ashley stripped naked in the seat across from her. Outside of her mother, Melina had never seen anyone else totally naked in her life!

"Did that hurt?" she asked shyly, admiring the butterfly tattoo just below Ashley's belly button."

"Just a little," she replied. "Oh Mel," whispered Ashley "it's okay for you to look at me. She should be shy when it comes to my body." "What happened to your hair?" chuckled Melina, pointing at Ashley's bald snatch. "Why did you shave it all off?"

"For your information, it's called a Brazilian Wax. It drives the men absolutely wild! They just love the way it feels around their cock! "Around their what?!" exclaimed Melina, as she giggled.

"You really have led a sheltered life, haven't you, little girl?!" said Ashley as she gently caressed the smooth area between her thighs. "You've got a lot to learn young lady."

"I'm so sure that I do, but for now, will you please put some clothes on?!"

"Ten minutes to the Brande Estate."

"I guess I should start getting dressed." She sat quietly and watched as Ashley got dressed and put on her make-up. Gazing at the dimly lit landscape, through the tinted window as it passed, Melina's face turned pale. She now realized where she was. "Melina, are you okay? You look as though you'd seen a ghost."

"If you only knew," she mumbled, as her voice trembled. There it was, the place in which she had spent so many years, filled with happiness and fond memories. Now it had become more of a curse, the place of her worst nightmares. The Sullivan Estate.

There it was, haunting her from the other side of the glass. Melina cringed with fear, as she slowly backed away from the window.

"What is it?" asked Ashley, as she watched Melina slide backward into her arms. Just as she had begun feeling good about herself, the harsh reality of the attack embraced her like an eerie fog.

"It's nothing," Melina mumbled.

"What do you mean nothing?" inquired Ashley. "You're

whiter than I am right now."

"I just don't want to talk about it right now, that's all." The rest of the ride was completed in silence, as Ashley respected Melina's wishes.

The mood changed quickly as they approached the Estate. The chauffeur smiled as he opened the door. Seeing the two beautiful women caused him to have a flashback. Reminiscing, he recalled one night, in particular, when he dropped off a guy, with six ladies, at the club. He did not have to guess what went on back there that night. The seats were soaked, and the smell of sex was unmistakable. He came to his senses when Ashley took his hand to assist her in getting out of the car.

Chapter 14
New Horizons: Welcome to My World

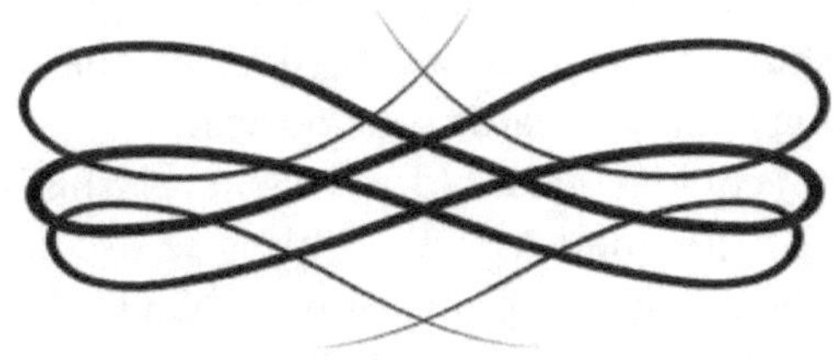

The walkway leading up to mansion was breath-taking! The floral bedding, along each side, was exquisitely illuminated! The soft lighting was carefully arranged and hidden to give a "glowing" appearance to the floral arrangements along the walkway. Neither of the women had ever seen anything quite like it! They marveled at the painstaking craftsmanship as they approached the steps leading up to the front porch.

"Oh my GOD, this place is incredible!" exclaimed Ashley, as she grabbed Melina by the arm.

"I can't believe I'm actually here again," Melina whispered.

"You okay being back?"

"I'll be alright. It's just the memory of **how** I got here in the first place that bothers me so." The women paused at the top of the steps, turned towards each other, then held hands.

"You know, I have the strangest feeling that this night is going to change **both** our lives," stated Melina.

"Remember this moment, Mel, because this is where your road to happiness begins. Just look at this place!" she exclaimed, as she surveyed the front lawn." "Now that's the most beautiful thing I have ever seen!" sighed Ashley, while clutching her hands against her chest. The heart-shaped shrine had caught her eye.

"I know. According to the Sheriff, that's where they found me. All I can really remember is Nate holding me in his arms. Besides being raped, it's the only thing I keep thinking about, I mean, I can remember about that day," explained Melina.

"I heard that! You want him, don't you?!" teased Ashley. "Nathan and Melina sittin' in the tree, k-i-s-s-i-n-g!

"Oh, shut up!" responded Melina, as she laughed, while playfully shoving Ashley towards the doorway.

"Damn, I could so grow old and die here! This is what heaven should look like." dreamed Ashley. "This is so exciting. Pinch me!" she said, slightly bouncing up and down. "Ow!" she cried out, as Melina pinched her on her plump ass. The front, main double-doors, were open. The soft music got their attention, comforting their ears. As they slowly approached the entrance, a voice rang out.

"Come in, come in. Welcome to our home!"

"Hi Monica, this is my friend Ashley."

"Nice to meet you, Ashley. I trust everything went well? No problem shopping, I see. Hum-m-m, very nice," said Monica while peeking into a couple of the bags.

"Thanks to Ashley," admitted Melina. "Without her help, I probably wouldn't have even made it here!"

"And the ride. . . did Brian take good care of things, as expected?" "The driver was a perfect gentleman, and the ride, oh, the ride was fantastic!" replied Ashley.

"Yes, it was," added Melina. "Quite an unforgettable experience!" Monica looked puzzled, as the two women giggled softly at the answers they gave.

"Here, take their things up to the fifth floor." Monica handed

Brian an envelope containing his pay and a "One Shot" key-card for the elevator. Once used, it would not work again. "Just leave their things outside the door."

"Thanks for everything!" said Melina and Ashley, as they followed Monica into the mansion. Monica paused for a few seconds, looking out the door. She then pressed the button on the wall, automatically closing and securing the mansion's entrance.

Meanwhile, Sheriff Melbourne was working diligently to dig up some new clues to his biggest case in years. "Hey Johnson, run that part back again, where she got out of the truck. Did you see that?! Run it again, slower. There! Stop it there! You see that?! I think she had something in her hand. Now take it slow, one frame at a time. Let's see now, her sweater falls from her waist, she staggers a bit, then loses her balance, falling up against the shrubs there and . . . Look!" exclaimed the Sheriff. "There's nothing in her hand now! I think we had better take a ride out to the Brande place. I'm sure I'll find what I'm looking for, right there in that bush."

"Johnson, place the disk back into the Evidence Locker and let's get a move on!" Johnson had only been with the County Office for a little over three months. He was still a rookie fresh out of the Academy and was thrilled to be involved in such a high-profile case with the Sheriff.

"Yes sir!" blurted Johnson. "I'll be right out! But shouldn't we be getting a Search Warrant?" he suggested, trying to impress his boss.

"Oh, I'm sure Mr. Brande won't mind us checking a few of his shrubs. After all, he has nothing to hide. I do suppose I should give him a call to let him know we're on our way through. Get the car."

The inside of the mansion was even more beautiful than the women could have ever imagined. The main entrance was huge and seemed to go on forever. The decor was magnificent. Straight ahead, at the end of the marble corridor, was the glass elevator. On either side was a spiral marble stair case, which went all the way up to the fifth floor. People were mingling and looking over the railing of the first few levels. It was so amazing! You could look straight up to the glass ceiling atrium area, just above the fifth floor. In the center of the ceiling, hung this massive crystal chandelier. The support lines were so thin, it appeared to be floating in midair. We were so taken by the decorative display, we did not notice the hundred or so people staring quietly, as we entered the Main Dining Hall. "Well, here goes nothing!"

"Everyone, these are our guests, Melina and Ashley," announced Monica. "Please, make them feel at home." You could see Melina's heart pounding through her dress. She had never seen so many people in her life, and she did not take being the center of attention very well at all either. After watching Ashley for a few seconds, she nervously began greeting the family members as they began introducing themselves. The crowd parted as Nathan and James entered the dining hall. Melina and Ashley stood there stunned as the brothers approached. Each wore a black tuxedo and wore them well too! They looked like something fresh off the cover of GQ Magazine! Suavely, both men approached the women and presented them with corsages.

Ashley's eyes twinkled as James took her by the hand, placed it upon her wrist, then escorted her to her seat. Nathan was so overwhelmed by the presence of Melina, he just stood there, momentarily speechless, while she shyly avoided making eye contact with him. Finally, he spoke. "Welcome to my world." whispered Nate, as he took Melina by the hand. "I pray that you will stay and make my home your own." His hands shook nervously as he placed the corsage upon her wrist. A smile beamed across Melina's face. She sensed that this was not something he was used to doing. "Could this **really** be my Prince Charming?" pondered Melina, as she inhaled then exhaled deeply. He led her to the head of the table where she was to be seated next to him. She looked away bashfully as everyone in the room looked on. "This is nerve-racking, but maybe, eventually, I could get used to it," she pondered.

Nate smiled. He was at a loss for words. He never dreamed she would be sitting next to him. And she looked so beautiful! The dress matched her eyes and was trimmed in gold. It looked magnificent against her smooth, bronze skin. Conservative, the halter style dress was just sexy enough without showing a lot of cleavage and just long enough to hide all of her assets. But it was still short enough to turn on every man (and a few of the women) in the house. It hugged her body as if it were painted on! Nathan's heart raced, and he began to get butterflies in his stomach. He was becoming a nervous wreck as he struggled to find a way to start a conversation.

Melina's long curly hair flowed over her shoulders and down her back. "Will you stop staring at me!" she blushed. "You act like you have never seen a woman before."

"But you are no mere woman." whispered Nate. "You are a Goddess, an Angel sent from heaven!" I can't believe I just said that. I'm such a nerd! thought Nate. However, Melina was looking deeply into his eyes, clinging to every word. She could see, and began to feel, the passion he held in his heart for her. She got a lump in her throat, and her heart fluttered wildly!

"That's enough you two!" interrupted Monica. "You're going to make me lose my appetite!" Everyone began to chuckle. The ice was finally broken, and the room was as it should be filled with the love, warmth, and laughter of a close-knit family.

Chapter 15
A Family Feast, Brande Style

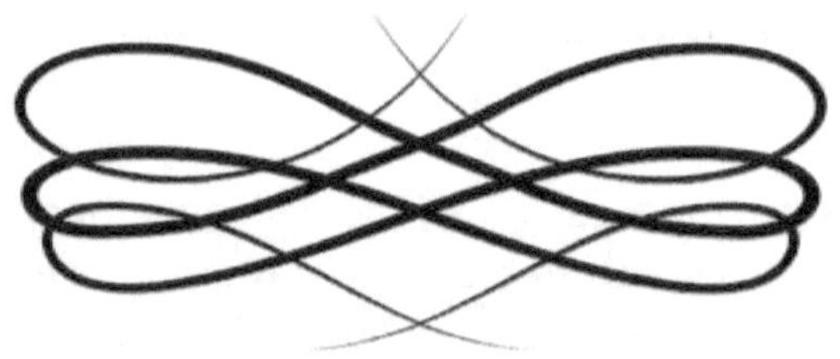

The enormous banquet table was set with the finest black china, trimmed in 18kt gold, and solid gold eating utensils. It was filled with all types of appetizers, everything from assorted fruits and salads to exotic cheeses and breads. As everyone began to snack, the doorbell chimed. "I'll get it!" replied Monica, as she rushed out of the hall.

"Oh, hello everyone."

"Now is that any way to greet your mother?"

"I'm sorry," moaned Monica, as she hugged her mother and aunts. "I was expecting someone else."

"You mean someone like **me**? Surprise!" shouted Dr. Marshall, as he caught the door just before it closed.

"Mom, everyone, this is Kenneth, my guest.

"So, **this** is the mysterious doctor you have been carrying on about for the past few days," teased Sheryl.

"Mom, shush!" scolded Monica.

"So, what have you been saying about me?" teased Kenneth, putting his date on the spot. Monica quickly looked away in an attempt to avoid further embarrassment. "That's okay, you can tell me later," whispered Kenneth, and he took her the by the hand as they entered the dining area.

Sheryl walked slowly towards the head of the table. Nate stood up and took Melina's hand, as she slowly rose to her feet.

"Mom, this is Melina. Melina, this is my mother."

"It's an honor to meet you, ma'am."

"The pleasure's mine. Nate can't say enough about you. I must say, he was telling me the truth. You are quite beautiful!"

"Thank you."

"I understand you will be staying with us for a while."

"Yes ma'am, if you don't mind."

"Then I guess you should start calling me 'Sheryl'". Melina smiled, as they hugged briefly.

During their brief embrace, Sheryl whispered into Melina's ear, "I love my son dearly and my son seems to care a great deal for you. Please don't hurt him."

"Yes ma'am," acknowledged Melina. She was not at all intimidated or upset by what was said to her. She understood all too well, the love a mother has for her child. After all, she recalled her own mother did show her the same type of love, at one time. Her mind began to drift, but Melina quickly blocked out the horrifying flashbacks. She wanted to enjoy the evening. Sheryl's words sounded sincere, not threatening. They were the words of a proud and loving mother who only wanted the best for her child. Melina admired this. Meanwhile, Nate's cell began to vibrate in his jacket pocket. The conversation was brief.

After a few more introductions, followed by the blessing of the food, everyone began eating.

"So **that's** who the empty seat was for!" teased James.

"Oh, shut up!" replied Monica. Some of the staff from "Dark Passions" were hired to cater the event. It worked out perfectly. Two of the suites had small parties, so it freed up some of the club's elite personnel, who were more than happy to do it. They all wanted a chance to see the inside of the mansion. Brande Manor was well known throughout the state for what it used to be and what it had become. Oh yeah, and double the salary was quite the incentive as well. The waiters and servers began entering the room carrying an assortment of golden, individually covered platters.

There was a choice of several varieties of chicken, beef, seafood and pasta dishes. All simple dishes exquisitely prepared by the chef that was hired to please the stars.

"I've never tasted anything quite like this before!" exclaimed Ashley. "This food is exquisite!"

"My complements to the chef!" added Kenneth.

"Melina, are you feeling alright?" asked Nate. "You seem very quiet."

"Oh, I'm fine. I just can't get over all of this, that's all," she whispered. "Your life is so different from what I've been accustomed to."

"What was your life like?" asked James.

"Well, let's put it this way. I guess you could say that I was always on the outside looking in."

"Well, not anymore," concluded Nate. Melina smiled slightly while looking into Nate's eyes. Then bashfully she looked away. She began to get a warm fluttery feeling in the pit of her stomach. "This must be the feeling Ashley spoke about," she thought. "Do I really have feelings for a man I barely even know, or am I just being taken in by his sincere kindness?" She glanced over at the man who had saved her life, in more ways than one. She was caught off guard to see that he was looking at her as well.

"What is it?" he inquired.

"Oh, it's nothing," she responded. "I was just thinking about something, that's all."

Melina was distracted by the nearby laughter of her friend. Ashley and James seemed to hit it off right from the beginning. She was infatuated the moment he approached her. "I hope she knows what she's doing," thought Melina, while trying to eavesdrop on their conversation. "She's fresh out of her tenth bad relationship."

"Want to stay with me tonight?" she heard James ask boldly. "Don't do it!" thought Melina.

"Believe me when I say that sounds very tempting, but I can't," answered Ashley. "Melina needs me right now. I really should look after her wounds."

"She seems fine," James noted, glancing over at Melina and Nate as they conversed.

"The truth is, I just got out of a bad relationship, and I'm not ready to start another one just yet."

"That doesn't mean you should deprive yourself of the good time I could show you," countered James. Ashley just smiled, looked down towards the table, then shook her head. She looked back up at James and said, "I'm not going anywhere. Can't you show me that 'good time' another night? I really want to get to know you first." **Now,** James knew where he stood with Ashley. She wanted to have sex with him, but just didn't want to seem like an easy lay.

"Okay, but if you change your mind, I'm on the second floor." "That's good to know," she whispered.

A voice interrupted Melina and Nate's conversation. Melina let out a sigh, relieved to be avoiding the next obvious question from Nate, one she was not quite ready to answer.

"If anyone cares for dessert, you will find a wide assortment in the back of the room on the buffet table, along with all the champagne any of you can possibly drink," announced one of the waiters.

"I'm sorry, but no champagne for you my dear. Doctor's orders," explained Nathan, as he got up from the table.

"Excuse me, but where can I go to freshen up?" inquired Melina. "I'll show you," stated Monica.

"Wait for me!" replied Ashley.

"What is it about women always going to the bathroom together?" asked James, playfully.

"It gives us a little time to talk about you men," admitted Ashley, looking back, while smiling and winking at James. He just laughed. "You think you're so slick, don't you Monica?" teased Kenneth. "You're still on the hook about what your mother said when I arrived."

"So, I talked about you. What's the big deal!" teased Monica. "At least I didn't tell her about how you were checking out my ass at the hospital!"

"Oh snap, how did you know that?!" chuckled Kenneth as he covered his mouth.

"The same way I could tell you're looking at it now!" teased Monica, while glancing back over her shoulder, as she walked away with the two ladies.

"Would you like to see where you'll be staying? You can freshen up there," said Monica. The women chatted as they entered the elevator. The men looked on as the elevator slowly moved from floor to floor. "Each of the upper floors has three full bathrooms, complete with Jacuzzis."

"Wow, this is something!" exclaimed Ashley.

"This is all a result of my brother's life-long dream. He has worked extremely hard to get where he is today. His only regret is that our grandparents didn't live long enough to see or enjoy it. Here we are, the fifth floor. It's all yours," announced Monica.

"This . . . this is my **room**?!" exclaimed Melina, as Monica opened the door. Ashley paused to gaze up at the stars through the glass ceiling, before entering the room behind the other women.

"I had everything cleared out. We were only using the space for storage anyway. Here. This is your key to the elevator. You can only gain access to this floor by using it in the slot next to the floor number in the elevator. It also unlocks the door, so keep it with you at all times. Over here is the private security system for this floor.

With it, you can control the motion sensors and alarms along the stairs."

"It's quite simple really." Monica slowly went over the basic instructions, and then watched as Melina went through the motions.

"This monitor was added so that you could see who was at the door. You're quite safe here and you have all the privacy you will ever need." Melina and Ashley walked around in a daze as Monica gave them a tour of the fifth floor.

"Monica?"

"Yes?"

"Would I be asking too much if I wanted Ashley to stay for a while? I mean, after all, she **is** my nurse."

"To be perfectly honest, I think Nate would say 'yes' to anything you asked of him." Melina blushed. "And as for James, I don't think he would have it any other way. He seems to have eyes for you," Monica admitted.

"And I see you have eyes for my boss!" Ashley pointed out. There was an eerie silence in the room as the three women looked at each other. Suddenly they burst out, laughing hysterically. Women; go figure!

"Listen, you ladies just relax and take your time coming down.

There is really no need for you to rush back to the party right now.

We have a little family business to attend to." The two women glanced at one another, then decided to sit on the sofa to rest bit. Melina nestled back into the soft, cozy fabric. She moaned as she slowly lifted her arms, then stretched them over her head. "So, what do you say Ash. Care to join me in starting a new life?"

"How could I say no to all of this, I mean to you?!"

"Yeah, you were right the first time!" chuckled Melina.

"Maybe James could be **my** Prince Charming." Ashley hoped.

Monica chuckled briefly at what she heard as she closed the door, then headed for the elevator.

"It's really going to get interesting around here!" she mumbled, as the elevator stopped to pick up guests on the third floor. "I wonder if Kenny would like to move in as well?" she pondered, smiling, as several people boarded.

The doorbell chimed. "James, come with me," requested Nate. "It's the Sheriff. He said that he needed to speak with me about something. It sounded important."

"Damn, I was hoping to talk to Ashley some more."

"You'll have plenty of time for that later," said Nate, as he opened the door.

"Sorry to bother you folks at this hour, but I have an urgent matter to discuss with you," stated the Sheriff. "This here is Deputy Johnson."

"Pleased to meet you," stated the deputy.

"We were watching the surveillance coverage you provided and discovered something interesting. It appears Ms. Delgado placed something in the bushes near the corner down there. Mind if we take a look?"

"Sure Sheriff, why not," responded Nate.

"Sounds like quite a party in there."

"We decided to take your advice," admitted Nate.

"It's more of a family gathering," added James. "Feel free to check it out Sheriff and when you're done, you and your deputy are welcome to join us, if you like."

"Thanks, we just might take you up on that." The two officers turned, then walked swiftly down the stairs.

"James, I want a close visual on everything the Sheriff does," requested Nate.

"I'm all over it," replied James. The two men maneuvered quickly through the crowd, then headed into the Monitor Room.

"Let's see now. She got out of the truck just about here, then staggered over in that direction," concluded the Sheriff. "Deputy, shine your light into the bushes here." The Sheriff put on his rubber gloves and began prying around the interior of the dense shrubbery. "I could have sworn she put it in, right around here," he complained, as he continued to feel around.

"Hey Sheriff, what's that?" asked the deputy as he pointed to an object just below the Sheriff's left hand.

"I knew it. Good eye, son!" exclaimed the Sheriff, as he removed a crumpled up small, black plastic bag from the bush. The deputy held open the evidence bag while the sheriff carefully placed his new-found clue inside.

"I guess we won't be joining the party, huh Sheriff?"

"Just get your ass in the car and let's get back to the station!" exclaimed the Sheriff, as he smacked the deputy on the back of his head.

"What do you think **that** was?" inquired James.

"Whatever it was, it doesn't involve us," answered Nate.

"The Sheriff **did** seem to be in an awful hurry though," noted James.

"Let's get back to the party. We can check out the coverage a little closer tomorrow. "Ashley seems like a nice girl. Not quite your type, huh," remarked Nate. "She and Melina have become really close, so don't mess this up for me!" he added.

"Look Nate, can't you see that I've changed over the years? I think I can really get into Ashley. She's fine as hell!"

"Is that all you can see? You haven't changed at all!" scolded Nate.

"Give me a break!" exclaimed James, as he grabbed Nate by the arm. "Just because I'm not all 'sensitive' and 'bitchified' like you, doesn't mean I can't like her for something other than her body!"

The door to the monitor room opened abruptly. "I can hear the two of you half way across the room!" Monica interrupted. "The ladies are upstairs, and it may interest you both in knowing that

Melina asked if Ashley could stay with us for a while. I think she likes you." James smiled, then chuckled sarcastically as he walked out of the room. "Nate, you need to come to terms with your brother. He is who he is."

"I know, but if he does the same thing to Ashley that he has done to hundreds of women in the past, it could jeopardize my relationship with Melina! Brother or no brother, I will not lose her due to his stupidity!"

"You both need to slow it down a bit," advised Monica. "It's their first night here, so don't push it."

"You just worry about your little doctor friend out there!" barked Nate.

"Don't take your frustrations out on me big brother!" They looked at each other, hugged, then said, "I love you."

"Let's get everyone back into the dining hall so we can give them the good news," requested Nate.

"What about Melina and Ashley?" Monica asked.

"We don't need to disturb the girls for this. It's a family matter anyway. You can call for them to come back down after the meeting."

"Okay then, let's do this," replied Monica.

"Finally, after a month of dead ends, I have some hard evidence! This needs to be taken to the lab ASAP!" explained the Sheriff as he carefully opened, then looked into the bag.

"That's totally disgusting!" exclaimed the deputy, as he took a brief look at what was retrieved.

"No, that's evidence," reassured the Sheriff, as he removed two spent condoms from the bag and placed them into separate containers. "Damn, it's three a.m.," noted the Sheriff. "Lock these up. I want you to run these down to the lab first thing in the morning! This is priority number one, understand?!"

"Got it Sheriff."

"Okay, let's call it a night, Johnson. I'll see you at seven sharp." "Night Sheriff. Damn, it'll be four by the time I get home. How's a man supposed to survive on a couple hours of sleep?" grumbled the deputy, as he walked out the door.

Meanwhile, back at Brande Hall: "First of all, we would like to thank you all for coming. I trust that you have all enjoyed the food and are having a wonderful time. This is something we should do more often. Not just for special occasions, but to maintain our family's togetherness."

As the crowd clapped, James whispered into Monica's ear, "I think I'm going to be sick!" he said.

"Quiet!" whispered Monica.

"I'm sure you've all noticed that production is up this season."

"Up by thirty-five percent," added Monica.

"We want you all to join in our good fortune. After all, you have all worked just as hard as we have to make this happen," continued Nate. "Therefore, starting next harvest, we will be increasing your shares by five percent," concluded James. The room was filled with the sound of cheers as the excited family members expressed their heartfelt thanks.

"We have just one last order of business before you get back to the party. Cameras are going to be installed throughout the fields. This is for two very important reasons. The first, is your safety. In the event someone gets injured, we can locate and assist you more efficiently. The other reason is to avoid theft. We can't monitor the fields twenty-four hours a day, and we don't want people sneaking into our fields, stealing our produce. I'm sure you will all agree that having an extra set of eyes out there will be a big help to us all. There will no longer be a need to stay up all hours of the night patrolling the fields. Each home will be equipped with monitors. Motion detectors will alert you to any activity in your fields and everything will be recorded. So, continue to work hard and we will continue to share in the profits," concluded Nate.

"Thank you everyone and enjoy the rest of the evening!" concluded all three, in unison.

"Please feel free to explore the mansion. All floors, with the exception of the fifth level, are available for touring," concluded Nate. "Do you think they bought it?" he whispered. The relatives conversed about what they had just heard, as they slowly filed out of the dining hall. Kenneth slowly approached the head of the table. "Nate, do you think it's possible for me to check in on Ms. Delgado? It **has** been a long night and she's been pretty active. I want to make sure that there is no excessive swelling or bleeding."

"Sure doc, not a problem. And by the way, thanks for all you've done for her." The two men politely shook hands.

Monica phoned the fifth floor to notify the women of the doctor's pending arrival. "Ken, I'll take you up," stated Monica. Nate handed her his key. He had the only key that gained access to every door and elevator destination in the entire mansion.

"What's **that** look for?" inquired James, as he finished off a glass of champagne.

"I don't know," Nate answered. "I guess by having her here, I had forgotten how sick she was, that's all."

"Aw-w-w, what's the matter?" teased James. "You jealous about the doctor sticking his nose where yours should be?!" he suggested. "Why do you always have to be such a major asshole?!" exclaimed Nate, as he picked up, then quickly downed his glass of Remi Martin.

Of course, James was right, but he did not have to be such an ass about it. The two men walked out and headed in the direction of the pool. "Where are the two of you headed?" asked their mother, Sheryl.

"Just walking and talking," answered James.

"What's wrong Nate?"

"Oh, nothing Mom. James is just being his old charming sarcastic self as usual."

"The good doctor went up to check the plumbing on his girlfriend!" joked James.

Nate exploded! "Back off! I am so sick and tired of your bullshit!" James, being twice Nate's size, was always trying to bully his older brother. It was clear that he was just jealous of his brother's success. "Take a walk with me James," suggested Sheryl, in an attempt to ease the tension between her two sons. "Why must you always do that to your brother?"

"Mom, you never came to my rescue when he used to pick on me!" whined James.

"That was when the two of you were kids. Now get over it! The three of you have given so much back to our family. I'm so proud of everything you have accomplished. This is a special night. Don't ruin it." "She always takes his side," James thought, as he and his mother rejoined Nate. "Why? Because he was so successful, and I was such a failure?" "Now you two play nice." Sheryl hugged her sons, then left to rejoin her sisters out by the pool.

"Get away from me!" grumbled Nate.

"You heard Mom. Play nice!" demanded James, as he gulped down another glass of champagne.

"You're turning out to be just like our father. Didn't all of that drinking help kill **his** career too?" James scoffed, then downed two more glasses.

Chapter 16
Turning Point: A New Lease on Life

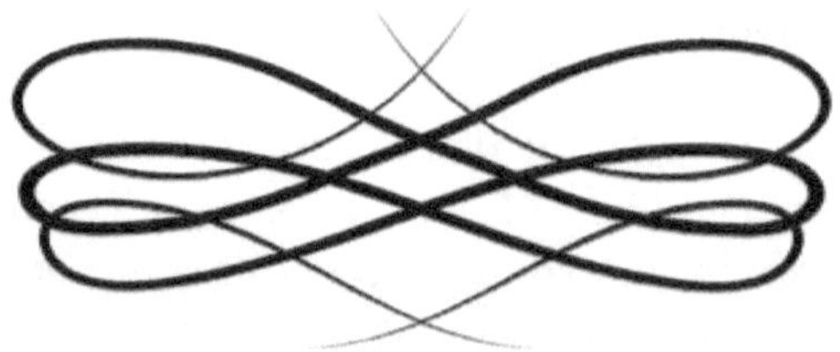

"Just lay back and try to relax Ms. Delgado. This will only take a minute." Melina turned red from embarrassment as the doctor knelt down between her legs. "Nice haircut!" he thought, as he gently spread her smooth lips apart to begin his examination. "Ouch," she mumbled, squirming, as he probed around her tender insides. Even though Kenneth was her doctor, she felt violated. It just wasn't the same as it was when she was in the hospital. There, she was always sedated, but here, she was fully aware of what he was doing.

She could see the look of disapproval on Monica's face through the slightly opened door.

"Did he really have to do that **now**?" Monica wondered aloud. "He's only looking out for her best interests," assured Ashley. "It **is** her first night out of the hospital and she has been pretty active," she continued.

"I know, but it's kind of awkward knowing my date is putting his face between another woman's legs."

"Tell me a little about your brother," requested Ashley, in an attempt to get Monica's mind off of what was going on in the bedroom.

A short time later, Dr. Marshall exited the room. "She's a little swollen and a bit tender, but there is no bleeding. All in all, she's doing fine."

"Nate will be glad to hear it," stated Monica. After washing, Melina rejoined the group. "Ready to get back to the party?" Monica asked, as she phoned Nate about Melina's progress. She did, however, realize how silly she was acting, as Kenneth took her by the hand and led her out of the room. But he could sense something was amiss.

"You seem withdrawn Monica. What's wrong?"

"It's nothing. I'm just a little tired, that's all." Melina and Ashley interrupted the conversation as they exited the room.

"My key!" shouted Melina, as she just managed to catch the door before it closed. "I'll be right back!"

"I'm going ahead. I'll see you all downstairs," said Monica. "What's **that** all about?" asked Ken. Ashley quickly explained why Monica had become distant. "But that's my job. How could she be mad about that?!"

"Because she really likes you dummy, that's why," explained Ashley.

"Why are women such babies?!"

"Oh really? How would you like to watch her examine another man's penis?" countered Ashley.

"I'll schedule Melina to see Dr. Graham, starting next week. Now I'd better catch up with Monica! Thanks for the heads-up Ash!" Ken headed for the stairs as Melina approached.

"All set?"

"I am now." The two ladies headed towards the elevator and back to their men.

"Ashley, if I tell you something, do you promise to keep it between us?"

"Sure I do. What kind of a question is that?!" she responded.

"I'm really grateful for everything he has done for me, but I don't think I can let Dr. Marshall examine me anymore. It really made me feel uncomfortable. I was so drugged up in the hospital, I didn't give it a second thought, but now . . ." Melina folded her arms and cringed, as if the very thought of it, gave her the willies.

"I don't think Monica took it well either," admitted Ashley. "She stormed off right after you went back into the room for your key. But don't worry. I explained why Monica was acting that way. He's sending you to see Doctor Nancy Graham, starting next week."

Melina slouched against the wall. "Maybe I should just stay up here for the rest of the night," she moaned.

"Oh no you don't! Dr. Marshall can handle his own problems. Take a look down there." said Ashley, glancing over the banister. "Don't they look simply delicious?!"

"Let's go!" agreed Melina. "There's no way I'm passing that up!" she confessed.

"Now **that's** my girl!" replied Ashley. "I knew you had a thing for Nate. But you can't give him any yet! Doctor's orders!" They giggled as they approached the elevator. Secretly, Melina was beginning to wonder what it would be like to be with Nathan. She was finally coming into her own.

Nate and James waited in anticipation, as the elevator slowly made its way down to the first floor. The music caressed their ears as it flowed smoothly from the speakers embedded in the walls.

"I'll bet the doctor can't get enough of probing that fine ass!" teased James, as the elevator doors opened. Nate tried to ignore his brother's comment, as Melina stepped out.

"Would you like to join me out near the pool?"

"Yes, I would," she whispered. Melina welcomed the feel of Nate's arm, as it slowly went around her waist. She smiled as she looked up at him, then did the same, as he slowly escorted her down the corridor towards the pool. As they neared the end of the corridor, Melina stopped, then turned to face Nathan.

"I really never had the chance to thank you properly," she said, as she held Nate's hands.

"You don't need to thank me. Having you here with me like this is more than I could have ever hoped for." They both began to breathe heavily as they gazed deeply into each other's eyes. Melina quivered as their lips inched closer and closer. The tension was almost unbearable! Melina's eyes began to close as Nate's lips approached hers. "This is it!" they thought. Their breathing became more intense the closer their mouths came together.

"Break it up!" shouted James.

"Kissy, kissy!" mocked Ashley. The embarrassed couple separated, as James and Ashley passed between them snickering.

Reluctantly, Melina and Nate followed Ashley and James outside, where people were still eating, drinking, dancing, and generally having a good old time around the pool. "Thanks a lot," whispered Melina, as she walked past Ashley. Nate guided her towards a beautifully decorated gazebo, just a few yards away from the pool. *"Aw Man, Heatwave! This is one of my all-time favorite ballads!"* Nate confessed.

"Always and forever, each moment with you-ou-ou is just like a dream to me-e, that somehow came true . . ." "Care to dance?" asked Melina coyly.

"Hey, I was supposed to ask **you** that." The soft lighting complimented the music inside the gazebo. It was hypnotic. The couple embraced closely as they danced. Melina opened her eyes briefly to ensure she wasn't dreaming.

"Come on, let's join them."

"No, I think we should give them some time alone," advised Ashley, who was now starting to feel guilty about ruining her friend's big moment.

"You're right. I have a better idea. Follow me!" James

suggested, also starting to feel bad about how he had been treating his brother. After all, he didn't have to offer him the job.

"Could this be our song?" Melina whispered, as she looked up at Nate.

"From now until the end of time," he replied.

"Just look at that," Sheryl said to her sisters. "After all this time, I think my son has finally found love."

"Just look at her. She's probably just after his money," said Jean. "Will you please shut up," Sheryl demanded.

"You know I'm just saying what everybody else here is probably thinking!"

"Just take a **good** look at them," Sheryl pleaded. "Do you see the way she's looking at him? She has **real** feelings for my son."

"You had better hope so, or she'll take him for all he's worth!" "Jean, what do you know about love anyway?" added Betty.

"Yeah, your idea of love is getting drunk and banging as many men as you can handle!" chimed Lorraine.

"Oh, and let's not forget the occasional female!" added Jerri.

"Whatever! You all can kiss my fat ass!" concluded Jean, as she got up from the table.

"Only if you've had all of your shots!" joked Jerri. The five sisters could never stay together for long periods of time. They always ended up picking on Jean. *I was led to believe, that, because of her, the family had lost most of their parent's belongings, which held such valuable memories. When their mother died, Jean was said to have sold everything in the house. Those items were now, gone forever.*

The song ended much too soon for Nathan and Melina. Even though their song had ended, they continued to embrace and sway slowly back and forth. Nate smiled as she rubbed her face cozily against his chest. Then, the swaying stopped. The nervous, heavy deep breathing began once again, as they each awaited the others next move. Melina could feel his heart pounding. Nate knew that this was his moment. It was now or never! He swallowed deeply as he sensed Melina was looking up at him. He looked down and gazed passionately into her eyes. She gazed hungrily back into his, longing for something she needed, and needed badly. The two of them were becoming absolutely love-struck!

"Please don't ruin this, James," Nate thought, as he lowered his lips to meet hers. Oblivious to their surroundings, the couple was unaware that almost the entire family was watching them with anticipation. And then it happened. Their lips met, melting together in one long, deep, passion-filled kiss.

"Now!" shouted Ashley, her voice filled with excitement. James flipped the switch, which ignited the fuse that sent fireworks souring overhead. "Now that's my girl," Ashley whispered, as she smiled. Holding James tightly around his waist, she could not be more happy and relieved, as they watched the couple engage in their first kiss. The moment was nothing short of magical. They both became weak in the knees, and got so dizzy, they thought they were going to faint! Wow, what a kiss! Everyone clapped and cheered.

The fireworks display could not have been timed more perfectly. As the couple slowly ended their first kiss, they became aware of what had transpired. They giggled with embarrassment as they tried to avoid making eye contact with the family members. They looked towards the warm evening sky to enjoy the rest of the fireworks display. Still engaged in their embrace, Nate smiled over at his brother and Ashley, nodding, to show his approval. Melina held Nathan tightly. She was in awe about the way her life had suddenly turned around, changing for the better.

"God truly works in mysterious ways . . ." About month ago, I experienced the worst day of my life," she thought. "**Now** look at me!" Tears of joy began to stream down her face. Nate didn't know what to think about that moment. He decided to just gently hold her

in his arms, never wanting it to end. What seemed like an eternity of pain and suffering had all but vanished from their hearts and all it took was a single kiss, the coming together of the lips of two people fulfilling the needs of one another, causing a chain reaction of feelings, which ignited the healing spark of love!

"Are you okay?" whispered Nate, feeling the warm tears as they soaked into his shirt.

"I couldn't be better," she answered, as she looked up at her mysterious savior. He dried the rest of her tears with a handkerchief, as she smiled up at him. Nate had also become overwhelmed by the moment, as his eyes began to tear up. Being a man, he quickly and discreetly wiped them, not wanting anyone to see his tears of joy. But **she** had seen. Melina knew, at that very moment, how Nate truly felt about her, but she kept it to herself.

"That was a nice thing you did for your brother," Ashley whispered into James' ear. She was so tall, she nearly stood eye to eye with him. "So nice, in fact, I think you deserve a little reward." She caught James by surprise as she gently pressed her lips against his. "WOW!" panted James, as he tried to catch his breath.

"I like seeing this side of you," Ashley whispered.

"What side is that?"

"The kind, loving side. You don't have to play the tough guy all the time you know."

"And what if I don't, then what?"

"Well, we'll just have to wait and see what happens," teased Ashley, as she slowly rubbed his muscular chest, slowly easing down to his stomach. She laughed as he flinched. "He's ticklish!" she noted. "Keep **that** up, and you'll be in trouble," warned James.

Ashley laughed as she broke the embrace. "Come on," she said. She took him by the hand, then escorted him in the direction of the gazebo.

"Hey, what's going over there?" wondered Monica, as she

and Ken also headed in the same direction. Melina turned and positioned herself in front of Nate as the other couples got nearer. "Oh . . . My . . . Gosh!" whispered Melina softly, as she backed up, pressing her back against Nate. She quivered ever so slightly, then moaned quietly, as she lowered her head. She could feel the warm juices, as they filled the padding in her panties. Melina struggled to control her panting, and keep her knees from buckling, as the other couples arrived. (Unknown to her, Melina had achieved her first orgasm!)

"Okay you two, that's enough of that!" declared Monica. "We do still have guests to entertain."

"I think we're going to call it a night," announced Sheryl, as she and her three sisters approached.

"Hey, where's Auntie Jean?" asked Monica.

"You know how she is," answered Sheryl. "She probably went off to find herself a few good men." They all hugged and exchanged pleasantries. "Good night. I'll see you in the morning," said Sheryl, as she hugged Melina. "You two were made for each other," she whispered. "Give him your heart. You both deserve happiness. Nate, don't keep her up too late. She just got out of the hospital."

"**Good night Mother**," urged Nate. The other family members also began to head out. However, there was still a lot of work to be done before the three siblings, and their new guests, could finally turn in.

By the time they re-entered the mansion, the staff had everything just about back to normal.

"Am I dreaming or was there just a huge party going on in here?!" questioned Ashley.

"You'd never know it," added Ken. "O-o-oh, four thirty," he groaned. "I've got a fourteen-hour shift starting at ten," he complained. "With an hour-long drive home, I should be calling it a night as well."

"There's plenty of room. Why don't you just stay here?"

offered Nate.

"I don't want to impose."

"Nonsense. There are two empty rooms on the third floor. Take your pick."

"Thanks Nate!" whispered Monica as she grinned, elbowing him in the side. "Come on party-pooper," teased Monica. "I'll show you to your room."

"Good night Mr. Brande, and thanks for everything," concluded Ken.

"Melina, don't you think **we** should be turning in as well?" suggested Ashley, as she and James slipped away, heading in the direction of the elevator. "You've been on your feet a lot longer than you should have. And you still have a lot of healing to do, so let's go young lady. You need your rest." With a sad expression on her face, Melina lowered her head, then conceded.

"I guess. But I'm not tired and I feel fine."

"It's okay. I'll see you soon. I promise." whispered Nate. He placed his finger beneath her chin, then slowly raised it. He then kissed her softly, but briefly on her lips. Melina thought she would pass out, as she began to sway.

Even though she wanted it to be longer, that kiss was actually the perfect way to end the evening.

"Your furniture won't be in for at least two days, so why don't you sleep in my room?" offered James.

"Nice try, but I don't sleep with **any** man on the first date," teased Ashley. "Maybe the second, but **never** the first!" she flirted. Once again, she caught James off guard as she kissed him. As the elevator doors opened, she called out to her friend. "**NOW Melina**!"

"Oh, all right. I'm coming, I'm coming!"

"Good night Ashley. I'll have a key-card for you in the morning." "Good night Mr. Brande, and thanks for letting me stay."

"Please, call me Nate; and you're so welcome."

The men smiled and watched as the women arrived on the

fifth level. The women waved over the banister as they walked towards the door. Ashley once again gazed up at the stars while Melina reached into her top and pulled out the key.

"That's real lady-like," joked Ashley."

"Where else was I supposed to keep it?! Hey, where are **you** going?" asked Melina, as she watched Ashley walk towards the unfurnished room.

"First, I'm going to hang up these clothes, then take a shower, and then make up the couch."

"Are you kidding me? The couch?! You're not sleeping on the couch!" scolded Melina. "That bed in there is big enough for six people! Besides, no matter how beautiful this place is, I still don't want to sleep alone, at least not on the first night. Please-e-e-e-z!" begged Melina. "Sleep with me?!" she asked, as they entered the bedroom.

"Huh, I turned down sex with James on the first date to sleep with you! Somehow, that just doesn't seem quite right!"

Melina laughed, then picked up a pillow and threw it at Ashley.

"Just for that, I'm showering first!" laughed Ashley, while tossing the pillow back at Melina.

"Boy, there sure aren't any secrets in this house," said Ashley as she entered the bathroom. It was one huge room. Everything was out in the open. Even the shower was encased in clear glass. "I hope you don't have anything to hide, because it's all going to be out in the open in here!"

"Well, can I get in there before you get into the shower?" asked Melina.

"Girl, what's wrong with you? We both have the same plumbing. Besides, there's enough room for both of us in here." Melina couldn't wait. The moist padding between her legs was beginning to irritate her vagina. She had to wash. As she entered, Ashley peeled her dress down and onto the floor. Melina shook her head and looked towards the floor.

"You just love being naked around me, don't you?"

"I told you I wasn't shy, didn't I?"

"A-a-a-ah," Melina moaned, as she slightly pulled down her panties and held the heated cloth between her legs. "That's much better." She closed her eyes and began to reminisce about her evening. She could still feel Nathan's hard-on pressing against her back. She removed the cloth and placed it into the sink.

"Damn, you sure look mighty irritated down there!" observed Ashley, who had finished her shower and was now kneeling behind Melina, looking up at her red, swollen snatch.

"What the hell?!" shouted Melina as she quickly closed her legs, catching her panties between her knees. "Didn't you look up my ass enough in the hospital?!" she complained.

"What happened? I thought Dr. Marshall said you were doing fine?"

"I am fine. I've just been spending too much time on my feet, that's all."

"Why don't you get in the shower. I'll be right back."

Four adjustable pulsating shower heads were embedded in the ceiling and walls. They relaxed every muscle in her body. She placed her hands against the wall and moaned as the beads of water gently massaged her neck.

"Here, try this," stated Ashley. "It's an antiseptic wash the doctor ordered."

"Thanks. Ow! It stings!" complained Melina, as she gently messaged the lotion between her legs.

"It should help you feel a lot better." Ashley admired Melina's body as she rinsed off. Melina turned to rinse her back, only to see Ashley still watching her.

"Will you get out of here?! What are you, gay or something?!" she joked.

"I've never tried it, but you do look mighty tasty!" laughed

Ashley. There just seemed to be something sexy about watching Melina through the wet glass. "Nate has very good taste, I'll give him that much," she muttered.

"You were right," sighed Melina, as she stepped out of the shower. "I feel much better, and my coochie also thanks you!" she joked. "Now, will you please put some clothes on? I'm so jealous of your body!"

"Oh please, Melina, you really need to take a good long look in the mirror."

"I can't believe we're both standing here naked like this!"

"I know, isn't it great!" exclaimed Ashley, as she hugged Melina from behind.

"Now that feels different," Melina whispered.

"What do you mean by that?" Ashley inquired."

"Oh, nothing," replied Melina, as she playfully wiggled free of Ashley's hold, then trotted into the bedroom. Ashley licked her lips as she watched. Both ladies began emptying the shopping bags, in search of the newly purchased sleepwear. Ashley slipped on a black teddy, while Melina slipped on a fresh pair of padded panties. "How long will I have to wear these?" she asked.

"Until you are completely healed, and believe me, you'll thank me for it later."

The women conversed about their evening while Melina put her clothes away.

"What do you think of James?" asked Ashley.

"He seems nice enough; maybe a little crude. He treats his brother so disrespectfully sometimes."

"Yeah, I know, but I can fix that," Ashley said. "It's hard to believe he's the "little" brother." She continued.

"Not really. I know who the big brother is!" Melina snickered. "What's **that** supposed to mean?!" asked Ashley. Melina groaned as she sat on the bed and placed a pillow across her lap.

Ashley laid on her back with her head on the pillow. "Okay, spill it girlfriend." Melina shook her head as she ran her fingers through Ashley's hair.

"I don't believe I'm telling you this," she mumbled. "After we kissed, I could feel 'it' get hard against me."

"What do you mean, 'it? Just say it: his penis . . . his cock . . . his dick . . . his third leg?!" teased Ashley. Melina blushed profusely.

"I could feel it from here, to here," she said as she placed one hand against her lower abdomen and the other just below her breasts.

"OUCH! Damn girl, you're going to need another surgery after he sticks you with that!" exclaimed Ashley. "Well, if **his** is that big, it only stands to reason, that his brother's is too!" Melina sighed, then laid back onto the bed, as the two ladies pondered the thought.

"Hey, I just thought about something," remarked Ashley. "You got further on your first date than I did, you slut!" she teased.

"Yeah and I can still feel it pressing against my spine!" laughed Melina.

"Oh, now I get it!" shouted Ashley, as she quickly sat up. "**That's** why you were so red and tender down there! Your poor little coochie had an orgasm, didn't it?! I thought you had a strange look on your face when we walked over to the gazebo! You are so lucky I didn't figure that out before I gave you that medicine, or I would have let you suffer, you little slut!" scolded Ashley.

Ashley laid down facing Melina.

"Thanks for staying with me," she whispered. "I never would have gotten through this without you," admitted Melina. They smiled sleepily at one another. Melina rolled over as Ashley snuggled up behind her, placing her arm across Melina's shoulder.

"This is really nice," whispered Ashley, "but I'm sleeping with James tomorrow!" she joked.

"**Now** who's the slut?" whispered Melina, giggling, as they eventually, drifted off to sleep.

Chapter 17
Mending Melina: Restoring Her Soul

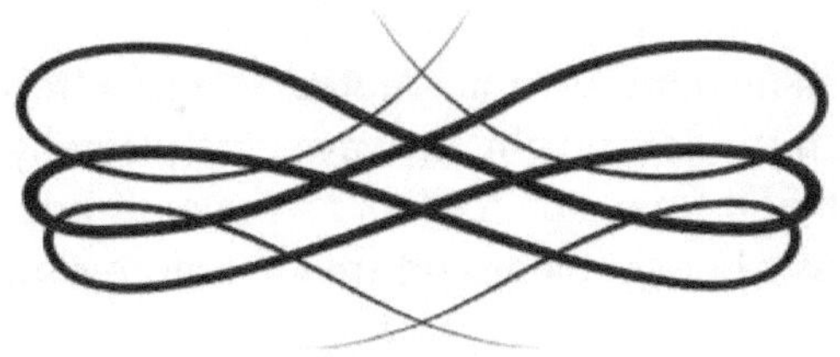

"Everyone out of the house?" asked Nate. "Yeah, the staff is just about finished out back as well," yawned James. "Good. I'll check around before activating the security system, while you take care of the perimeter."

"What do you think Melina's up to right now?" inquired James.

"I don't even want to think about it," responded Nate, as he shook his head while rubbing his temples. "By the way, thanks for not ruining the moment a second time."

"You can thank Ashley for that. I wanted to."

"The fireworks were a nice touch," said Nate.

"You know, I really do like her, Nate."

"I think she likes you to. I hope it works out."

"Back at you bro."

"Man, it's been a long day. See you in the morning," said Nate, completely exhausted. Love between these two was complex, as it usually is with most siblings. One minute, they're friends; the next minute, they're enemies. One day, they're close; the next, they can't stand to be in the same room with one another. They play together; then they fight with one another. However, through it all, they stay close at heart because that's what brothers do.

"Wow, that was quite a kiss!" whispered Monica.

"That's for showing me such a good time," answered Kenneth. "Good night," replied Monica, as she walked towards her room. "Where do you think **you're** going?!" she asked, as Ken approached her from behind. "**Your room** is that way."

"But . . ."

"Speaking of butts," interrupted Monica, "You can look, but you can't touch . . . not tonight anyway." She playfully stuck out her ass and switched it from side to side, as she entered her room. She looked back over her shoulder and smiled before slowly closing the door.

Kenneth groaned while giving her the saddest look he could muster, as she slowly and gently closed the door. He lowered his head, tapping his forehead against it. "Go to bed, Doctor Marshall, you have a long day ahead of you. I'm naked and I'm about to get in the shower. Now be a good boy and just go to bed."

"Aw damn!" groaned Kenneth. Monica laughed as she listened through the door. "I want you so-o-o bad," he admitted.

"I know you do." she responded. "The feeling is mutual."

"Damn, she locked it!" cursed Ken, as he tried the handle. "I just wanted a little peek," he whispered.

"Another time. I promise." Ken slowly turned, walked into his room, then plopped onto the bed. He tried to imagine Monica naked and, in the shower, as he dozed off.

"Wake up sleepy-head," whispered Monica, into Ken's ear.

"What time is it?" he asked as he yawned and stretched. Still annoyed by her rejection a few short hours ago, Ken decided to get even. He jumped out of bed and walked slowly past Monica towards the bathroom. Monica's eyes nearly popped out of her head as she glared at his naked body. She was speechless as she watched his "stuff" swing freely, as he passed by. "That's just the expression I was hoping for! You can look, but you can't touch!" he teased, as he wiggled his finger at her. "Does that sound familiar?!"

"Now **that** was just mean," said Monica, waving her hand in front of her face as though she was having a hot flash. She sat and watched as he showered. It took every ounce of willpower she had not to get up and join him.

"Where are my clothes?" he asked as he re-entered the room, wrapping the towel around his waist.

"They're in the Multi-Task Cleaner, on the "dry clean" cycle. They should be ready in a few minutes. In the meantime, have some-thing to eat." He smiled as she pointed to the glass top table out on the balcony.

"Aren't you going to join me?"

"No, I can't. I need to get your clothes ready. Besides, I'm starting to regret the decision I made last night. I'll be right back." She giggled as she stood up, kissed him, and then waltzed out of the room.

The warm gentle breeze caressed their bodies as they slept.

Ashley moaned slightly, as she began to awaken from her slumber.

She smiled when she noticed that the two of them were still snuggled together. She gently kissed the back of Melina's neck. Feel-ing frisky, Ashley decided to take advantage of Melina while she slept. She gently began to caress Melina's firm breasts. They felt so good through the silk top. Melina moaned, and her nipples began to harden as she awakened. However, she didn't let Ashley know it.

Ashley began softly squeezing Melina's nipples. Something about her made Ashley want to experiment with a woman. Sud-denly, Melina reached back and slapped Ashley on her tender white ass. "Ow, that hurt!" laughed Ashley.

"That's what you get for waking me up! Now play with your own titties!" laughed Melina.

"I do, all the time!" admitted Ashley. After a quick trip to the bathroom, both women headed downstairs in search of breakfast.

"Good morning you two. How'd you sleep?" asked Monica.

"Just fine." "Heavenly." replied both women.

"You still here Dr. Marshall?" teased Ashley.

"Um-um . . ." Dr. Marshall cleared his throat, smiled, and then muttered, "I was just about to leave." Ashley chuckled, aware of the awkward position her boss was in.

"Where are the others?" inquired Melina.

"Well let's see. Ashley, **your** man is in the fields and your man is making his daily delivery to the club," answered Monica, as she pointed to each woman. "Oh, and my man is heading out to work, so excuse me!"

Monica walked Dr. Marshall to the rear exit, then out to the doublewide drive-way which surrounded the entire mansion. After a passionate kiss, she watched as he got into the car and slowly drove away, before re-entering the house.

"Well, I'm off today, and now that we are all without men. What do we do until they return?" asked Ashley.

"Sorry, but you two are on your own for a while. I have finances to review and bills to pay. Why don't the two of you relax out by the pool for a while? Maybe we can go shopping later. I need to stock up on groceries and I'm sure you both will be needing a few more things to get settled in. As much as I would love to hang out, I must get to work. Just make yourselves at home." The women enjoyed the rest of their continental breakfast as they reminisced about the previous night.

"What do you say, want to clean up this mess, then head out to the pool?" asked Ashley.

"I really would like to see the rest of the house, but I guess I can wait until Nate returns."

"Come on, let's lay out for an hour or two. I could use some sun." "Why not," conceded Melina. Monica approached the women just as they were about to board the elevator. "I'm glad I caught you. I have your new keys." Monica handed each woman a platinum bracelet.

"This is a new type of key, much better than carrying around a card. James wants you to try them out. They are encoded with a computer chip that gives you access to sixty percent of the property. It works the same way as the card. Just hold it up against the sensor. The key slots will soon be obsolete and are in the process of being removed. Green light you're in . . . red you're not. You never have to take them off. They are completely shock- and water-proof. You are the first to use these, so let us know how you like them. Ours are still being programed. See ya!"

"Damn, these are nice! I may never leave this place!" stated Ashley.

"This is one heck of an expensive house key!" noted Melina.

Both ladies went up to their floor, changed into their swim wear, then headed out towards the pool. It was already eighty degrees outside and it was only nine-thirty. Since there was no one around, both ladies opted to wear thong bikinis. The water was warm and felt fantastic as the women dove in for a quick dip. They took turns putting lotion on each other's backs, as they prepared to lay out.

"Just . . . my . . . back!" scolded Melina, as she felt Ashley venture down and across her plump, soft, golden ass. "Are you sure you've never slept with a woman? Because you sure are working **me** over!"

"There's just something about you that turns me on, that's all." Melina chuckled as she closed her eyes and just let Ashley indulge herself. Besides, that little massage was really on the money!

Chapter 18
Melina's Torment: Facing Her Demons

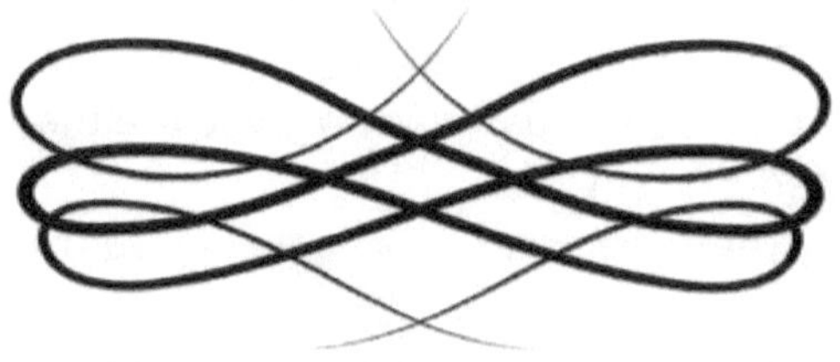

"Ready up there?" asked the voice over the intercom system. "We'll be right down," answered Melina.,

"I could use a nap. The sun really wiped me out!" said Ashley. "Well, you should have used that time at the pool to sleep instead of trying to get in my panties," scolded Melina. "I really hope that you have sex with James soon, so you can leave me the heck alone!"

"Well, after what you told me about Nate, I'm a little apprehensive about making **that** move!"

"Yeah right! You can't wait to ride that . . . well you know." responded Melina.

"You are such a baby! Just say it! Ride that dick!"

"**You** are so nasty!" scolded Melina.

"You're just mad because you have to wait another six to eight weeks to get some," teased Ashley. The two women laughed as they headed towards the elevator and down to the first floor.

"What do you feel like riding in?" asked Monica as she

opened the door to the garage.

"Wow!" Both ladies were amazed as they checked out the collection of vehicles.

"How about that Caddy Coupe over there?" suggested Ashley. "Nice choice. I don't think Nate has even driven that one yet. He just got it in a week ago."

"He's not going to be angry, is he?" asked Melina.

"He said, and I quote, 'Take your pick.' Besides, just look at us. We deserve no less!" Monica was right. All three women were wearing short sun dresses and they looked fantastic. The Cadillac was a perfect compliment.

"I get the front seat on the way back," said Ashley as she climbed into the back.

As they drove out of the garage, Ashley glanced at Melina. She could see a faint glow on her face that was not there before. She smiled, understanding that her new-found friend was beginning to get over being molested just a few short weeks ago. She still had a long way to go, but she was headed in the right direction. The real test would be how she would react to Nate's advances. Well, one step at a time I guess. However, in Melina's case, its baby steps.

The lot was half full as they pulled in at the marketplace. Monica decided to park catty-cornered, half way back, taking up two spaces. As the ladies got out, and began to walk across the lot, they got just about every man's attention. A group of women gave them nasty looks as they entered the store. One woman even slapped her husband as he accidentally ran into her with the shopping cart. The women giggled at the way the men, and some of the women, were reacting to their arrival. It's just the reaction they were going for. They knew the dresses were a bit sheer and that you could see the outline of their bodies through them.

"We'll each take a cart. I'll get what we need for the house and you two just get whatever you like. Drive 'em crazy girls! Monica suggested. They all chuckled, then set off in different directions.

Melina hummed as she headed towards the fruits and vegetables section. She was as happy as could be. After all, this was the first time in her life she had ever been in a super market, let alone able to shop for herself. There were so many things she wanted to try! She smiled as she came across the display featuring "Brande Mangoes". They were much more expensive than the others were, so she decided to see if she could smell the difference. "U-m-m," she moaned. There was no comparison! Nathan's were, by far, the better-quality fruit, and worth every penny. (And no, she didn't come to that conclusion just because liked him.) She continued along the section, picking up an assortment of fruits and a few vegetables.

Satisfied with her selections, Melina decided to head down the next aisle. She smiled as the men went out of their way to speak. Her new-found confidence was slowing beginning to show.

Melina's heart pounded as she stopped abruptly. Her face turned pale as she looked into his eyes! She was terrified, and her body began to tremble!

"Melina, is that you?! Damn girl, I almost didn't recognize you! We were wondering when you were going to turn up!" exclaimed Junior. "Hey, dad, look who's here!" Melina could not move. She was petrified!

"You sure have been a hard one to track down, little lady!" sounded a familiar voice coming from the direction of the Manager's Office. Tears ran down her cheeks. She could not control herself as urine trickled down her legs.

"Now you don't have to be afraid of us, does she daddy!" chuckled Junior. The men stood alongside of her as they ushered her down the aisle a bit.

"Do you know what kind of trouble we're in?!" mumbled Ray. "The Sheriff has been all over us! You had better drop those charges before something bad happens to you! Do you hear me girl?! Get where I'm coming from?! Get that Sheriff off our backs, or else!" Melina stood between the two men trembling. She tried to scream for help, but nothing came out. "I know you're staying at the Brande Place. Don't make me do something you'll regret!" As other patrons entered the aisle, the men quickly walked away.

Ray knew there was nothing more he could do at the time. "That's it?!" complained Junior. "You're just going to let her walk away?!"

"What do you propose I do, drag her out kicking and screaming and take her with us? I'm sure your mother would enjoy hearing her story about what we did, not to mention the commotion we would cause in here. Just take it easy. Did you see how scared she was?! She pissed herself when she saw us!" chuckled Ray. "Don't worry. She'll do what's best!"

"I hope you're right, or we'll be spending the next twenty-five years getting raped ourselves!" The thought of what his son said, wiped the smirk right off Ray's face.

"Come on, let's get out of here!" he grumbled.

Melina collapsed to the floor in tears. She was so terrified, she could hardly move! The store manager came running over, after being notified by several patrons of a hysterical woman in one of the aisles. Word spread quickly around the store, and it wasn't long before Monica and Ashley, who were only three aisles over, heard about the incident. They decided to locate Melina to make sure that it wasn't her. They turned, then looked down the aisle to see Melina on the floor in tears.

"Oh my God, Mel. What happened?!" exclaimed Ashley, as she and Monica ran over to assist their friend.

"They were here! The two men who raped me were here!" she sobbed. "They threatened me to drop the charges, then they just left me here! I tried to scream! I really tried!" The two women helped Melina up off the floor, then tried to calm her down.

"I'm calling the Sheriff!" exclaimed Monica. "Is there somewhere we can wait?" The manager escorted the women to his office. "Cleanup in aisle four!" announced a voice over the store's intercom system.

"Hey Nate. Where are you? Oh my God! Melina was just face to face with the men who raped her! We're at the market on 5th, waiting in the Manager's Office. The Sheriff is already on his way! Okay, see you soon. Nate's just a few miles away. He will be here shortly." Still in shock, Melina just sat there quivering, while staring nervously at the door to the office.

"Melina, why did they just walk away? They know that you will be able to give the Sheriff a description." Melina knew there would be no turning back. She had to come clean with everyone. Even though she hated her mother for what she did, she still didn't want to see her go to jail.

"I know them," Melina mumbled.

"What?!" replied Monica.

"What did you say?!" Ashley responded.

"I will explain everything when Nate gets here." Monica and Ashley just stood there stunned. Melina buried her face in her hands, as she wept uncontrollably.

"**What the hell?!**" was the only response Ray could give, as he and Junior entered the house to find it in complete disarray.

"Where's mom?!" shouted Junior. "She could be hurt!" The two men searched the house frantically, fearful that someone may have broken in.

"She's not here!" Ray concluded. He entered the bedroom to find the closet and dresser drawers open and empty. "Junior, all of your mother's things are gone: her clothes, jewelry, books, computer, everything!" Ray stood in the middle of the room dumbfounded.

"Dad, what's going on?"

"How the heck should I know! I've been out making deliveries with you all day!" Ray decided to call her as they headed back downstairs. Junior stated, "Look dad, don't bother. She left her phone here on the coffee table."

"We had better have a talk with Valencia. Maybe she knows something!" suggested Ray.

The two men hurried down the path. Ray didn't bother knocking on the door. He just barged right in.

"Valencia!" he shouted.

"Ray, what the hell?!" she responded, as she exited the bathroom, wrapping a towel around her naked body.

"Where the hell is my wife?!"

"She told me she was taking a vacation and that I would not be needed for a couple of weeks."

"Taking a vacation?! What vacation?!" demanded Ray.

"How should I know, she's **your** wife!"

"Dad, I've got a bad feeling about this! Something tells me we should take a vacation too!"

"What's he talking about Ray?!"

"We were out making deliveries when we ran into Melina at one of the local markets. We told her to drop the charges, then left her there on the floor crying! When we came home, it looked as though we 'd been robbed!"

The room became filled with nervous tension. "Junior, you may be right. We **should** all take a little trip," said Richard. "Go pack a few things. We'll stay at the cabin for a couple of weeks."

"But Dad, what about the farm and all of the workers?"

"I'll let them know we'll be away on a family emergency or something and pay them in advance for the harvesting. I'll put Pete in charge of deliveries until we get back." Valencia just stood there in a daze as the men ran out the door.

"Wait. What about me?!" she stammered.

Chapter 19
The Truth Revealed

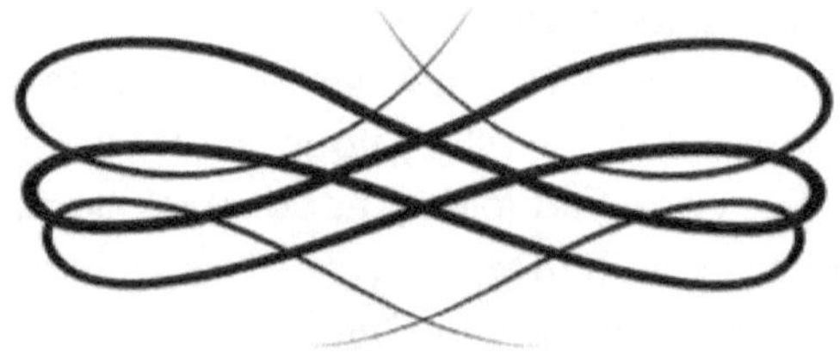

"Wait here. I'll only be a minute." Mrs. Sullivan got out of the cab, then hurried into the Sheriff's Department.

"How may I help you?" inquired the Desk Sergeant, sitting behind the glass.

"I'm here to see Sheriff Melbourne."

"I'm sorry ma'am, but you just missed him."

"That's alright. I'll just leave this here with you." She handed him a sealed envelope and a box. The Sergeant briefly checked the contents. "Please see that he gets this the moment he arrives. It's very important."

"Yes ma'am. I'll call over the radio to let him know to pick it up, just in case I'm off duty before he returns."

"Thank you, Sergeant. You have a nice day."

"Bye ma'am." Mrs. Sullivan smiled briefly, then turned and walked out of the precinct.

She relaxed as the cab continued on its way to the airport. "There's no turning back now," she thought as she took a deep breath, then exhaled. Upon arrival, she sat patiently while the driver unloaded her Gucci Luggage. Tears began to stream down her cheeks as she thought about her son. He was so young, only twenty-two years old. Junior admired his father so much, he would do anything he asked. She hoped that with all the arrangements she had made, he would be with her soon enough. "All set ma'am?" asked the driver.

"I should have done this a long time ago," she answered, smiling, as she got out of the cab. She then slowly entered the airport lobby.

"Melina, are you okay?!" asked Nate as he rushed into the office. Ashley was on the phone with James when he entered.

"Nate just arrived, so I'll talk to you later, okay? Bye."

"I'm so sorry. I should have told you the truth weeks ago!"

"Told me the truth about what?! What are you talking about?!" "Calm down Nate. She knows the men who raped her."

"WHAT?!" he shouted. Sheriff Melbourne walked in just as Nate was about to question Melina in detail about her last statement. "What's all the shoutin' about?" he asked, as he entered the office.

"I know who raped me, Sheriff," mumbled Melina. "It was Mr. Sullivan and his son, with the help of my mother." Melina closed her eyes as she prepared to go back in time, back to the day that would haunt her, and yet change her life forever. With their mouths gaped open, everyone listened as Melina gave a detailed account of the attack.

"It was around four-thirty in the afternoon, right after we had finished working. Thursday, June 19th, was my twenty-first birthday. Mrs. Sullivan had left the house and gone into town about a half hour before the attack. My mother and I had just finished the guest room when we heard singing coming from down the hall. . . Happy birthday to you, happy birthday to you . . ." Melina's voice cracked as she sang the all too familiar lyrics. She fought back the tears, cleared her throat, then paused a few seconds before continuing.

"Mr. Sullivan and Junior entered the room carrying a huge cake draped with twenty-one candles. You should have seen my face. I was so happy!" she chuckled, as the tears ran freely down her cheeks. Nate picked up a box of tissues from the desk and offered them to her. She dried her eyes, then continued. "Junior placed the cake on a table in the corner of the room, then said, 'Make a wish!' My mother just stood there with this strange look on her face. When she saw me glancing over at her, she tried to smile, but I knew something wasn't quite right."

"I walked over to the table, closed my eyes, made a wish, and then blew out the candles. My mother asked what I had wished for. 'If I tell you, it won't come true!' I happily answered. "I recalled the nervous tone in my mother's voice when she spoke. Then I heard Mr. Sullivan say, 'I'll bet you didn't wish for this!' Melina chuckled as she said, "I thought he was offering me a birthday present! I even remember smiling as I turned around! I was utterly shocked to see them both standing there with their pants down! Embarrassed, I turned my head, then asked what they were doing."

"My own mother walked over, grabbed me by the arm and began pulling me towards the bed! When I began to struggle, she told me to calm down and just co-operate, that it would be the best thing for all of us. Can you believe that! My own mother! When he saw that my mother couldn't control me, Mr. Sullivan crept over, grabbed me from behind, picked me up and carried me over to the bed. I was crying and pleading for him to stop, and not to do what I feared was about to happen! Then I heard Junior say, "Dad, maybe we shouldn't . . ." His father told him to shut up and get my panties off. I pleaded with Junior, but his father had such a strong influence over him. I was kicking so much, Junior couldn't get near me! My mother stood in the corner as they struggled to get control of me."

"Finally, Mr. Sullivan just fell onto the bed with me, using his weight to hold me down. I could feel his 'thing' getting hard against my butt! He called to my mother, ordering her to help hold me down. She hesitated at first, but then he yelled at her to move her ass or 'the deal was off.''

"What deal?" interrupted the Sheriff.

"Hold on, let her finish!" demanded Nate. Melina looked at Nate for the first time since starting her horrific tale. Even though there were tears in his eyes, his face was filled with hatred and rage. All he could manage to say was "Go on Melina," before getting all choked up. Melina could feel every bit of his pain and anger, as she paused briefly before continuing.

"My mother walked over to the opposite side of the bed, then grabbed me by my wrists. After a short time, she managed to pull both my arms up over my head. Mr. Sullivan sat up and put all of his weight on my back. I remember him shouting, 'Junior, get your ass over her and grab her legs!' Now, with Mr. Sullivan on my back, I could hardly breathe and was completely helpless. Junior pulled on my legs until I was only lying on the bed from my waist up. I tried pleading with my mother, but she just frowned, closed her eyes then turned her head. Mr. Sullivan barked, 'Son, if you can't get her panties down, then rip 'em off!' I screamed as the material tore into my flesh! My mother told me to just relax and let it happen and that it would be over quickly. Junior raped me first. I screamed as he forced his way inside of me. He tried to be gentle about it, but when he couldn't get penetration, he just shoved it in! The pain was excruciating!"

"After a few moments, Junior shouted 'Damn, daddy, she's bleeding all over the place!' But Mr. Sullivan ordered him to just keep going! He said that it was normal because I was a virgin. Even with all that blood, Junior just kept going and going! My insides were on fire, and I was filled with pain as he continued to violate me! Finally, he was finished. He made three or four short hard jabs inside of me. I was in so much pain, all I could do was lay there while Mr. Sullivan climbed down off my back, anxious to take his turn. By that time, I was starting to go numb from the waist down and could barely feel a thing as he pounded away at my insides. Since I had little or no fight left, he told Junior to take another turn. By then, I was nearly unconscious from all of the pain."

"Just before he entered me again, Junior whispered, 'I'm so sorry for this,' into my ear. This time, it took him and his dad a lot longer to finish. Finally, my mother, who was kneeling on the floor, let go of my arms. I just laid there waiting to get some feeling back in my legs. After they left the room, I managed to push myself off the bed and onto the floor. I almost passed out from all of the pain, and there was so much blood on the side of the bed, I thought I would throw up! I noticed the condoms they had used discarded on the floor. I put them in a small plastic bag and planned on taking them to the police. After confronting my mother, I grabbed my sweater and stumbled out of the house. I was so afraid they would catch me, I hid the bag in the shrubs back at your house, after an old man offered me a ride. The next thing I knew, I was in the hospital."

The office was completely silent, as Melina slowly opened her eyes. With the exception of the Sheriff, everyone was wiping his or her tears. Ashley knelt down and hugged Melina tightly. "It's okay. It's all over now. You did good baby," she whispered.

"I'm going to need you to come in and give a written statement," said the Sheriff, as he reached for the phone. "I'm going to need a couple of patrol cars dispatched to meet me at the Sullivan Estate. I'm arresting Richard Sullivan, Richard Sullivan, Jr., and a Miss Valencia Delgado for the rape of Melina Delgado." The Sheriff covered the phone while he awaited a response as to who would be dispatched.

"You sure could have saved me a lot of trouble if you had told me this from the very beginning," complained the sheriff.

"Even though I hated my mother for what she had done, I didn't want to see her go to prison."

"Why the sudden change of heart then?" inquired the Sheriff. "When I saw them here, I was terrified! I knew that I would never be safe once he told me that he knew where I was staying. And I didn't what to bring trouble or harm to anyone else."

Monica took Melina by the hands and assisted her in getting to her feet. The three women embraced while Nate struggled with his emotions. The raspy voice returned on the other end of the phone.

"Sheriff, I'm sorry, but I forgot to mention, a Mrs. Sullivan left a sealed envelope and box here for you. She said it was important you got it, as soon as you got back."

"Give it to Johnson and tell him to lock it in my desk. And have Reilly bring a female officer with him. I'm on route."

"Yes Sir!"

"Oh, one more thing Ms. Delgado, what was all that business about 'the deal being off?'"

"In exchange for my virginity, my mother was given the deed to the house behind the mansion. I tore it up and threw it in her face."

"Head over to the station and complete the statement. I'll see you soon."

"Sheriff, can't she go home and get cleaned up first?!"

"Okay fine. Just get her there before five. I need that statement on file today!" demanded the Sheriff, as he quickly rushed out of the office.

"Do you mind if I ride with Nate?" asked Melina.

"We'll see you back at the house," acknowledged Monica. Most of the ride was completed in silence. Melina sat there petrified, as Nate sped home.

"Please slow down, you're scaring me!" she begged. His face was filled with rage, as he replayed her story over and over in his mind.

Nate glanced at the speedometer to find he was doing over ninety miles per hour. He eased his foot off the gas and slowed to around seventy-five. "Talk to me Nate. What are you feeling?"

"Fine, I'll tell you what I'm feeling. If I ever see those bastards I'll . . ."

"Don't say that Nate!" interrupted Melina. "I can't lose you too! If I do, I'll just die!"

"I'm sorry. I just keep thinking about what you said. I can almost picture what you went through. They need to pay for what they did to you!" Melina placed her hand on Nate's leg, as he began to speed up again.

"Just think of it this way. If it had never happened, we wouldn't have met." She smiled as he placed his hand upon the one she had on his thigh. He squeezed it firmly, as he began to calm down. Nate's rage began to subside as he glanced over at her. There was no denying she had captured his heart. Nathan was completely in love with Melina.

James was waiting outside of the garage as the car arrived. He assisted Melina in getting out. "Thank you," she whispered. Embarrassed, she hurried to the elevator to go change clothes. "I'll be right back," she said as she scurried away. Nate grabbed the Armor All and a cloth, to clean the passenger seat of the Corvette.

"Everything okay?" asked James.

"It will be, as soon as they arrest those bastards!" Monica and Ashley slowly pulled into the garage shortly thereafter. James walked over to greet Ashley as she got out of the car.

Chapter 20
A Woman Scorned

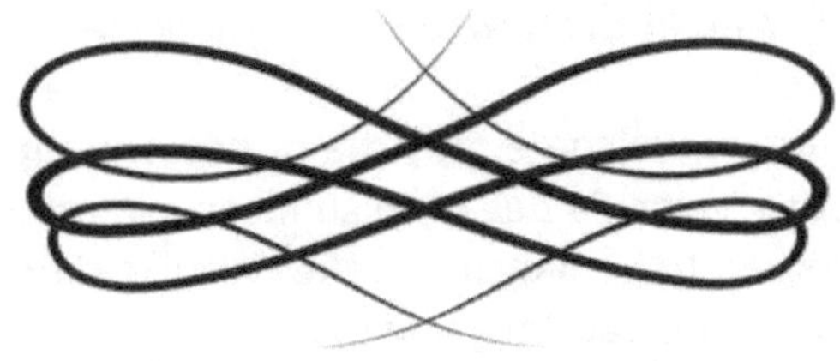

Valencia stood in the driveway as the men quickly loaded the SUV.

"What about me Ray. What am I supposed to do?"

"I suggest you get as far away from here as possible!"

"But this is my home. It's all I know!"

"Then you'd better enjoy it while you can! The Sheriff's probably on his way here, right now! And don't even think you're coming with us! You had better come up with something, because we are so out of here!" He and Junior climbed into the SUV as Valencia wept.

"Ray, please don't leave me here!" she begged.

"Here, take the pick-up!" said Richard, as he tossed her the keys. "But you know I can't drive!"

"Well, for your sake, I hope you're a fast learner!" With that being said, Richard stepped on the gas. Valencia choked from the cloud of dust, as they sped away. Valencia slowly climbed into the truck. All she could do was sit there and cry. She began to reminisce about all the good times she had spent with her daughter as she was growing up.

Flashback eighteen years ago: "Read me the story about Cinderella again, please mommy!" asked three-year-old Melina. It was her favorite bedtime story.

"Once upon a time . . ."

"Hi mommy, how was your day?" asked five-year-old Melina, as she ran and jumped into her mother's arms.

"I'm so glad you're home. I missed you so much!"

"Thank you for the new dress, Mommy! Doesn't it make me look like Cinderella?!"

"You are so welcome my little princess. Happy tenth birthday! I love you!" Valencia began to smile as she remembered how they would pretend to be dancing at the ball, like Cinderella.

"Mother, one day I'm going to take you away from here, and you will never have to work again!" promised sixteen-year-old Melina, as she and Valencia walked up the path to the main house. It was Melina's first day working at the mansion.

The roar of a jet flying overhead snapped Valencia out of her flashback. She got out of the truck, ran into the house, then into the kitchen and over to the sink. She got down on her knees, opened the cabinet door and quickly removed the cleaning products stored underneath. She then removed the bottom panel and took out a small metal container. She opened it, took out the taped-up deed to her home, then dumped all of the money they had managed to save over the years into her handbag, which was a Christmas gift from Mrs. Sullivan a few years ago.

Along with some food, clothing and bedding, she quickly placed everything into several plastic trash bags. After a quick look around, she took them out to the truck. She could drive a little but did not have a license. Richard would sometimes let her drive his old pick- up around the fields to collect the produce ready for delivery, from the farmers. "Just one last thing before I go." She removed a pen and a piece of paper from her purse, then quickly wrote a note. Hoping someone would find it, and someday give it to her daughter, she ran back into the house, placed it on the coffee table, then left.

"What am I going to do?! Where am I going to go?!" she pondered, as she started the truck. She thought about what Richard had said about the Sheriff, then decided to get moving. "Maybe I'll hide out in the fields for a day or two until I can figure things out. The sheriff probably won't check out there," she thought. "I should be safe until the early morning hours." She maneuvered the truck through the narrow paths between the trees. After parking, she got out and began to walk around while trying to gather her thoughts.

"I know it's around here somewhere. Here it is!"

She recalled the old tool shack some of the workers would take breaks in from time to time. She opened the door, paused a moment to look around, then slowly walked in. Inside were a couple of chairs at a card table, assorted tools, and some fishing rods. An old twin size mattress they would use to take naps on was propped up in the corner.

Valencia cringed in disapproval as she noticed some familiar stains splattered about its surface. "Men are so disgusting!" she mumbled, as she carefully turned the mattress around. "At least this side looks clean." She grabbed an old broom, swept down the mattress, then laid it on the floor. "This will have to do for tonight," she thought.

She went back to the truck, grabbed the keys and all her belongings, then returned to the shack. After placing a sheet over the mattress, she laid down. She thought of her daughter and the terrible thing she did to her. She cried herself to sleep, wishing she had done things differently. "I'm so sorry, my little Princess!"

Sheriff Melbourne and his back-up arrived at the Sullivan Estate within minutes. After knocking several times and getting no response, he decided to try the door. "Damn it!" cursed the Sheriff, as he found it to be unlocked. Upon entering, he called out, "This is the Sheriff's Department. Is anyone here?!" An eerie silence echoed what he had already known; he was too late, they were gone. "Look around. See if you can find a clue as to where they may be headed." The two deputies, that had gone to arrest Valencia, arrived at the main house. "The place was empty," announced one of the deputies. "Shit! Let's get going!" stated Melbourne, as he reached for his radio.

"Put out an APB on Richard Sullivan, Richard Sullivan, Jr., and Valencia Delgado!" As he walked out the door, he gave a detailed description of the suspects from a photo he picked up off the mantle.

"Sir, here's a photo of Valencia and her daughter, and this letter was also on the table," said the deputy. It simply read, "To anyone reading this, please see that my daughter, Melina, receives it. I can never express the sadness I feel for the part I played in what happened to you. How could I do such a vile thing to my own daughter? I can only hope and pray for your forgiveness. I pray that one day I can find a way to make it all up to you somehow. I love you 'My Little Princess.'" signed Valencia.

"No Melina! Don't. I'm sorry!" shouted Valencia, as she raised her arm to shield her face from the ax her daughter was wielding. She prayed for forgiveness as it came crashing down into her scull! Valencia quickly sat up on the mattress. "Oh shit!" she sighed. "It was only a nightmare!" She sat there motionless, wiping the sweat from her brow, while feeling about her head. The sound of nearby voices caught her attention. She peeked through a crack in the wood of the old shack, to see a couple of farmers hanging around the deserted pickup truck. Quickly, but quietly, she removed the sheets from the mattress, and stuffed them back into the bag.

She grabbed the bags, picked up the mattress, then hid behind it in the corner. She could vaguely make out what they were saying. It was something about the truck. They were wondering why it was in the fields. One of the men thought, since it was rather old, it must have stalled, and Mr. Sullivan decided to leave it there. The men conversed, laughing, as they entered the shack. Valencia's heart pounded as she tried not to breathe. They noisily moved about the shack, knocking over some of the tools. After a couple of minutes, the men walked out carrying the fishing poles and a tackle box.

Valencia took a deep breath, then exhaled as she listened to the voices slowly fade away. She eased out from behind the mattress and placed the bags on the table. "That was **too** close," she sighed.

"I can't stay here. I'll definitely get caught! I'll have to leave when it gets dark. She sat at the table to ponder her situation. She went into her purse, removed several bundles of money, and began counting. "I was saving this for Melina's future, but right now, I need it more than she does. Twenty-four-thousand-seven-hundred dollars. Not much of a life savings, but it **will** hold me over for a while. All in hundred-dollar bills. It was smart of me to ask to be paid this way. Easy to conceal, easy to carry. F--ing Richard! He could have taken me with him! After all I've done for him. All the secrets I've kept. I deserve better than hiding out in this dusty old shack!"

She gathered her things together, got in the truck and drove slowly towards the back end of the fields. She was aware of the old service roads behind the property and hoped that the Sheriff would not be waiting for her. Valencia had no idea where she was going to go. She cursed the fact that she had spent most of her life on the estate, without venturing off to learn her way around while she had the weekends off. It wasn't like she was actually a prisoner there. She could have had her license and lived life differently. Instead, she became content with staying in servant's quarters, pleasing Richard, and raising Melina. When she reached the road, she let out a sigh of relief to find that the Sheriff was nowhere in sight.

The service road went on for about three miles. It was

mainly used by over-sized trucks and tractors. When she reached the main highway, Valencia decided to drive over to the next small town to find a cheap motel. With the money she had, she could stay there for quite some time. But she needed to get rid of Richard's truck. She needed to find a place within walking distance of a shopping center, so she stopped for gas and asked the attendant if he knew of a place.

As directed, she drove two miles west. There was the shopping center, just as the gas station attendant had described. She made a right at the light, then drove about two miles down the road. Valencia smiled as she drove up to the remote motel, which sat back off the road. The place looked a bit rundown, but it was just what she was looking for. Just across the road were several stores and a Laundromat. "Perfect," she mumbled, as she parked near the office of the motel. "I can hide the truck around back. You can't see it from the road parked back there, so it will never be spotted."

"Hello, may I help you?" inquired a soft voice from a room behind the front desk. An elderly woman, using a walker, slowly inched out to greet Valencia. They exchanged pleasantries while she paid for the first month in advance. "You'll be staying in number ten. Just as you requested, the room's 'round back." As she walked out of the office, Valencia took a deep breath and looked around. "It's not exactly home, but it'll do for now," she thought. She got into the truck, then drove it around back.

As she opened the door, the smell of mildew got her attention. "I suppose no one has stayed in here for quite some time." She switched on the air conditioning to alleviate some of the odor. She turned on the television, then began stripping the bed. "I may as well go do some laundry. I need some food and cleaning supplies anyway." She wet one of the wash cloths to wipe off the table. She removed the items from one of the bags and placed them on the dampened surface.

After placing all of the linen inside the empty bag, Valencia removed two one-hundred dollar bills from her purse, then locked the rest of her money in the safe. She left her room, then headed across the street. Valencia froze in her tracks, as she noticed a State Trooper driving through the lot of the small grocery store. She quickly entered the Laundromat, hoping that she wasn't spotted. Valencia sighed in relief, as the car continued on its way. "If this is any indication as to how my life is going to be, I'm in a lot of trouble!" whispered Valencia. The only downside to having all of these hundred-dollar bills is needing change. Valencia stuffed her things into the washers, then headed over to the mini-mart.

The Sheriff returned to the Station in a very foul mood. He was pissed that every one of his suspects had flown the coop just before he arrived. Even though he had left Johnson on stakeout, he knew that the odds of anyone returning were a long shot. His gut told him that they were all long gone. "I may as well take a look at the stuff Mrs. Sullivan left." He opened the box to find an assortment of DVD's, all dated by month. With the exception of the first disk, they were all in order by year, and there was at least five years' worth.

He placed the disk from September into his desktop computer. After five or ten minutes, he decided to press fast forward, as there was relatively nothing of interest on the beginning of the disk, just cameras skipping from room to room, showing the Delgado's as they went about their cleaning. "I guess she didn't really trust them," he thought. "Maybe someone was stealing . . . What the hell?!" He quickly played back the previous few minutes. "Well I'll be damned! It wasn't the maids she was spying on. It was her own husband!" deduced the Sheriff, as he watched Mr. Sullivan screwing the crap out of Ms. Delgado!

His eyes widened as he watched Junior later enter the room and take his turn with Valencia. "Why those dirty little sons-a-bitches. Screwing the help! No wonder Mrs. Sullivan left! I would have shot that bastard in the ass on the down stroke! It had to break her heart watching her husband, **and** her son, both screwing that slut. I really don't need to see this," he thought, so he switched the disk, replacing it with the first one in the box, which was not dated. "Holy Shit!" he shouted as he pressed play. He watched anxiously as the Sullivan boys entered the guest room with a birthday cake. "Is this what I think it is?!"

The Sheriff recalled the cake scene from the story Melina had told him about earlier that day. "Hell yeah! Your ass is mine!" he shouted as he slammed both hands on his desk. "Now I got you all dead to rights!" Mrs. Sullivan had provided the Sheriff with all the evidence he needed. He was in sole possession of the complete rape video, from start to finish! "All I need to do now is find your perverted asses! THANK YOU, MRS. SULLIVAN!" exclaimed the Sheriff as he gently kissed the disk. "I'll look at the rest of this stuff later." He copied it, then placed the original disk in an evidence bag and labeled it before having it taken to the precinct's Evidence Room.

"I had better give the Brandes a call."

"Hello? Oh, hi Sheriff."

"Listen Mr. Brande, there's no need for Ms. Delgado to rush over. She can come in tomorrow to give her statement."

"Thanks Sheriff. She'll appreciate that. Have you made any arrests yet?"

"When we got there, everyone was gone. I believe they're on the run, but don't worry, we'll catch up to them. Count on it!"

"Damn it! I hope Melina doesn't freak out! Alright, Sheriff, see you tomorrow."

Melina had showered, changed clothes and was out by the pool, relaxing alone and sipping champagne to ease her nerves. She took the news better than I had expected. I suppose there was a part of her that still loved her mother and didn't want to see her get arrested. She just stared at me, with a blank expression on her face, as I filled her in on what the Sheriff had said.

"I just want a normal life," she whispered. Melina got up from the lounge chair and headed back inside. She poured herself another glass of champagne.

"No thank you," said Nate, as she offered it to him. "Take it easy with that. You're still on medication."

"It's my last one," she promised.

Startled, Melina laughed nervously as Nathan scooped her up in his arms. "Are you trying to sweep me off my feet, Mr. Brande?!" The champagne was taking its effect on her, as she dropped her glass while they gazed deeply into each other's eyes. Just for a moment, Melina had forgotten all about her troubles, as Nate carried her into the family room. Her hardened heart was slowly softening up for this stranger who had somehow found the key to unlocking it. His words of wisdom and comfort were slowly winning her over.

He gently placed her upon the couch, then kissed her softly on the cheek. "Just relax here a minute. I'll be right back." Melina closed her eyes, as the soft music caressed her broken spirit. Of course, it was Bootsy . . . *"Love vi-brations; love vi-brations, love vi-brations moving 'round and round . . . we have love! . . . we have love! . . ."* Melina smiled as she thought, "Where does he get this stuff?! I've never heard music quite like **this** before, but I think I like it!" When the song ended, she slowly opened her eyes. Her eyes teared up as she noticed Nathan standing there holding a huge bouquet of freshly cut flowers.

"They are so beautiful. Thank you," she cooed.

"Yet they still pale in comparison to you." Melina carefully set the vase full of flowers on the table next to her, then held out her arms.

Nathan smiled as he got down on his knees in front of her. Melina inched forward onto the edge of the couch, greeting him with a hug. They embraced tightly, holding each other with the passion of a kindling romance. The small flicker would eventually ignite the flame of love between two unlikely souls destiny had seen fit to bring together. It seemed only fitting that Heatwave would emanate from the speakers next . . . *"Happiness, togetherness, lovingness, foreverness Now I guess, that's is why I'm blessed, with peace-full-ness . . . well!"*

"Nathan, what are you doing to me?!" she whispered, while holding him ever so tightly. "I don't really even know you. Yet here I am, holding you in my arms! I thought that the day would never come when I would **ever** embrace a man. How is it that I have come to trust you so easily, practically overnight? Nathan, I'm scared," she admitted, "but being with you seems so right."

"Melina, trust me when I say, I know how you feel. This is new to me as well. I don't quite understand it, but I think I knew right from the beginning that we were meant for one another."

Melina didn't say another word, and this made Nathan quite apprehensive. He wondered if he had overstepped his bounds.

"Did he say too much? Did he frighten her back into her shell?" Nate was beginning to panic! That is, until Melina gently kissed him on the neck! If it was dark, the glow from Nathan would have lit up the room! He was beaming with a new-found confidence! "Thank you, Jesus!" he whispered softly. That moment defined their relationship, and Nathan brought her fresh cut flowers almost about every day, just to relive and renew that feeling for both of them.

Over the next few weeks, the couple acted like a pair of teenagers. Both were shy, finding it hard to even complete proper sentences in the presence of one another. The attraction was obvious, but neither of them knew how to process or proceed with it. They were like a couple of newborns learning to take their first steps. But regardless of the awkwardness, they still managed to slowly win over each other's heart.

Chapter 21
Time Heals All Wounds

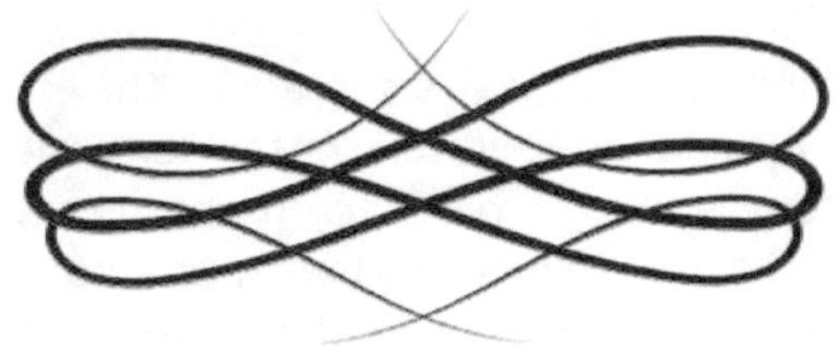

It has been three longs months since her vicious attack. Melina and Ashley have settled in nicely at the Estate. It was beginning to feel like home. Nathan and James were doing all they could think of to win the hearts of the two women. They showered them with gifts and gave them intimate tours of the special places in their home. Dr. Marshall had also gotten cozy with the Brandes. Even though he was not staying there, he came over every chance he got. The long hours he kept at the hospital annoyed Monica, but she understood his dedication. The Sheriff checked in from time to time, just to keep everyone up to date on the fugitives at large.

Sheryl and her sisters were on their way to tend to the shrine when they spotted Ashley and Melina relaxing on the porch.

"You two ladies have lounged around long enough. It's time we put you to work!" announced Betty, as she awaited Sheryl's response. After a long pause, Betty elbowed her sister, urging her to speak.

"You're right. We really should give them something else to

do. Would you ladies come with us please?" asked Sheryl.

"Sure!" responded Ashley, as she and Melina got up from the table and walked over to the steps. Neither of them knew what to think, or what to expect, as the group of ladies walked across the front lawn.

Now, it had never been suggested, let alone allowed, to let anyone outside of the group of sisters work on the family shrine. Jean handed the girls some pruning shears and gloves. By looking at the expression on her face, you could tell Sheryl was still struggling with the idea. She stepped just inside the shrine, while the rest of the women lined up just outside the area. They all bowed their heads as Sheryl said a brief prayer. At the conclusion, she turned back around to face the group. "It has never been appropriate for anyone, other that the immediate family, to step foot inside this shrine. To be honest, I still struggle with the thought of it to this very moment. However, Nate, James and Monica have opened their hearts, and our home, to both of you very special ladies. Therefore, I would be honored if you would join us in the Brande Women's Family Tradition of 'Honoring Our Ancestors.'"

"Even though someone has already broken that tradition," mumbled Lorraine, glancing in Melina's direction. Jerri tapped her on the hip,

"Stop it!" she said.

Nervous, Ashley and Melina stood in silence. They knew that this was a very big deal to Ms. Brande.

"It would be an honor," said Melina, with pride. They listened carefully, as the sisters took turns telling the story of their Ancestors. It was a sad tale of slavery, treachery, and betrayal. It gave a clearer understanding as to why Nate did what he did for his family. The story brought tears of sadness, as well as tears of joy, to every woman's eyes. Melina, Ashley, and the four sisters, held hands tightly, until the family's tale ended. Both ladies understood that this would be one of the single most important moments of their young lives.

Nate stepped out onto the balcony to get a little sunshine. The air conditioning was a bit too chilling, so he decided to warm up in the sun. As he glanced over towards the west side of the lawn, he could not believe his eyes! He called Monica and James and asked that they hurry up to his room. Upon arrival, they hurried over to the balcony doors. Nate opened them then said, “You are never going to believe this.” The siblings stood in disbelief, as they watched the ladies working **in** the shrine **together.** Nate put his arms around his brother and sister, as they could do nothing but watch speechlessly, as the women worked.

“Nate, if you start crying, I'll toss your oversensitive ass right off this damn balcony!” teased James.

“I just can't believe it!” whispered Monica. “Is that **our** mother with the girls **inside** the shrine?! Man, if the two of you don't marry those ladies, you'll have to kill 'em!” teased Monica.

“I can't believe my eyes! This is really big!” added James. They were **both** right. It took everything inside of her for Sheryl to do what she did. I couldn't find the right words to describe just how big of a deal this really was! That area of land was more important to my mother and her sisters than all of the property we owned, combined.

“Should we join them?” suggested James.

“No, I think we should give mom some time alone with them,” said Monica. Not wanting to be seen, Nate suggested that they all go back inside.

“What do you have planned for today?” asked James.

“I'm going to teach Melina how to drive. She needs her license. It's time she learned a little independence,” said Nate.

“And which car do you plan on letting her wreck?!” teased Monica. “I think we should go out and find something used, while they're busy working.”

“Let's get something for her and Ashley to share,” added

James. "After all, they go just about everywhere together anyway."

"Then I'd better go with the two of you since you're buying them a car. This calls for a bit of a woman's touch."

"Oh. What are you trying to say?" asked Nate.

"Oh nothing, just that the two of you would probably come back with a Hummer! Trust me. I have the perfect car in mind."

After nearly three hours, the ladies had finally finished the tedious task of maintaining the shrine. "Thank you so much for allowing us to join you. I now understand why this land means so much to all of you," stated Melina.

"I'll never forget this moment, or what I've learned here today," added Ashley. The women all took turns embracing. As they gathered up the clippings, Betty whispered into Sheryl's ear, "Mom and Dad would be really proud of you Sis."

Sheryl smiled and simply said, "Thanks, I think your right. I do feel good about letting them in."

"We do this once a month," announced Jean. "You are now officially part of the family. As women, you are obligated to join us."

"Thank you for the privilege," said Ashley.

"And thank you for accepting us into your family," added Melina.

The two ladies returned to the house with a newly enlightened attitude about the family. This was not about owning land or having money. This was about maintaining a family's all-but- forgotten-heritage, remembering how hard it was to get where they were today. It was about the struggle, the sacrifices, and the hardships of those before them, that paved the way for the family's survival.

"Wow, that was really intense," whispered Ashley, as they entered the house. "Do you think they really want us here?"

"I think they are genuinely happy to have us," stated Melina. "We were officially accepted into the family today. This is bigger than either of us could comprehend. Couldn't you feel it? There was this aura around us as we worked, like there was someone watching over us."

Ashley was completely taken in by what Melina had said. She pondered the thought of what it all really meant. Her family came into her thoughts. They were never this close. Maybe that is why she and her brother were spread out across the country and didn't stay in touch.

"What's wrong Ashley?"

"Oh nothing. Just something you said made me think of my brother and how completely opposite we are from **this** family." Melina put her arm around Ashley's waist, as the two tired souls headed for the elevator.

After a quick shower, the ladies went looking for the rest of their newly acquired family. Anxious to talk about the events of the day, their voices rang out in an echo, as they ventured about the house.

"Where **is** everybody?!"

"I don't know, but I'm starved!" responded Ashley. "Let's get something to eat!" They strolled into the kitchen for a late breakfast. They then went back out onto the front porch where their day had originally begun.

"Boy, this fresh fruit salad really hits the spot."

"I know, and the mangoes really set it off," responded Ashley.

"I've never had anything that tasted so delicious," said Melina. After finishing off the salad and croissants, they sipped on coffee and began chatting about the Brande Family History. "You know, I could never imagine being cut off from my entire family just because I married outside my race," admitted Melina. "That's so sad, not being able to enjoy the company of your mother, father, sisters, brothers, nieces, nephews . . . know what I mean?"

"Ashley! Melina!" rang out familiar voices from inside the house. "Hey, where have you all been?!" questioned Ashley, as she and Melina went inside.

"We've had quite the morning workout!" stated Melina.

"Yeah, we noticed," replied Monica.

"You knew and didn't try to rescue us?!" joked Ashley.

"What! And go up against my mother and her sisters . . . no thank you," chuckled James.

"You appeared to be having so much fun!" replied Nate.

"You know something, it **was** nice, and we learned so much about your family," admitted Melina.

"Well, for putting up with our family, we thought the two of you deserved a little reward. Now close your eyes and hold hands." They carefully led the ladies down the corridor and out towards the garage.

"What's going on?!" laughed Melina.

"Just be a good girl and keep those pretty green eyes of yours closed!" said Nate. "Now, I wanted to surprise you by taking you out and teaching you how to drive, but we decided to let Ashley do the honors. Monica thought you would be more comfortable with her."

"The only problem was deciding whose car was going to be sacrificed!" interrupted James.

"Ha-ha, very funny," said Melina.

"With all of those cars, you would think Nate would offer to give one up," teased Monica.

"However, we couldn't agree on which one to let you use, so there was only one logical conclusion. We had to buy you one," admitted Nate.

"You can open your eyes now," stated Monica. "SURPRIZE!!!"

"We figured, that since the two of you go practically everywhere together, you wouldn't mind sharing the same car for a little while."

"A Mercedes Coupe?! You bought us a Benz?!" The two ladies screamed and jumped for joy as Nate handed Ashley the Starting Sensor.

"Oh my God! I can't believe this!" exclaimed Melina. The ladies hugged and kissed each of the siblings, then ran towards their new car.

"Look, it isn't exactly brand new. It's a couple of years old," admitted Nate.

"He didn't think it was right to let you wreck a new one!" joked James.

"Yeah, well, it looks new to me!" said Ashley. The car was beautiful, pearl black with beige leather interior. It was gift wrapped in red ribbon with a big red bow on top.

They each grabbed a side, then pulled off the ribbon. Ashley got in, while Melina stood there watching in admiration. Melina turned around, shaking her head. She ran over to Nate, hugged him, then kissed him passionately. She shook her head again as she looked deep into his eyes. Try as she may, she could not find the words to express her gratitude. Monica and James eased away and joined Ashley in the car.

"Nate, I really don't know what to say. This is too much. Why would you buy us such an expensive car? I would have been just as happy with something older and less flashy."

"Before you say anything else, I really want you to understand something. This is one of the safest cars on the market. I want to protect you in every way possible. Please let me do this for you and Ashley. A pretty lady deserves nothing less than to be seen in a pretty car."

"Okay, but please, you don't have to shower me with expensive gifts. You've given me so much already! I owe you my very life!"

"Hey, hold on a second. You don't owe me anything. But if you like, when you're feeling up to it, and the time is right, there **is** one way you can repay me . . ." Melina smiled and then blushed. She lowered her head, to break eye contact, then giggled like a little kid as she felt him start to harden. Playfully, she pushed Nate away.

Embarrassed, she tried not to look, but she just could not resist. She could feel her heart pound, as she gawked at what was stiffening down Nate's pant leg. She caught Nate by surprise when she asked him, "What's that?" as she pointed coyly at the bulge in his pants.

Nate laughed as he watched her turn red, embarrassed by what she had said.

"Why don't you come over here and find out!" he countered. She again looked into Nate's eyes and said, "Someday I will, I promise."

With that, she turned, walked over to the car and got in. "Y-y-y-yes!" Nate said cheerfully, as he pumped his fist. Unknown to him, Melina smiled, as she discretely watched his celebration.

"Want to go for a ride?" she called out.

"Maybe later. I've got a lot of catching up to do."

"So do I," admitted Monica. "You two have a good time."

"Be careful Ash, we still have some unfinished business to take care of," hinted James as he leaned into the window to give her a kiss.

"Look Melina, I don't know how much longer I can hold out."

"What do you mean?"

"I'm ready to screw James' brains out, that's what I mean! It's been three months. Isn't that coochie of yours all better yet?"

"I suppose so, but I'm just not ready. Besides, who said you had to wait for me?"

"Well, I don't want to seem easy."

"Can we continue this conversation when we actually **leave** the garage?" suggested Melina. Ashley started the car, then eased it out. "Damn this is nice," moaned Melina, as she settled into the soft, plush seating.

"Don't change the subject. After all he has done for us, it's time someone put out, I mean, showed him a little gratitude!"

"Very funny. Nate really understands me. He's not rushing me into anything I'm not ready for."

"Well judging by the way he reacted a few minutes ago, I'd say he's ready to explode!" Melina turned and looked at Ashley with an expression of utter shock.

"Keep your eyes on your own man!" she exclaimed.

"O-o-oh, someone's getting mighty touchy! Don't get the wrong idea. I just meant that the way he looked at you, the way he hugged you, and looked into your eyes, gave all the signs of a man in heat, that's all!"

"I'm sorry Ash. I know you're right. It's just that seeing that big thing growing down his pant leg doesn't help my cause at all. To be honest, I think I'm ready to try, but I'm kind of afraid of it."

"Don't worry Mel, it won't bite!" teased Ashley.

Both ladies laughed hysterically as they cruised down the street. "Don't worry, it'll be fine. Take it slow. You'll know when the time is right. If there is one thing I do know, it's that Nathan Brande is a true gentleman. He won't hurt you."

"I know. He's the type of man most women can only dream of finding. I won't let him get away."

"Wait a minute . . . that tone in your voice . . . Is that lo-o-o-v-e I'm hearing?"

"Oh, just shut up and drive," mumbled Melina.

"No way!" shouted Ashley, as she abruptly came to a halt. "Seriously, are you really falling in love with him?!"

"Don't be silly. It's only been a few months. How could I be in love already?" said Melina, unconvincingly.

"Come on, girlfriend, spill it! I've seen how the two of you act together. You act like a couple of newlyweds, all lovie-dovie and what not. It's just so sickening sometimes!" Melina could do nothing but blush.

"Well you and James aren't much better! Come to think of it, Monica and Dr. Marshall are becoming quite an item as well."

"I'll admit it. I do have strong feelings for James. He makes me feel like no other man ever has. I could see myself being with him." The ladies sat quietly and pondered their thoughts. "Wow, enough of that! How about some driving lessons?" Ashley concluded.

Melina hummed as she pulled down the visor to shade the sun from her eyes. "Hey, what's this?" She noticed a sticky note attached to the back of the visor. "What's it say?" asked Ashley.

"Check the glove compartment . . . and it's in Nate's handwriting." Inside were two gift-wrapped boxes containing Gucci Sunglasses and a single red rose!

"Aw-w-w, that is so sweet!" said Ashley, while clutching her chest. Both ladies donned the glasses. Melina held the flower to her nose, then inhaled deeply. "God sent you the perfect man. Never have I encountered a man with such a heart for romance. He always finds a way to make you smile. He is most definitely your Prince Charming, that's for certain."

Melina couldn't speak. Her stomach was churning and her heart was fluttering once again. She felt hot, so she turned up the air conditioning.

"Girl, look at yourself. You've got the bug! Love is written all over your face."

"I think you're right Ash. Even now I wish I was in his arms. He makes me feel as if nothing or no one could ever harm me again. But when we're together, I just can't seem to find the right words to express myself. I feel like such a dunce sometimes!"

"Yeah, love'll do that to ya sometimes. But don't worry, it will all work out in the end. You'll see."

Chapter 22
A Sullivan's Family Reunion

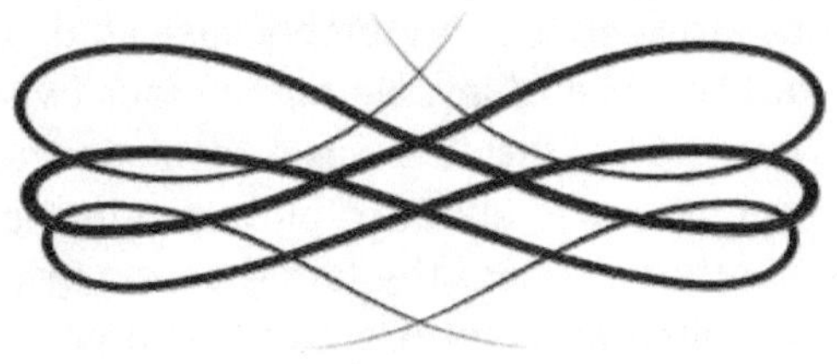

"Let's get a move on son. By the time we get back to the cabin, it'll be time for lunch." They broke down the camp site and gathered up the fishing gear. Junior stopped to make sure the fire was out, while his dad loaded up the SUV.

"What do you think mom is doing right now?"

"I really have no idea. She's been so distant the past few years." "Do you think she found out about what we did and decided to leave?" Richard could hear the sadness in his son's voice.

"Junior, look, whatever happens, we will make the best of it. And if your mom has any say in the matter, she will do what's best for you." Richard smiled at his son, in an attempt to give him some much-needed reassurance, as they got into the SUV.

It began to rain lightly as they approached the cabin. "Junior, grab the fish. We'll just leave everything else in here until the rain passes."

"**Mom?!!!**" shouted Junior, as he entered the cabin.

"What the hell?! How did you find out about **this** place?!"

"Richard, you'd be surprised. There is very little I don't know about you and what you do. Junior, please go upstairs while your father and I have a little chat."

"It's good to see you mom," said Junior, as he slowly walked up the stairs. "Dad and I have missed you so much." She smiled until he disappeared up the steps.

"Listen honey . . ."

"Don't you honey me! Just shut your mouth and listen up! I have known about your relationship with Valencia for over ten years. I just chose to keep it to myself because I didn't want to hurt my son. But you! You had to involve him in your twisted little love fest! Do you know how difficult it was to smile in that bitch's face every day, knowing she was about to blow you in the next room?! **That,** I can deal with, but I hate the fact that you involved our son. You screwed that bitch in every room of our home, including our own! I had to watch it all, just about every single day. But I did it and taped it too. Why Richard?! Was it worth it?! And now you've dragged my son right down and into the gutter with you."

"Even though you don't deserve it, I'm going to give you a chance to make things right." Richard sat quietly as she walked over to the closet and removed a large yellow envelope. She sat in the chair across from Richard and handed him the paperwork. Patricia sat quietly as Richard read through the legal documents.

"You expect me to sign my land over to you just like that?! That land has been in my family for three generations!"

"You should have thought about that **before** you started screwing the help! The way I see it, you have only two options: one, you sign it over to me, or two, you lose it to the state when you go to jail." Richard was dumbfounded.

"Yes, that's right. I know what you and Junior did to Melina. The poor girl nearly died! Did you know that?! I captured each and every disgusting moment of the way you raped her, on film! I just wish there was a way I could have kept Junior out of it." She fought back the tears as she continued. "Shit, it was her twenty-first birthday Richard! It was supposed to be one of the happiest days of her life and you raped her and took away her innocence!"

She fought diligently to maintain her composure. "Listen, just sign it over to me and I'll sell it to get the money for Junior's attorney fees. I'll keep the cabin so he will have a place to stay when he gets out."

"What about . . ."

"What about you?!" she interrupted. "You can rot in jail for all I give a shit! At least our son will be okay!"

"Hear me out Patricia. You don't have to sell the land. I've got some money saved, more than enough to pay for any lawyer. You can live off of the fruit profits for the rest of your life. Just don't sell my land!"

"By the time **you** get out, you'll be too old to run a farm! That is, if you live long enough!"

"Okay, I get it. You hate me. But Patricia, what you can get for selling the land, you could make five times over in just a few short years."

"Don't you get it?! I don't want anything else to do with it, Richard! I want to forget that I ever knew you! There is nothing left between you and me. We're done."

"This part of my life is over! I'm getting as far away from here, that place, and the memory of you, as I possibly can!"

"Come on, Patricia, let me keep my land. It practically runs itself. The farmers do all of the work. All you have to do is collect the money. You don't need to be there for that, do you? Take the money I have saved. It's more than enough to start a new life. You can continue to collect the profits until I get out, then we can split the difference. My attorney handles all of the bills and salaries for the workers, so you really don't need to do a thing. Just let me call and set up an appointment. He'll make all the necessary arrangements and you'll have power of attorney over the estate until I'm released."

Patricia thought long and hard about the proposition. It made sense to keep the money coming in rather than settling for one lump sum. As much as she wanted to put it all behind her and start a new life, the offer was way too sweet. Besides, if she wanted, she could still sell the property while she had power of attorney. Richard would be powerless to do anything, while sitting in jail.

"Okay, Richard, you can keep your property, but on one condition. I want seventy percent of the profits, if, and when, you get out." "I'll split that with Junior." Richard was hot!

"Seventy percent?!" Even after all the money she stood to make while he was in jail! There was nothing he could do.

His land meant everything, and he really didn't want to lose it. He reluctantly contacted his attorney and made the appointment.

"I just have one other question. What did Valencia get out of it? There had to be a reason why she did what she did for all of those years. And to let you screw her daughter on top of everything else?! She wasn't in it just for the sex; you're not **that** good!" Richard had no more fight left in him, so he decided to come clean.

"I gave her a deed to her house."

"You what?!"

"In exchange for everything, as part of our 'agreement,' I gave her a deed."

"She screwed you for the deed. That's just perfect!"

"There **is** one other thing I think you need to know."

"You know what Richard, I don't even care anymore. If it doesn't affect my money, I don't want to hear about it."

"No, it has nothing to do with that."

"Then keep it to yourself. I'm going upstairs to see my son."

Junior was listening to the entire conversation from the top of the stairs. The thought of going to jail was scaring him to death. He quickly walked to his room when he heard his mother coming up the stairs.

"Junior, I know you were listening. Open the door." He opened the door with tears in his eyes.

"Mom, I don't want to go to jail!"

"Listen Junior. What you and your father did was a horrible and unforgivable thing. Melina was like family to me. You had no right to violate her that way."

"I know Mom. I felt so guilty, I actually apologized to her. Can I ask something of you?"

"Sure baby, what is it?" she answered softly.

"Mom, will you please help daddy? I know he doesn't deserve it, but I don't want to see him die in jail!"

"I'll do what I can, that I promise you." Patricia wept as she hugged her son. "If I had only put a stop this a few years ago, my son wouldn't be going through this today," she thought.

As she walked down the stairs with Junior, Patricia noticed Richard was no longer sitting in the living room.

"Richard, where are you?" she called out.

"I'm in the wine cellar. Can you come down here and bring Junior with you, please?

"Where are you?"

"I'm in here. Just walk past the wine racks." Neither she nor Junior could believe their eyes. Richard had a huge wall safe hidden in the wine cellar.

"Here, take this." He handed Junior a canvas bag. Junior undid the latch to discover that it was filled with hundred-dollar bills. "There's about two-hundred-fifty-thousand dollars there. That should cover a fresh start and any attorney fees you may have."

"Here Pat. I had been saving these for you." She slowly opened the small black box. Her eyes widened, as she stared speechlessly, at the thousands of diamonds sparkling inside. "I had been collecting them for years. I was actually going to have the jewelers make you something special with them, but now there's no need. There's nearly two-million dollars worth of diamonds in there. That should be more than enough to start over with, I suspect."

"For what it's worth, I'm sorry for ruining our life and our family. I hope that one day, you can forgive me. I have about another three-hundred-thousand dollars in the safe. If you want it, take it."

"No Richard. As a matter of fact, you can put these back as well. If I need them, I'll get them later." Junior smiled as he sensed a little compassion in his mother's voice.

"I've been saving money as well, enough to get started over." Patricia handed the box filled with diamonds back to Richard so he could return it to the safe.

Patricia put her arm around her son's waist as they walked upstairs. "This is really hard for me to say, but Junior, I think you should turn yourself in. It's the right thing to do and it will help your case a great deal."

"Your mother's right son. The judge will take it under consideration when the time comes for sentencing."

"What are **you** going to do dad?"

"I have some other things to take care of first, but I'll turn myself in in a week or two."

"The longer you run, the worse it's going to be for you."

"I know, but this has to be done, for you **and** my son."

"Okay, Richard, but you know it's only a matter of time before the Sheriff finds out about this place as well."

"Come on Junior, let's go. I'm parked out back."

"I'll call my attorney to set up an appointment first thing in the morning. We'll go to the Sheriff's Department after we see him." Richard walked over to his son and hugged him tightly. "I'm so sorry I got you into this. Please forgive me." He didn't respond. Junior was so afraid; he was in shock. Patricia grabbed, then pulled him by the arm, to break his father's embrace. Richard could do nothing but watch helplessly as his family turned and walked away. He just stood in the living room as they walked through the kitchen and out the back door. He plopped into the chair as he heard the car start. He lowered his face into his hands as he listened to them drive away. "Well, I can't stay **here** much longer," he thought. "When she eventually makes her way back to Florida, the Sheriff will definitely find out about this place."

"Damn! I'm going to lose everything because of those two bitches! There's no way Patricia is going to give my farm back to me once she gains Power of Attorney! She must really think I'm a stupid jackass. Someone's going to pay!" Richard was so overcome by rage; his anger got the best of him. He grabbed his tackle box off the floor, stood up and threw it through the bay window. "They won't get away with this! That little cunt's living it up with the Brandes, while I have lost just about everything! Well, I'm going to fix both those bitches before I go to jail. Count on it!"

Richard returned to the basement, removed some money, and another box he had stored inside the safe. Just before he closed it, he decided to remove everything he had saved over the years. He put everything into the empty burlap bags he had stored on the floor of the safe. "Screw that, I'm not going to jail. I hear Mexico and Puerto Rico are nice this time of year, and I can live like a king with the money and jewels I have! I'll give things some time to blow over, then come back for those two bitches that ruined my life."

He began gathering up the things he would need for the long drive across the border. "The less I have to stop, the better." He filled a cooler with water, sodas and cold cuts then covered everything with ice. He placed other food items in an empty box, then tossed in a handful of assorted tableware. "Next stop, Cancun! I'll party there for a while, get laid, then come back here to handle business. I'll get back in, and then back out, of the country, before that stupid hick of a Sheriff even knows what happened!"

Patricia and Junior arrived back at the estate around ten-thirty the next day. She was exhausted. Even though she and Junior shared the drive back, she had driven to South Carolina on her own. She was relieved to see that the Sheriff was no longer staking out the house. "Junior, I'm going to take a shower. Your father has a wall safe in his den. The combination is fourteen, two, nineteen, each of our birthdays. That's the one safe I **do** know about. Check to see if he left anything behind that we can use."

"We rushed out of here so quickly, he never went into the den, so whatever he left behind should still be there," stated Junior. He removed the family portrait from the wall, which covered the safe, then slammed it to the floor, destroying it completely. Junior took a deep breath, in an attempt to curb his anger. Seeing the portrait only reminded him that he would be on his way to jail, very soon.

He entered the combination, then opened the door to the safe. "Jackpot!" Junior began removing an assortment of valuable contents. "Will you look at this! Six Rolex Watches, books and books of collectible coins and stamps. Damn, gold and platinum bars and a stack of savings bonds. Wait, they all have **my** name on them!" Junior began flipping through the stack of bonds. He then realized they were worth fifty-thousand dollars apiece. Junior slowly sat down at the desk and stared at the wealth of items in front of him.

"He left this here on purpose. Dad had planned ahead and left this here for my future." He looked over at the shattered glass and torn portrait he had thrown in the corner. "Damn it, Dad!" He fought back the tears and got out of the chair. "I'll just ask Mom to put this stuff away for me. Maybe in a safe deposit box or something. She can keep the rest. I can live a lifetime off of this stuff alone. Maybe she can liquidate everything except the bonds and one of the watches. She could open an account so it could gain interest while I'm away. Aw hell, I don't know. She'll figure it out."

Just as he was about to close the safe, Junior noticed a small envelope he had overlooked wedged in the back corner. "What's this?" Junior cut open the sealed envelope with the letter opener lying on the desk, then removed a single piece of paper. He turned a pale shade of white, as he stood in shock, reading its contents.

He fell back against the wall, then slowly slid down until he was sitting on the floor. "I can't believe it! I just can't believe it!" he muttered, as he continued to stare at the legal document. "This **can't** be right! There is no way this can be true!" Junior stared blankly across the room, as he tried to make sense out of what he had read. He began to massage his temples, as his head pounded.

"Was there anything in the safe?" asked Patricia, as she entered the den. "Junior? Junior?! What's wrong?!" There was no response from her son. He just sat there staring into space. Junior thought briefly about concealing the truth from his mother to spare her the pain. But she too, deserved to know his father's dirty little secret. She didn't even notice the fortune sitting on the desk as she hurried to her son's side. Patricia called to her son once more, as she knelt down, shaking him gently by the shoulders.

He didn't even flinch as the tears flowed from his eyes. He held onto the document tightly, while Patricia attempted to take it from his trembling hands. Reluctantly, he released his grip. The room was filled with a gloomy silence, as his mother read its contents. "OH . . . MY . . . LORD!!!" Patricia fell to her knees, then hugged her son tightly. "I RAPED MY OWN SISTER, MOM!" Junior shouted.

"MY SISTER! MY OWN SISTER!" He sobbed uncontrollably onto his mother's chest.

"I should have known it was his child," mumbled Patricia, as she began to recall the day Richard returned to the house, very upset. "I was about eight months pregnant with you at the time. He claimed he had just caught Valencia, and one of his farm hands, having sex in the tool shed. Shortly after Melina was born, I found out about the affair, then had cameras installed throughout the house. I understand how you must feel son, but you've got to pull yourself together. We have a lot of things to talk about and take care of, before the attorney arrives."

"I deserve everything I've got coming to me **and then** some! She's my sister," he mumbled.

"Don't be ridiculous! Even though what you did was vile, you didn't know it was your step-sister. Maybe this can help your case somehow. Now come on, get up. We need to get moving." "Was there anything else in the safe?"

Junior pointed to the top of the desk, as they slowly helped one another to their feet. "I think dad left this stuff for me. Look, the bonds all have my name on them."

"So, he planned ahead."

"Mom, could you do something for me?" Patricia stood quietly as Junior explained what he wanted to do with his sudden wealth. "Sure, honey, I understand, and I'll take care of everything. But like it or not, I will still be adding money to your accounts as time goes on. I have more than enough already. What am I going to do with it all?"

The doorbell rang, startling both of them.

"Ready?"

"Yeah Mom, I guess so." They walked hand in hand to the front door.

"Come on in," announced Patricia.

"It's good to see you again," stated the attorney. "Hello, Richard, my name is Peter Crawford. I'll be handling your case. Have you spoken with the Sheriff at all?"

"Not yet," answered Patricia. "I wanted to sit down with you first."

"Give him a call while I speak briefly with Richard. Advise him that we will be in his office by three o'clock sharp.

"Richard, I want you to understand that I'll be working to

get you as little time as possible. I know you are afraid, but the fact that you are turning yourself in, will only work in your favor. Now, start from the beginning. I want to know how this all started with your father pressuring you into having sex." Junior got an idea as to where this was headed. He was going to place the blame on his father. Junior didn't say a word as he slid the piece of paper across the table. The attorney took a very close look at the document.

"Did you know about this?"

"No Sir. I just found it in back of dad's safe about an hour ago." "Good, now tell me everything." Peter listened carefully, taking notes, as the story unfolded." Patricia walked into the room just as Junior was finishing up.

"Alright, first the bad news. You are over twenty-one, which makes you responsible for your own actions."

"Then what's the good news?"

"Unless we can somehow shift the blame onto your father, I really don't have any. Where is he anyway?"

"Probably heading for the Mexican border as we speak," joked Patricia. (Little did she know how right she was!)

"Well, with him on the run, one of two things will happen. The judge will hit you with the full sentence or he'll be lenient. I'll reach out to the Brandes' Attorney. I'm sure we can work something out in your favor. Your father hid the fact that she was your sister. Maybe this could work for you somehow."

"If I had known, I never would have done it."

"I'm sure Richard realized this. That's probably why he kept it a secret. I'll work on it. Now let's get you to the Sheriff's Department. It's important we arrive as scheduled."

"Mom, what about the accounts?"

"Don't worry about that. You go with Peter, and I'll get to the bank."

"What accounts?"

"Dad left me a lot of valuable collectibles and I wanted to

put it all in the bank until I got out."

"I suggest that any assets be left in your mother's care for now. There's a good chance they will sue you, so anything in your name would be vulnerable."

"That's just it. I wanted to split what Dad left me with my sister.

I just wanted to show her how sorry I was for what I did. Don't get me wrong, I'm not trying to buy her off or anything. I just want her to know just how much I regret my decision."

"If that is what you want, then I suggest you present it to her after you are sentenced. That way, it doesn't seem like a bribe."

"I'm putting everything back into the safe," said Patricia. "I'm going with you to see the Sheriff. There is no way I'm letting you face this alone!"

"I'll need to keep the Birth Certificate to submit as evidence," suggested Crawford.

After returning everything to the safe, Patricia and Richard, Jr. joined the attorney at his car.

"I'll be right behind you," she said, as she hugged and kissed her son. That ride was the longest one of his life. Junior pondered different scenarios to help keep his mind off of where he was headed. "Why didn't I just say 'no'?!" I probably could have stopped him. My God, there was so much blood! Why didn't Mom put a stop to it from the very beginning?! None of this would have ever happened if she had done something about it years ago!" Ultimately, he realized that what he did was his own decision, and he was now ready to pay the price for raping his sister.

As they arrived at the station, the Sheriff and two of his deputies, were waiting outside. They walked over to the car as we parked.

When Junior opened the door, the deputies instructed him to turn around and place his hands on the roof of the vehicle.

"Is this really necessary?" asked his attorney.

"It's standard protocol," answered the Sheriff, as he stood back gloating. After patting him down, Junior was read his rights, while he was being restrained. He was then escorted inside the precinct for processing.

Patricia struggled to get out of the car. She just could not stop the tears, even after she finally got up the courage to go inside. After being processed, Junior recorded his sworn statement. "You did fine," said Mr. Crawford, as the Sheriff walked out. "You can have ten minutes. Don't move from this spot, deputy. I'll be back in ten!" instructed the Sheriff. "Yes Sir," answered the deputy, standing at attention outside the locked door of the Interrogation Room.

"Now don't you worry about a thing. I'll get to work on your defense immediately." Patricia just sat there numb with guilt.

"I could have stopped this years ago. Why did I let it go on?!" she mumbled.

"Mom, don't blame yourself. I knew it was wrong, yet I did it anyway. I know you were just trying to protect me. Just take care of yourself. I'll be home before you know it. If you don't want to help dad, I'll understand. He should have told me Melina was my sister."

"We both deserved to know," whispered Patricia, as she thought back to what Richard was trying to tell her back at the cabin, before she cut him off.

"Due to the fact that you turned yourself in, I should be able to get you released until your trial," interrupted Peter. "That should give you time to get all of your affairs in order."

"How long do you think he'll have?"

"At least a week. Your bail may be pretty steep, but you'll get it all back after he appears in court."

"Do you think it'll be okay if I reach out to Melina, just to apologize?"

"Whatever you do, do not attempt to contact Ms. Delgado. Don't speak to her, don't write to her, or even if you run into her on the street, don't look at her. It is imperative you understand that. I'm sure the judge will make that clear to you on the date of your arraignment. If you make any attempt to contact her in any way, you will be in breach of your restraining order. You will then be arrested, and your bail will be forfeited. Do you understand?"

"Yeah, I get it, Stay away."

"Your time's up!" announced the Sheriff, as he and the two deputies re-entered the room. "I'll see you soon, mom," said Junior as he got up from his chair. As he attempted to walk over to hug his mother goodbye, Junior was immediately apprehended, shoved against the wall, and then placed in chains by the deputies.

"I said your time was up, rapist. Save it for the arraignment!"

"That's no way to treat my son! After all, he did turn himself in!"

"It's okay, mom," said Junior as he was forced out of the door.

Patricia began to cry as she watched her son being taken down the hall. "He'll be fine. Go home and take care of whatever you need to take care of. I'll have him out in a few days."

"Thank you, Peter. I don't know what I would do without you." He smiled as she kissed him on the cheek. Peter then removed his handkerchief from his breast pocket. "Here you go. Dry your eyes. You'll **both** need to stay strong. This is only the beginning."

Chapter 23
Turning Up the Heat

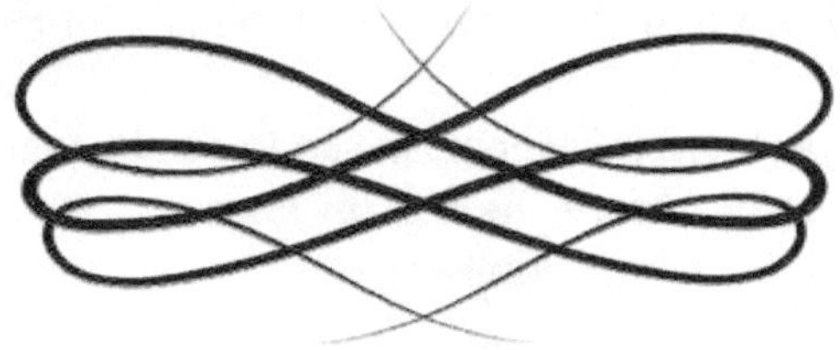

Over the next several days, Nathan began getting closer to Melina. They began taking long early morning walks together. A bond was forming between them even though they hardly held conversations. They were both still so shy the only thing they did was hold hands from time to time. Whenever they looked at one another, they would quickly glance away. A couple of nights a week, Nate would prepare meals just for the two of them and invite her out to the gazebo for a dinner beneath the stars. Slowly but surely, Nate was gaining her trust, and winning over her heart.

James was in the Surveillance Room changing disks when Nate walked in.

"Morning James."

"Hey, what's up?"

"Ready for another harvest?"

"Always up for getting paid!" responded James.

"Is sis up yet?"

"Haven't seen her. She's probably still asleep. I think Dr.

Marshall came over late last night."

"Speaking of the good doctor, how are things going with you and Nurse Ashley?"

"About the same as you and Melina. If she holds out any longer, she'll be treating me for the worst case of "Blue Balls" known to man!"

"I hear you bro!" chuckled Nate.

"When you have women around, taking care of it yourself just doesn't seem like an option any longer."

"What's it going to take to get these women to put out?!"

"Well, we already know what Melina's problem is. What's Ashley's?"

"Her problem **is** Melina. She seems to be waiting for her to get over everything before she has sex with me. So, do me a favor and turn up the heat, why don't you?!"

"Good Morning!" sang Monica.

"What's so good about it?" grumbled James.

"Aw-w-w, what's the matter boys. Still not getting any?!"

"Judging by the way you just floated in here, I'd guess the good doctor made a house call and took good care of his favorite patient!"

"Will you two please shut up!" pouted Nate. "If you don't mind, I'd rather not hear about my baby sister's sexcapades!"

"Oh, loosen up big brother. At least one of us is getting laid!" giggled Monica. "Nate's used to waiting. How long has it been, five, six, ten years? But James, this has been the longest you have ever gone without gettin' some!" acknowledged Monica. "I'll bet you're about to explode!"

"Don't remind me. I can barely walk as it is!"

"Well, if you two insist on continuing this conversation, I'll be in the kitchen." Nate exited the room, embarrassed, as his brother and sister laughed.

"Oh great. Just what I need! Will you two please go back upstairs and put some more clothes on?! You are driving me absolutely crazy!" complained Nate, as he walked into the kitchen to find Ashley and Melina half dressed. They were wearing very short silk robes over top of even shorter, skimpier, and very revealing lingerie.

"Wow, **someone's** grouchy this morning!" teased Melina, while bending over in the frig.

"Will you please stop that!" begged Nate, as he reached past her, grabbing a cold bottle of champagne, and placing it gently against his swollen scrotum.

She walked over to Nate, then kissed him good morning.

"Where's **my** man?" inquired Ashley.

"In the Surveillance Room," said Nate nervously, still trying to recover from watching Melina bend over in the fridge. "Look baby, I appreciate how good you look and all, but you are driving me out of my mind! I don't mind waiting, but you make it so hard . . . in more ways than one!"

"Oh, I'm sorry, but believe me, it'll be worth the wait. I promise." Nate trembled as she ran her hand under his shirt to rub his chest. He quickly pulled away as her hand ventured down to his lower abdominals.

"See, **that's** what I'm talking about!" he scolded, as he shook his finger. "You know how easily I get . . .well, you know. Yet you still tease me!"

Melina cornered him against the refrigerator. "Can't you see I'm falling in love with you?" she whispered. Nate was stunned, and his eyes widened! It took several seconds for what he had just heard to register. She smiled at the expression in his face before lightly kissing his lips and turning to walk away.

"Melina," whispered Nate. She reached back and lightly pressed a finger against his lips.

"Sh-h-h-h, don't say anything. I just thought you should know, that's all. I'll go put some clothes on now." She smiled, then slowly walked away, purposely teasing him, by slightly pulling up the back of her robe to expose the lower part of her cheeks, causing Nate to nearly drop the bottle of champagne.

"I'll see you all later!" announced Dr. Marshall, as he headed towards the front door. Monica ran from the Surveillance Room to kiss him goodbye.

"Have a good day," she whispered.

"It could never be as good as last night," he answered. Nathan interrupted their passionate kiss, as he exited the kitchen.

"Oh, take it upstairs why don't you?!"

"Don't mind him. I'm sure you can figure out what **his** problem is. Oh, Nate, by the way," added Monica, "I was thinking about taking the girls to the beach today."

"**Shit!!!**"

As they entered the foyer, Ashley and James chuckled to see a look of despair on Nathan's face.

"Now, James, should **you** really be laughing at **me**?!" teased Nate. James turned his attention back to Ashley.

"You really do need to do something about this," he said, motioning down at his crotch. "I'm really in a lot of pain here."

"Um-m-m, can we talk about that **elsewhere**?" she asked, with a look of embarrassment on her face. Dr. Marshall laughed as he walked out the door. "Hey, where's Melina?"

"She went up to put on some clothes."

"That's not a bad idea. I don't think it's proper for guests to walk around half naked," hinted Monica.

"I'm sorry. I didn't know he was here," apologized Ashley.

James walked Ashley to the elevator.

"Do you need some help getting dressed?"

"Oh, I think I can manage. Look James, just be a little more patient with me. We're getting very close. Soon okay?" He smiled then kissed her softly. James watched as the elevator slowly rose. He could see her lacy thong lingerie panties beneath the tiny robe. Ashley giggled, then playfully hid her goodies from his prying eyes.

"Oh, she is so going to get it!" he mumbled, as the elevator arrived at its destination. He watched longingly, as she walked to the door, opened it, then went inside.

"Come on, big brother, let's get to work. You look like you could use something to do before you go nuts," stated Monica.

"Oh, shut up. Just because **you** got some last night," grumbled James, sarcastically. "And please, don't mention 'nuts!'" They shared a brief laugh.

"See you in a couple of hours," interrupted Nate. "I need to make a delivery to the club."

"Why don't you take James with you. I think he could use the fresh air."

"Just for the record, air has nothing to do with it!" grumbled James.

"What do you say. Want to ride?"

"Why not. I've got nothing better to do."

"Oh, did sis mention she was taking the girls to the beach?" asked Nate.

"Oh great! Will someone please just cut my balls off now!" stated James.

"Yeah right, that's just what I need too, more sexless torture." The brothers headed back upstairs to get their beach gear.

Nate turned on the intercom link to James' room.

"This is going to be so-o-o bad! I think I'll spend my time in the ocean, **away** from Melina!" joked Nate.

"I know that's right! There is no way I'm putting myself through that again!" complained James. "What Ashley had on this morning was so bad for my heart!"

"And bad for other things as well!" added Nate. After some quick packing, the brothers headed for the garage. "Give me a hand with these," asked Nate. "I didn't expect company." They unloaded the Corvette, then put the cases of mangoes in the luggage compartment of the Caddy SUV.

"I told Nate I was falling in love with him."

"No! You didn't. What did he say?!"

"He kinda went into shock."

"I'll bet he did! Why did you tell him?!"

"It just came out. It just felt right, know what I mean?" said Melina, as she sat on the edge of the bed.

"Uh oh, you've got that look in your eyes," noticed Ashley. "You really do love him, don't you?"

"I just told you I did."

"You know what comes next don't you?"

"Yeah, I know."

"Are you ready?"

"Dr. Graham said I was over a month ago, but I'm still not quite sure yet."

She cringed at the thought, while placing her hands between her thighs, pressing firmly against her smooth mound. Ashley just laughed.

"Well, I'll be glad when you make up your damn mind! James has been putting some heavy pressure on me! To be completely honest, I don't think I can hold out much longer myself. My kitty-cat is thr-r-r-robbing! And she's so-o-o hungry!" said Ashley, clenching a fist and moved it back and forth between her shapely legs.

"You are so nasty!"

"Whatever! All I know is you had better do it soon, or I'm going to jump on you myself!"

"Wait, what are **you** waiting for?!"

"Isn't it obvious? I'm waiting for you. I want to experience that special moment the same time that you do," admitted Ashley. Melina smiled.

"Thank you, Ashley. Thank you for everything. I would have never made it through all of this without your help." Ashley hugged her friend, then whispered in her ear.

"And thank you for helping me to become a better person." After a brief pause, she continued. "Now, will you please do your man so I can do mine!" Melina chuckled as she playfully pushed Ashley away.

"Thanks for ruining the moment!"

"What are 'sisters' for?" chuckled Ashley.

"Yeah, I love you too!" Ashley turned, then walked into her room to start getting ready for the beach.

Ashley had, carefully and systematically, gotten Melina past her devastating ordeal. She did it by first, getting her past all the horror of both the physical and the emotional damage she had sustained. While her body was healing, she kept Melina's mind preoccupied, refusing to let her give up on happiness and the joy of sex. You can call it destiny or divine intervention, but either way, the fact still remains, Melina found her way into the arms of a good, kind, and loving man. Instead of allowing herself to become distant, cold, and unloving, she slowly allowed him to warm, and then jump-start her broken heart.

Even though Melina was afraid, she began to trust in the man that would change her life forever. A man who would protect her, heal her wounds, and help her to become a whole woman once again. Soon, she would feel the way all women longed to feel, and that's - loved. She would be safe from those who wanted only to cause her pain by taking the very thing any woman would gladly give freely. Her heart, her body and her soul is reserved for the one and only deserving person: the man who would take the time to reach deep inside of her very essence, to caress and nurture her heart with loving kindness. "Well, I've done all I can, Nate. The rest is up to you, God willing," pondered Ashley.

"Looks like another huge harvest this year, huh Nate? Nate, did you hear me? We're going to make a ton of money this season!" Nate just glared ahead, unresponsive.

"If I had known this was what riding with you was going to be like, I would have just stayed at home." Nate turned off the radio. "Melina told me she was falling in love with me."

"Hold up. she said **what**?!"

"You heard right. We were in the kitchen this morning when she hugged me and said she was falling in love. I was so stunned, I couldn't speak!"

"And the problem with that **is**? I would be doing cartwheels if Ashley had said that to me!"

"I guess I'm still in shock. She really caught me off guard."

"That's what you wanted, isn't it? I know you love her."

"Of course I do. I just can't believe it, that's all. It's been so long I guess I'm a little apprehensive about letting my guard down again. Getting your heart broken really sucks!"

"Look, it's a little late to be having second thoughts. You should have contemplated that before you spent a million dollars on her medical bills."

"It wasn't about the money."

"I know that. It was love at first sight. I saw the way you were looking at her that day. There's nothing wrong with that. She appreciates everything you have done for her and she loves you for it. So what's the problem? Don't be afraid of her love, Nate. I've seen the way she looks at you, too. It's for real. I've known this day was coming right from the very start. Embrace it. She's not going to hurt you." Nate grinned, then interrupted.

"Okay, who the hell are you and what have you done with my **real** brother?!"

"I know I like to bust your chops a lot, but honestly, it's just because I'm a little jealous of your success. My career went down the tubes, but look at all you've accomplished," admitted James.

"Don't sell yourself short. I couldn't have done this without you and Monica. I almost lost everything. Don't you remember?"

"Yeah, but you didn't."

"You know what, I think 'Mom-mee' was watching over us." Both brothers smiled, as they thought of their grandmother. "By the way, what's up with you and Ashley? I thought you would have tapped that ass by now and moved on."

"Believe it or not, I really do have strong feelings for her."

"Not you!" chuckled Nate.

"Yes, me! I'm capable of loving a woman too, you know."

"Yeah, I know, but I just didn't think you ever would! The way you like to hit and run, I mean."

"Yeah well, thanks for your vote of confidence. Besides, I think she's going to hold out until Melina is ready to give it up to you. I believe she wants to compare notes."

"Yeah, they do spend a lot of time whispering about us, don't they?"

"And how do you like our little sister getting laid before we did?!" "I don't want to talk about it. Time to change the subject." He chuckled as Nate turned the radio back on.

"What do you think?" asked Ashley, as she walked into Melina's bedroom.

"You are not going to wear **that**, are you? You are going to make me look like such a prude." Ashley was wearing a black thong bikini with lime green trim. "That thing barely covers your coochie and your entire ass is out! I don't want Nate gawking at you all day!"

"It's you he has eyes for, not me. Besides, look at what you're wearing. You've got tits and ass hanging out all over the place!" "Not like that! I just think it's too soon to be showing so much skin around the men, that all."

"What about the lingerie we had on this morning?! Oh alright, I'll go change, you big baby."

"Thank you."

"Aren't you ladies ready yet?!" asked the voice over the intercom. "We'll be right down!"

The doorbell chimed as Ashley and Melina descended in the elevator.

"Certified Letter for a Ms. Delgado," announced the Courier.

"I'll take it," said Monica, as she walked out onto the front porch.

"Sign here please."

"Thank you and have a nice day. It's for you Melina. It's from the County Court House. I wonder what this could be about." Melina's hands began to shake as she read its contents. "Richard Sullivan, Jr., is in custody. He will be sentenced in two weeks."

"Are you okay?" asked Monica. "I guess so, but his father is still out there somewhere, along with my mother."

"Should we cancel the trip to the beach?"

"No. I'll be alright. The two of them are probably on the run somewhere. Besides, it's time I took my life back. I mean, as long as I have all of you, it'll be a lot easier to move on with my life." "We're here for you Mel." After a brief group hug, the ladies headed for the beach. "I had better let Nate know," stated Monica, as she reached into her purse for her cellphone.

Melina hadn't been to the beach since she was a little girl. As they drove, she reminisced about the times Mr. and Mrs. Sullivan would take her along to keep Junior company. For some reason, they never went to Miami. They always went to a smaller, more secluded suburban beach, just a few miles away. She thought about all of the fun she and Junior would have, making sandcastles and collecting seashells. It was the closest thing she had to a real family. The Sullivan's treated her as if she was their very own child. Whatever they bought for Junior, they got for her. She was never left out of anything. She smiled as she recalled Mr. Sullivan taking them out in the ocean on rafts. They would shout and wave back at Mrs. Sullivan, who was usually tanning. She would occasionally join them, just to cool off a little, before returning to her blanket.

"Nate really loves the beach! Whenever we would come here as kids, mom couldn't get him out of the water. Have you ever been to the beach, Melina?"

"Huh? Oh, only when I was a little girl. Sorry, but you actually caught me daydreaming about going to the beach as a child."

"Did your mom take you a lot?"

"I never went with her. She was always working. But the Sullivan's took me and Junior just about every weekend. When I got old enough to work, they started giving her and me the weekends off. That's when the trips to the beach stopped."

"Well, here we are, and I'll be right back," stated Monica, as she got out of the car, then walked in the direction of a small hut.

"It's so beautiful here," noted Melina, as she and Ashley got out, then leaned against a palm tree.

"We were here a few months ago. Don't you remember?"

"No, not really."

"After leaving the hospital, we did a little shopping right up the street there. Don't tell me you've forgotten about our limo ride!" Melina blushed as she bumped up against Ashley's side.

"I don't think I could **ever** forget that night!" she giggled.

"Ashley, can you call James and let them know where we'll be?" asked Monica, when she returned, after paying for the parking.

"Sure, no problem." The ladies gathered their gear and headed towards the beach. "Yeah, that's right. We're parked near the street in the corner space. Monica reserved a space for you, right next to us. Just see the attendant. Okay. See you soon."

It was ninety-eight degrees without a cloud in the sky. The men along the strip gawked and whistled as the women crossed the street. "I really hate it when they do that! They treat us like a slab of meat. It's just so sickening!" complained Monica.

"I must admit, it really is a curse to be this fine," said Ashley, as she rubbed her hands up and down her waist and over her hips.

"Would you rather they didn't notice us at all?" asked Melina.

"No, but couldn't they just speak or wave or something?"

laughed Monica.

"The beach doesn't look very crowded today," noticed Melina. "That's because most people are working this time of day. It's one of the advantages of owning your own business. We're not locked into any of that boring everyday corporate drudgery. That's the main reason I'm so glad I didn't become an Attorney," admitted Monica.

As they stepped onto the grass, Melina removed her sandals. The trio paused as they scouted for a good spot to lay out.

"There's a good spot!" pointed Melina as she darted, excitedly, towards the sand.

"Melina, wait!" shouted Ashley, but it was a little too late.

"Ooch! Ooch! Ouch! Ouch!" cried Melina. Monica and Ashley watched, laughing hysterically, as she dropped her gear, then quickly hopped back towards the much cooler grass. "Stop laughing at me!" pouted Melina, as she leaned against a palm tree to caress her dainty little toasted tootsies. "I didn't realize the sand would be so hot!" she pouted.

"I'm sorry. I tried to warn you, but you took off so fast!" Melina gently slid her feet back into her sandals then went back out to retrieve the items she had dropped in the scorching sand.

The ladies located a quiet area about fifty yards away from a couple of families with kids playing along the shore. Melina smiled, as the memories of her childhood days at the beach were being played out right before her very eyes. She shaded her eyes from the sun as she looked around. She laughed as two children stomped at an incoming wave. It washed away the sandcastles they were working on, just a bit too close to the ocean.

"Here you are," interrupted Monica as she handed Melina the bottle of sunblock. "You had better put this on. You can burn rather quickly out here in this Florida Sun."

They each stretched out a blanket and began placing their items on the corners.

"Wow, its hot! I think we need some umbrellas," complained Ashley.

"The guys should be here shortly. They'll get them for us. Besides, I want to work on my tan," said Monica. "But you're black. You're tan enough already, aren't you?!" joked Ashley. The ladies stood up laughing, as they removed their beach raps, to begin applying the lotion.

"You know what annoys me more than the Neanderthals whistling at us?"

"What's that?" inquired Melina.

"The fact that I'm here with a White Girl and a Puerto Rican, who both have more ass than I do! What's up with **that**?!" joked Monica. "I thought white girls were supposed to have **flat** asses!"

"It's a new age!" joked Ashley, as she turned and playfully bounced her fat booty. Monica and Melina laughed and playfully smacked Ashley's round, jiggly ass. "I know what it is. Your ancestors found out about black guys, **you know** . . ." She held up her hands, about a foot apart, smiling, while bobbing her head up and down. "Once they had some of that, it was all over with! So now everyone has ass, lips and hips! Damn! Can't a sister catch a break any more?!" They all laughed while preparing to soak up some rays.

"I wonder what's keeping the boys?" thought Monica. "It's been about an hour now." She sat up and reached for the lotion.

"Can I help you with that?" inquired an approaching voice.

"No thank you, I can . . . Ken! What are you doing here?!"

"He came with us!" announced James, as he and Nate approached, carrying the umbrellas.

"I thought you were one of those annoying guys who had been whistling at us! **You** can rub me anytime!" she cooed. "I thought you were working!"

"What and leave your nearly naked body here alone on the beach?!"

"But how did you get off?! You're a doctor. It's not like you can just take the day off."

"To be honest, Dr. O'Shea wanted to stay a few more hours. Something about buying a new boat. He's covering for me. I have about three hours before I need to get back."

Monica quickly got up and jumped into Ken's arms, wrapping her legs around his waist.

"Hey, knock that off you two. There are children out here!" teased Ashley.

"Yeah, no one wants to see that!" remarked Nate. After greeting their men, the ladies turned over and ask them for a little assistance in putting some of the lotion their backs.

"D-a-a-a-m-n!" cried all three men, as they stared down at the abundance of beautifully sculpted ass lying before them. "I don't know whether to rub it or smack it!" cried James, as he knelt down beside Ashley.

"I just want to take a big bite out of that tender, juicy ass of yours," whispered Ken, into Monica's ear.

"You did that last night, and I still have the teeth marks to prove it!" teased Monica.

Nate stood motionless over Melina. Even though he had seen just about every inch of her body while she was unconscious on the lawn, he still couldn't get over how sexy she was.

"You okay?" she asked.

"I just can't get over how beautiful you are. It's stunning," declared Nate. Melina smiled, then whispered "Thank you" as she untied her bikini top, exposing the sides of her abundant breasts. "Damn, now that's just wrong!" he mumbled, as he applied lotion to his hands. Nate carefully straddled her hips and began gently rubbing her shoulders. Melina moaned, as he moved from her shoulders, to her neck and then down her back.

"Now, **that's** just wrong," she whispered, as she felt Nate begin to harden against her ample bottom, while gently applying the tanning lotion on the sides of her breasts.

Nate noticed her breathing getting heavier and more frequent, so he continued to massage the sides of her breasts. She didn't complain, so he rubbed them a little harder. Melina was getting so turned on, she couldn't control the way she squirmed. She slowly began grinding her ass against his erection. She could hear as he began to take shorter and heavier breaths, so she continued to squirm beneath him. Nate quickly moved from her back, down to her legs. "A-w-w-w, why did you move? That felt kind of nice."

"Another minute, and I would have . . ."

"You would have what?"

"Never mind, I'm finished anyway," he mumbled.

"No you're not. You missed a spot," she said teasingly.

Melina reached back, then pulled the sides of her bikini bottom up between her cheeks, exposing the majority of the roundest, juiciest assets Nathan had ever seen in his entire life! James's eyes bulged as he struggled to keep his attention focused on Ashley, and off the Latina beauty. Nate could only shake his head, as he stared hungrily, while preparing his hands for another adventure. As he rubbed, Melina moaned a little loader, then slightly raised her hips.

"What's going on over there?!" asked Ashley, as she turned her head to face Melina.

"Nothing," whispered Melina. Ashley smiled to give her friend some added confidence.

"James, your eyes had better be on me," she demanded.

"Where else would they be?!" he lied, as he took another quick look at Melina's exposed rump roast.

"Screw this, I'm going for it!" thought Nate, as he watched his brother lay down beside Ashley. Nate began deeply massaging her soft cheeks, gradually working his way inward, until his thumbs reached the material wedged in between them. He worked his thumbs until they were beneath her bikini bottom. He could feel the heat flowing from her vagina as he rubbed the sides of her swollen lips.

She quietly begged him to stop, as her body stiffened, jerking uncontrollably. "Please. Please Nate, don't!" she pleaded. Melina buried her face in the blanket as she erupted in an orgasm. He could feel the warm juices flow out onto his thumbs as he lightly pressed her wet, swollen lips together. Her body continued to spasm as Nate gently stretched her moistened bikini bottom back out across part of her exposed backside.

Melina struggled to get her breathing under control as Nate laid down beside her. Completely embarrassed, she refused to turn her head in his direction.

"It's okay baby. Please, look at me." She took a final deep breath, then turned her head to face the first and only man she ever willingly let touch her body in a sexual way. As she slowly opened her eyes, neither of them said a word. Their eyes said it all. Now Nate knew for sure Melina loved him and Melina knew it as well. As Nate moved closer, she rolled onto her side and held out her arms, to welcome him with a hug.

A few guys had gathered in the area, pretending to toss a football, just to get a better look at the women while they tanned. Suddenly, several of them froze in their tracks and stood with their mouths hanging open. Melina had forgotten she had untied her top! Her erect nipples stood out proudly upon her firm breasts. Nate's eyes widened as he took a good long look at them. "Heads up!" shouted one of the guys from down the beach. The football struck his buddy, who was staring at Melina's breasts, right in the face, knocking him into the sand. The lucky men began to applaud and cheer to show their appreciation for what they had just witnessed.

After realizing what she had done, Melina quickly pressed her body against Nate's in an attempt to cover her exposed breasts. The football bounced, then landed right next to their blanket. The dazed man got up, then slowly staggered over to retrieve the ball.

"I'm sorry about that," he mumbled, as he slowly picked up the ball, while attempting to get a closer look.

"Are you okay?" asked Melina.

"I sure am! This is the best day at the beach **ever**!"

"I know just how you feel!" answered Nate. "Next time, keep your eyes on the ball!"

"Yeah right, I'll try to remember that!" said the happy young man, as he jogged away.

"Damn! Did you see those tits?! They were perfect!" exclaimed the injured man, as he checked his nose for blood. Nate chuckled lightly, as the group of friends walked down the beach, talking about what they had just seen. Melina was so embarrassed!

"I can't believe I did that!" she exclaimed, while keeping an eye on the men.

"Well, you sure made a lot of guys happy today, including me!"

"That wouldn't have happened if you hadn't . . ."

"If I hadn't what?!"

"Oh, shut up and help me put on my top!"

"Hold on a sec, I kinda like this." Nate looked down at Melina's breasts, as her nipples pressed against his chest. Melina cupped her breasts in her hands, then sat up. "Okay, pervert, help me put on my top," she grinned.

"You can't even go to the beach without causing a commotion, can you?" teased Ashley.

"Well, half the men on the beach just saw me topless, so I think it's time to go!" she laughed.

"With all the strange sounds you were making over there, I'm surprised we didn't get thrown off the beach already!" teased Monica.

"We could hear you way over here!"

"Yeah, get a room you two!" added James, as he turned on his side to snuggle against Ashley. "Damn, Nate's doing better than me over there," he whispered, as he grabbed one of Ashley's butt cheeks.

"Aw-w-w, is my baby jealous?"

"No, I'm just horny as hell! So, screw me already!" Ashley laughed as she sat up to stretch, then change tanning positions.

"Thanks a lot!" grumbled Melina, as she playfully smacked Nate on his chest. "Not only did half the people on the beach get treated to an X-rated show, but now I'm all wet and sticky!"

"You are so welcome!" teased Nate.

"I guess I should go cool off." Melina got up, then headed towards the ocean. The men, who were now playing ball a few yards away, stopped and stared, as she slowly walked towards the surf. Nate just glared proudly at his goddess. She ran her fingers through her hair, from her scalp, down the back of her neck, tying it up with a scrunchy. Her hair flowed down her back, all the way down to her ass, and she didn't want to get it wet. He watched lustfully as her butt jiggled with each step. "I had better cool off too." he thought, glancing down. Nate quickly grabbed a towel and held it in front of his shorts to hide his growth.

Ashley, who had turned over on her back, was shading her eyes from the sun.

"Holy Shit!" she mumbled, as she glanced over at Nate. "No wonder she's too scared to have sex with him. That thing has to be over a foot long!" She drooled as Nate dropped the towel and headed for the water.

"Did you say something?" asked James, who had been distracted by Melina as she walked towards the ocean.

"Um, no. I didn't say anything," she mumbled, as she slowly slid her hands between her thighs, while pressing them tightly together.

"Want to get wet?" she asked.

"If that means what I think it does, hell yeah!"

"I mean, do you want to go for a swim?"

"Alright," groaned James. Ashley chuckled.

"You never know. You might get lucky."

"Well alrighty then!" He jumped up, ran towards the surf, and dove into the oncoming waves. Ashley laughed as she walked out to join him. "I hope I'm as lucky as Melina," she thought, as she slowly submerged herself. The water felt ice-cold after lying in the sun for so long. As she surfaced, her nipples protruded proudly against the inside of her top.

"Well, hello there!" said James, as he reached out and gently pinched one. Ashley playfully smacked his hand away, smiling, as she wiped the salt water from her eyes. "Ow, that kinda stings!"

The two couples played together for a while before slowly drifting apart. Ashley and James slowly drifted out about shoulder high into the ocean. It was easy to tell what was on their minds. They were both turned on from watching Melina and Nate just moments ago. While they hugged and kissed, Ashley became curious about what James was packing. She could feel it harden as they hugged. She turned around and rubbed her butt against it.

"You had better stop teasing me."

"Why, what are you going to do about it?!" Ashley could feel James pulling down his shorts. She slowly reached back, grabbed his swollen member and began to stroke it against her ass. She turned around, then looked down into the clear blue waters. Her eyes widened.

"What's wrong?"

"Nothing. I've never seen one quite this big before. At least not in person, anyway!"

"Don't get scared now!"

"Oh, don't get it twisted. I'm not afraid of anything!"

"Hey, what are you two up to over there?" shouted Melina, who had her legs wrapped around Nate's waist. "Don't put me down. I can't swim!"

"Are you kidding me?! Do you know how long I've waited to

get you in this position?!" admitted Nathan. Melina blushed while giggling. Ashley continued to stroke James's swollen member as she turned around. James reached down and slid his hand into her bikini bottom.

She squirmed as he slid his fingers in and out of her hungry vagina. Her eyes closed as the feeling became more intense. James's body became rigged as the moment of truth arrived. Ashley's head fell upon his shoulder as she climaxed. She had to bite her bottom lip to keep from groaning too loudly. James began to groan. She looked down, watching, as he ejaculated streams of thick white goo, into the clear blue waters, which quickly dissipated into the salty seas.

"Boo!" shouted Monica. The couple was startled to see Monica and Ken in the water. Ashley tried to quickly pull up James's shorts, as they got closer.

"Well you two sure look guilty. What have **you** been doing out here all alone?" teased Ken. "You looked like you were having so much fun, we decided to join you." Thirty yards away, Melina and Nate were in a world of their own as they held each other tightly. She liked the way his erection felt as it pressed against her vagina. It took every ounce of will power Nate had not to try to slide it inside of her. After a long and passionate kiss, she whispered, "You want to make love to me right now, don't you?" (Are you kidding me?!)

"Oh no. Oh we men just love standing in the water with a boner while hugging a beautiful woman! Who would ever be thinking about sex at a time like this?!" (That was sarcasm, by the way!)

The look on his face said it all.

"I want you too, baby," she admitted, as she slowly lowered her legs and stood in the water, which was up to her chin. She looked deep into his eyes as she slowly reached down into his shorts. Nate took her by the hands, then slowly guided them the entire length of his swollen member. She swallowed deeply, as her hand finally reached his enlarged testicles.

"It's been over five years since a woman has touched me there," he admitted. She cringed as he guided her hands back up his abundant shaft. As much as she wanted to, Melina couldn't bring herself to look down. A part of her was still afraid of its enormous size. Never the less, touching it felt really nice!

As she slowly removed her hands, Melina whispered, "You won't have to wait much longer." With that, Melina and Nate began to make their way over towards the other couples.

"Why are you blushing?" asked Melina.

"I'm not blushing," replied Ashley. "My face must be getting a little sun burnt."

"She got caught with her hand in the cookie jar!" joked Monica. "Didn't think we saw you pulling up James' shorts, did you?!" As her face turned beet red, Ashley quickly looked to James for support. All he did was chuckle. To hide her embarrassment, she quickly swam away.

"What did we just miss?" inquired Nate.

"We were just fooling around, that's all." answered James. He then swam away in Ashley's direction.

"I think it's about time I got back," said Ken. "Time sure does fly when you're having fun."

"It's time to get packed up!" shouted Nate to his brother. The couples slowly made their way towards shore.

"Do we have to leave so soon?" asked Melina, with an expression of sadness her face.

"We can always come back, anytime you like, with or without the others." Melina smiled as she took Nate by the hand. She began stepping gingerly across the hot sand, so Nate picked her up, then carried her to the blanket. Ashley couldn't help but notice the look of love gleaming all over her friend's face, as the couple approached their blanket.

"Look at those two. They really are falling in love," cooed Ashley, as she put her arm around James's waist.

"And what exactly do you think we're doing?" he asked. Ashley looked at James and smiled. That's just what she needed to hear. She was beginning to get a tad envious, watching Melina and Nate fall in love. She wanted the same for herself. But James was different. He was hardened, always keeping up tough appearances. Nate, on the other hand, was very sensitive, kind, and not afraid to express his feelings. He was just the type of man Melina needed in her life. After everything she had been through, it's easy to understand how she fell in love so quickly. We were each blessed with the type of man we needed in our lives.

Nate chuckled as he watched the same group of guys make a final pass. They watched sadly as the couples packed up to leave. Even though what the guys were doing was kind of disrespectful, he refused to catch an attitude. "I can't get mad at them for looking," he thought. "After all, she **is** beautiful, and I would probably stare at her too." One of the guys gave Nate the "thumbs up" sign as he passed by. Nate smiled and gave him a nod. "James would be in a brawl with them all right now!" he thought, as he folded the blanket. He dug into the sand and pulled out a small plastic container. "What's that?" asked Melina.

"It's just a little trick we use to hide our valuables from thieves.

"All set?" asked James. The group slowly walked back up the beach towards the sidewalk. They stopped briefly and took turns under the showers. Watching Monica, Ashley and Melina, as they rinsed, was like watching a sexy Playboy Video Shoot as the cool water ran sensually down their bodies. They seemed to turn in slow motion as they rinsed away the last of the sand. A driver passing by slammed on his brakes, narrowly avoiding a collision with a car in front of him that had slowed to watch the sexy show. "Will you three hurry up before you cause an accident!" teased James, as he watched the women finish up.

"We'll meet you back at the house after we drop Ken off at the hospital." They kissed, then got into the cars. "Oh look. How cute!" shouted Melina, as the guys drove off. On the corner, was an elderly woman selling puppies. Melina got back out of the car, then rushed over to get a closer look at them. "Wait a minute!" shouted Monica, as she turned off the ignition, then got back out of the car.

"What kind of dogs are they?"

"Shih-Tzus." answered the old lady.

"Aren't they the cutest?! I always wanted a puppy! May I hold one please?"

"Take your pick."

"Melina!" shouted Ashley, as she and Monica approached. Melina turned, holding a little beige and white puppy against her chest. "Look, isn't she the cutest little thing?!"

The look on Melina's face was priceless. She was like a kid on Christmas! "Can I have her?! Please, please, please!" she begged. Now Monica and her brothers loved dogs. But they hadn't owned one since their last dog died, over twenty years ago. *She recalled how painful it was, watching her brothers cry as they buried their German Shepard in the back yard.* "Oh baby, I don't know about that." Melina's face saddened as Monica explained. She could see the tears building in Melina's eyes as she knelt down to return the puppy.

"Nate's going to kill me for this. Okay, how much are you asking?" Monica handed the old lady three-hundred-fifty dollars, as Melina ecstatically retrieved her puppy. Melina danced the waltz all the way back to the car, while holding the puppy between her ample breasts. (Lucky dog!)

"Aw-w-w, look how happy she is!" said Ashley, as she

watched Melina head joyfully towards the car.

"Yeah well, let's hope it lasts. *After "Tiger" died, we swore to never get another dog. Losing him was just too painful."*

"Do you really think Nate would get mad about anything she does?"

"Yeah, good point. I guess we may as well head for the nearest pet shop." Melina's life had completely turned around. *GOD is always watching over us*. . . Melina is living proof of that.

Chapter 24
Skeletons in the Closet: Secrets Revealed

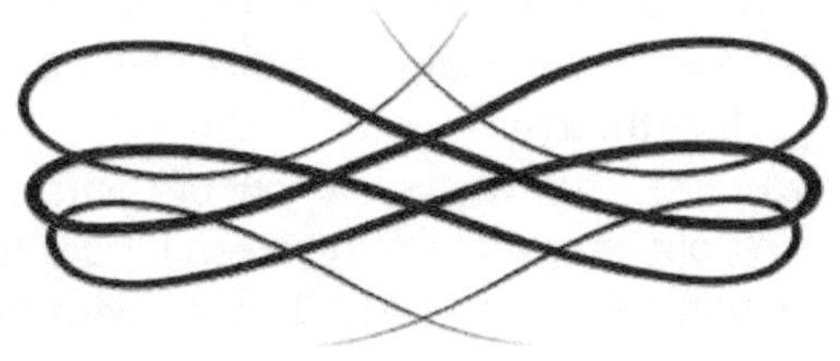

"Are you sure you want to do this?"

"She deserves to know the truth. It may even help my son."

"Alright then, I'll take care of it right away." Patricia walked out of her attorney's office filled with hope. Junior's arraignment is next week. Please GOD, let this work! She walked up the street towards the bank. Patricia was about to open the accounts, just as her son had requested. It was a lot harder than I expected to get rid of some of Richard's rarest collectibles, but it was done at last.

"Good Morning, Mrs. Sullivan. How are you today?" asked the Bank Manager, as she walked through the door. The Greenbergs were longtime friends of the Sullivan's. They all went to high school together. She was the Prom Queen and Mr. Greenberg was the Prom King.

"Just fine. And how's Vivian doing these days?"

"Much better. Thank you for asking. What can I help you with today?"

"I'll be opening two accounts and a safe deposit box for my son, Richard."

"I hope everything works out for him."

"Thank you, Hank. Oh, and thanks again for letting me use your cottage. I really needed to get away to collect my thoughts."

"Don't mention it. It's yours to use anytime you like."

"How do you feel about RJ being arrested?" asked James.

"I'll feel much better when they catch his father. I'm sure that with all **his** money, he's well out of the country by now, but Melina won't be able to relax completely until that bastard is caught and safely locked away," complained Nate. "I sure wish I could get my hands on him first though."

"I feel you bro. That was really low of them to do that, and on her twenty-first birthday no less. It's even harder to believe that she was still a virgin all those years. I mean with her being that beautiful and all," said James.

"Yeah well, I'm just glad to see how well she's bouncing back," added Nate. "I need to make a stop before heading home."

"No problem. I don't have any plans."

"By the way, what **were** you and Ashley doing out in the water? It seemed pretty intense."

"Well, let's just say, we were relieving some stress."

"So, you finally tapped that ass, huh?"

"As much as I want to brag, I can't. But she does have great hand skills though!" As they laughed, the news of the arrest caught their attention.

"How do you like that, using his wealthy influence to keep his name withheld from the press. What bullshit!"

"Look Nate. Don't let this ruin such a good day. Where **are** we going anyway?"

Nate parked in front of one of the most exquisite jewelry stores in South Beach, then turned to his brother.

"James, how do you **really** feel about Ashley?"

"What do you mean by that?"

"Just what I said. I know how I feel about Melina. I've known since I first laid eyes on her. I truly love her, I love her with all of my heart and soul! Oh, and hopefully, soon, with my body as well," he joked.

"I guess you could say I'm falling in love with her," admitted James. "But as you know this is uncharted territory for me. I don't stay with one woman for very long."

"Very long?! Don't you mean overnight?!"

"Screw you Nate! And why the hell do you want to know so badly anyway?!"

Nate pointed, directing James's attention to his right. He glanced back at his brother with a puzzled look on his face. "You are not going to do what I think you are, are you?"

"I love her James." For the first time in his life, James was speechless! "What, no witty comebacks or smart remarks?!"

"Not this time bro. I'm just glad you finally found someone to make you happy again. It's been a long time." Now **Nate** was puzzled! "Look man, I know I like to give you a hard time, but not today. Go ahead and do what you want big brother."

"Thanks man. I knew bringing you here with me was the right thing to do. I love you bro."

"Right back at you."

"Ah, the Brande Brothers. Good to see you again, my friends! It's been a few years."

"Five to be exact," stated Nate as he shook hands with the owner. "To what do I owe the pleasure?"

"I'm in need of your one-of-a-kind expertise. Nothing too over the top. Just keep it simple. I need a matching set of Engagement Rings. Five or six karats for her and maybe three for me." James decided to look around the shop while Nate explained what type of design and setting he was looking for.

"Hey Nate, what do you think about the girls having matching diamond necklaces?"

"Include sis and I'm in. The three of them have become practically inseparable over the past few months."

While James asked about some prices, Nate decided to take a short stroll down the boulevard, while making a call.

"Hello?"

"Hey, Tony, it's me."

"What can I do for you, Sir?"

"I'll be needing your special services a month from Saturday night. I know we're booked solid, so I will be utilizing the rooftop lounge, decorated and set up for a romantic party of eleven. It's for me, so really hook it up."

"No problem Mr. B. Would a staff of four be sufficient?"

"That's fine. We should be there around eight. Plan for it to run until around midnight."

"I'll see you tomorrow during delivery to discuss the details. "Thanks."

As he completed his arrangements, Nate turned around and headed back towards the shop. Mrs. Sullivan exited the bank as he was passing by. "Excuse me, Mr. Brande. I believe you know who I am."

Patricia's voice was raspy as if she had been sick or crying recently.

"I'm sure that I am the last person you wish to be speaking with right now, but I have some important information I wish share with

Melina."

"I have nothing against you Mrs. Sullivan. It's the rest of your twisted family I have a problem with."

"Understood. I also understand Melina is staying at your estate." "What's it to you?"

"Could you please see that she gets this. It's very important."

Mrs. Sullivan reached into her purse and removed an envelope. Nate took a step back and put up his hands.

"I think that anything you have for her, should be handled through our attorneys."

"Mr. Brande, this is about a personal family matter. I would rather not air this out in court. Please, I'm begging you. Please see that she receives this." Reluctantly, Nate accepted the envelope, then slowly began to walk away.

"Tell your husband to turn himself in."

"I have no idea **where** he is, and I really don't give a damn. He's dead to me now. Tell her I'm sorry about what happened." Nate stood and watched as Mrs. Sullivan walked away.

"Oh, there you are! What the hell are you doing hanging around out here?! Renaldo is waiting. Come on!" As Nate turned around, James could see a look of concern on his brother's face. "What's wrong? Did something happen?"

"I . . . I just ran into Mrs. Sullivan. She asked me to give this to Melina."

"Are you nuts?! Call the attorney!"

"She said that it was personal, and she seemed sincere about it." She has no idea where her husband is, and I really don't think she wants anything else to do with him."

"Can't say I blame her for that. I just hope you know what you're doing."

The brothers returned to the store to make the final arrangements.

"Sorry about that," apologized Nate.

"Don't worry about it. Now, when do you want to pick this up?" "This time next month."

"I know we're old friends and all, but don't you think that's kind of pushing it?"

"We have special plans, so I really need it to be ready. Add an extra five grand, for incentive."

"Would three o'clock be okay?!"

"That would be fine. Thanks, I owe you one."

That goes for everything, right?" asked James.

"It'll all be ready," assured Renaldo.

"What did you mean by that?" asked Nate, as they exited the store. "Oh nothing, I went ahead and ordered the necklaces for the girls, mom **and** our aunts."

"Man, I forgot all about them! Good looking out!"

The boys barely said a word to one another during the ride home. Nate couldn't stop thinking about Mrs. Sullivan. She must be going through hell right now. She lost everything: her life, her family. . . Nathan had actually begun to feel sorry for her. Her life was turned upside down by a man who had it all: a successful career, a wife who loved him, and a son to carry on his legacy. James was thinking about the purchase he was about to make. Little did Nate know, James had also ordered Engagement Rings for him and Ashley as well. He couldn't believe he was ready to settle down with one woman. He was nervous, yet happy about the direction his life was heading in. And he owed it all to his brother. He looked over at him, then smiled. If it were not for Nate's obsession with keeping the land, there would be no telling where they would all be today.

The silence was broken as they neared home.

"So, what are you going to do with that?" asked James, nodding in the direction of the envelope.

"I'm going to give it to her, what else."

"You don't even know what's in it. It could be more bad news. You don't want her to have a mental relapse, do you? She's been doing so well. . ."

"I've thought about this all the way home and I think it's the right thing to do."

"It's not sealed. Maybe we should take a look at it first."

"She said it was personal. How bad could it be?" Nate gradually slowed, then pulled over. "I don't know about this," he said as he picked up the envelope.

"Look, if it's bad news, she doesn't get it."

"But it's personal. We shouldn't be looking at it."

"Look at it this way. If she didn't want you to read it, don't you think it would have been sealed.

Nate looked at James as he slowly removed the document. "Whatever it is, it looks official," said James, as he noticed the seal stamped on the bottom.

"It's a Birth Certificate," said Nate, as he began to unfold the document. "This **can't** be right! Do you see this?!" Both men carefully read over the contents.

"Son of a bitch!" shouted James. "She's his **daughter**?! Sullivan raped his own daughter?!" Nate just sat there stunned. He could not believe that a person could be so vile as to rape his own child!

"You **cannot** let her see this! I can hardly handle it myself!" stated James.

"That Bitch!" exclaimed Nate. "She's trying to gain some sympathy for her son! I'll bet she's hoping Melina begins to feel bad for him and accepts a charge reduction when she realizes that he's really her half-brother!"

Nate put the SUV in gear, stepped on the gas, then spun it around in the opposite direction. "What the hell! Nate, will you please slow down?! You're going to kill us both!" But Nate never heard a word his brother said. He was filled with blinding rage! All he could think about was the hurt on Melina's face if she read the Birth Certificate. Nate didn't slow down until he pulled into the Sullivan's driveway. "You'd better think about this Nate. You're asking for trouble."

"All I want is some answers, and if she can't give them to me, then Melina never sees this. I'll burn it first!"

The front door opened as they got out of the car. "I thought you might be stopping by. Please come in. You must excuse the mess. As you have probably guessed, I'm moving and putting this place up for sale. I just want to put all of this ugliness behind me and start a new life, far away from here," she explained, as she walked into the living room. "Please, have a seat. May I offer you something?"

"No thanks," declined James.

"I just have some questions," said Nate.

"I suppose it's safe to assume that you read Melina's birth record," guessed Mrs. Sullivan.

"How could you ask me to give her that after all she's been through?! We are all doing the best we can! As it is, helping her to maintain her sanity is hard enough! Have you any idea what this will do to her!?! I'll bet this is just some kind of a sympathy plea for you son, isn't it?!"

"Nate, will you calm down!" interrupted James.

"Please, let me explain, Mr. Brande. Yes, you're right, I am looking for some sympathy for my son, but I also feel that Melina deserves to know the whole truth. I know you don't feel he deserves it, but he is my child, my only son. Junior didn't know she was his sister. We just recently found the records hidden in a safe. I know it doesn't make it right, but do you think my son would have done that if he had known?" Mrs. Sullivan reached for a handkerchief in her purse, then wiped her eyes.

"Do you honestly expect us to believe that?!" said James.

"I have nothing to gain by lying to you. I'm risking our entire case by telling you this."

After a few moments, she continued. "The other thing is that, well, I feel partly responsible for what happened to her. You see, about fifteen years ago, I began to suspect Richard and Melina's mother, Valencia, of having an affair. Several years later, I had cameras installed in all of the rooms. I even had one hidden in Valencia's home for a short time." James and Nate looked at one another. They could not believe what they were hearing. "My intentions were to give the videos to a divorce lawyer, but I decided to keep the affair to myself, for the sake of my son. I let Richard continue with his affair for over fifteen years. To tell you the truth, we spent very little time together as it was."

"When he wasn't working in the fields, he was managing the business and making deliveries. He didn't trust his workers. He thought they were stealing from him already. I gave the Sheriff a copy of everything that had occurred over the last ten years, including the rape footage."

"So, you basically turned in your own husband and son," muttered Nate.

"If I hadn't, I would never have seen my son again. Richard has a great deal of influence over him and could pressure him into doing just about anything he wanted. His plans were for the both of them to hide out at his cabin in South Carolina. He had no idea I had discovered some of the account deductions for his little hide-away.

I left for a few days to get my head together. When I returned, he and Junior had already gone. I suspected they had gone to the cabin and drove to see them. They weren't there so I waited. When they finally arrived, I told him that I knew everything about his affair, and in fact, that I had video of it all. I even told him that the Sheriff had a copy of it."

"Why didn't he turn himself in? Better yet, why didn't you notify the local State Troopers?" complained James.

"My only concern was for my son. Richard can rot in hell for all he has done to me and my family.

I was able to persuade Junior to turn himself in. He returned home with me to make the final arraignments. While waiting for the attorney, I had Junior check the only safe I knew about at the time.

He found the birth records hidden under a stack of stocks Richard had locked away. My attorney wanted to submit it into evidence, with hopes of swaying the judge, but I decided against it. Family affairs should not be aired out in court like someone's dirty laundry. So, there you have it. The whole twisted truth."

Nate sat quietly, staring at the floor. He didn't know whether to be angered or saddened by her story. Finally, he raised his head and asked, "Where is he?"

"To be completely honest, Mr. Brande, I have no idea. For all I know, he could be out of the country by now."

"I appreciate your honesty, but you still let your husband go free while your son sits in jail. I really don't see any justice in that. He gets to live out the rest of his days chillin' in another country somewhere, while Melina trembles in her sleep. James let's get the hell out of here." Mrs. Sullivan sat weeping, as Nate and James walked out.

"What a sick bastard! How do you rape your own daughter?!" said James as they neared the car. "And how on earth does your own mother help him do it?!" he added. Nate slowly pulled out of the Sullivan's driveway, then headed for home. "What are you going to do now?" asked James.

"I don't know," sighed Nate. "Let's see what Monica's opinion is concerning this mess. One things for sure, Melina **is not** getting this. Here, put this in the glove compartment for now," he said, handing James the Birth Certificate.

"Do you really believe that story about Junior not knowing Melina was his sister?" asked James.

"It doesn't matter. He did what he did, and that's all that matters to me. But for what it's worth, yeah, I do believe everything she told us."

"Just think. If she had divorced Richard, Sr., when she first found out, none of this would have happened," said James.

"True. But I would have never met Melina, and you would have never met Ashley. Talk about twisted fate," concluded Nate. He didn't say another word as he drove along, contemplating what should be done next. Before either of them had realized it, they had arrived at home, and were pulling into the garage.

Chapter 25

Two Down, One to Go!

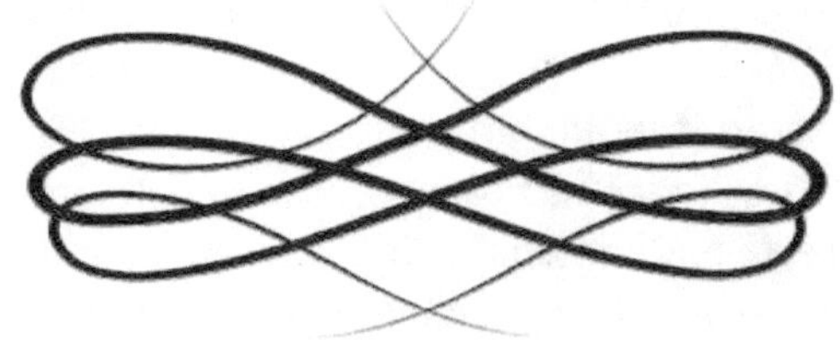

Another two weeks has come and gone, and there has been no sign of Richard Sullivan or Valencia Delgado. The sheriff had passed on information to all local and statewide authorities. It's as if they had just dropped off the face of the earth. "You did get the photos out to the Border Patrol, didn't you? "Yes sir, Sheriff. I faxed them out over six weeks ago, when you first asked me to," confirmed Deputy Johnson. "Well, send them again. Where the heck could they be?!"

Meanwhile, on a beach in Cancun, Mexico, Richard was stretched out in a lounge chair, enjoying another sunset. "Ah-h-h-h, sorry Junior, but this is so much nicer than a jail cell," he thought, as he sipped on a Margarita. "I just have to wait until the right time to make my move. Until then, I'll just have to lay low and try to enjoy life. That Bitch! I can't believe she videotaped me for all those years and then gave it all to the police!" Richard was so angry at the thought of what his wife had done, he threw his drink into the surf. "She had better watch **her** cute little ass too!" he pondered.

Junior's arraignment went as expected. The southern judge was a good old boy who didn't seem to take the charges surrounding the rape all that seriously. Despite the pleas made by Melina's attorney, including the fact that he had fled the state with his father, Richard's bail was set at a mere two-hundred-thousand dollars. He was released into his mother's custody within the hour. Throughout his entire arraignment, Richard refused to make eye contact with anyone other than the judge. He maintained a look of regret as the charges were read. It became obvious to us all that he would be receiving the minimum sentence. Melina took it well though. She seemed to be relieved that everything was finally underway.

"I expected it would go that way," stated her attorney, Michael Stone. "That judge has been on the bench longer than even I can remember. He has known the Sullivan's for a very long time. But don't worry, at the very least, Richard will have to do ten years."

"Yeah, but he could be out in five on good behavior," noted Monica.

"I don't care," moaned Melina. "I just want to put all of this ugliness behind me. And besides his father, **and** my mother, are still out there somewhere. They're the ones that really need to pay."

Melina thought back to that day, the day her life would be changed forever. "I can still see the look on his face," she explained. "Junior was reluctant, but his father kept pushing and pushing. He finally gave in to the pressure and raped me time and time again. He whispered an apology in my ear, and I could see the tears in his eyes as he . . ." She cringed at the thought, so Nate tried to console her.

As the couple hugged, Nate thought about the secret he was keeping from her, the fact that it was her very own father **and** brother who had violated her. He wondered if finding out would crush her spirit. She had recovered well considering the fact that her attackers were still at large. "Let's get out of here," whispered Sheryl. "Have faith. We will have our day." Melina smiled softly, as they all walked out.

"Saying 'thank you' could never begin to express the way I feel about what you have all done for me," whispered Melina. "You took me into your home and opened your hearts to me. You have become my family and GOD only knows where I would be without you . . . dead most likely. How do you repay someone for all of that?!"

"Just stay at my son's side. That is all you need to do," answered Sheryl. "He loves you very much. He has never told me, but a mother can always tell. Our family has never been this close before. Just look at us. My two sons **and** my daughter have all found love. What mother could want more for her children? I should be thanking **you**!" As Sheryl and Melina embraced, everyone looked on in awe. This was the family's defining moment.

"Mom, if you and your sisters aren't busy, James and I would like to take you all out to dinner next weekend."

"Well I'm sure we can clear our busy schedules. That would be nice."

"James and I will meet you all back at the house. We need to check with a couple of places and make the reservations." Mom, you and the girls can ride home together. We'll be there shortly."

"Okay baby."

After briefly hugging and kissing their girls, James and Nate walked over to the SUV where they stood by and watched as the limo drove off. "You can drop me off at the hospital," said Monica, into the intercom.

"You sure have been spending a lot of time with your doctor friend," noted Sheryl.

"Dr. Marshall and I are just having lunch, Mother. Please send the car back for me when you get home." Sheryl smiled, as Monica struggled to avoid the subject.

"What a way to start the day," yawned Ashley, as she

stretched.

"When we get home, I'm going right back to bed."

"How do you like being a nurse?" asked Sheryl.

"It's what I've always dreamed of doing," replied Ashley. "When I was a little girl, my grandmother was always ill. I would stay by her side and help the doctors take care of her. She would always tell me to follow that path. The doctors said I was very bright, and extremely helpful, for someone my age. I was nine or ten, I believe. Anyway, seeing this, my grandmother made me promise I would always help someone in need. A year later, the doctors moved her out of our home and into the hospital, so she could receive detailed care. My grandmother died seven months later from an inoperable brain tumor. It was her dying wish that I become a nurse and care for others, the way I had taken care of her."

The car was so quiet, you could practically hear their hearts beating. A tear rolled down Melina's cheek. "That was the saddest, yet most encouraging thing I have ever heard," whispered Sheryl. Melina grabbed a napkin from the wet bar to wipe her eyes. Her heart went out to her friend.

"And here I am today, taking care of your sad, sorry behind!" she joked, bumping against Melina.

"Your grandmother is watching over you with pride," announced Sheryl. "You have fulfilled your promise. I strongly believe Melina was the one she wanted you to save. It's time you moved on with your life. All of the events that have happened were predetermined the day you were conceived. Your reward for all of your determination, hard work and dedication, is love and happiness. GOD placed you in this position as a reward for all the good you have done. My sons have welcomed you into our home and James has fallen in love for the very first time in his life. **We** are your new destiny."

Silence had once again fallen upon the occupants of the limo. "Are you saying she should stop working at the hospital, Mrs.

Brande?" inquired Melina. "All I'm saying is that she has fulfilled her promise. The choice is hers to make. We have all been placed together for a reason. This is GOD's plan. We all have choices in life. HE wants us to make the right ones. The decisions are simply ours to make." Melina and Ashley looked at one another, as they considered what Sheryl had said.

"That's really deep, Mrs. Brande."

"Will you two please stop calling me that. I asked you some time ago to call me Sheryl."

When they arrived home Sheryl said, "Well, I don't know about you two, but I'm starving. Care to join me?" Sheryl removed several small dishes from the refrigerator. One contained sliced mango, cantaloupe and strawberries and the other, cut croissant and muffin pieces. "There's Apple Juice, Orange Juice, Milk and coffee. Please help yourself. The ladies sat quietly, enjoying another beautiful day in South Florida.

"I could really use another trip to the beach," sighed Melina. "I've loved going there ever since I was little."

"Nate was such a pain in the butt whenever his father and I took him and James there," recalled Sheryl. "I could never keep him out of the water! His father would literally have to go out into the ocean to get him!"

"If you don't mind me asking, what happened to his father?" asked Melina. "Well, that's a long story my dear, so here's the short version . . . *His father, James, Sr., was one of the most sought-after athletes in the country. All throughout high school, he played every sport available and excelled in them all. Baseball, football, track and field and his favorite, basketball. He received numerous scholarships, from some of the most prestigious colleges, from all around the country . . ."* Knowing a little of James's history, Ashley was particularly interested in what Sheryl was disclosing. She was finally beginning to understand her new found love's passion for the game, and also, what eventually ended his career. She sat forward, hanging on every word . . .

"Unfortunately, the schools weren't the only ones interested. I, and every other girl in the state, had a crush on the All-Star Athlete. We dated our entire senior year. I got pregnant with Nate shortly before graduation. Even though offers continued to pour in, James would not commit to a particular college. Soon afterward, I found out he was not committed to our relationship either. Rumors began to spread about him sleeping with dozens of women. Shortly thereafter, he began drinking and partying quite extensively. Six months after we graduated, Nate was born. Instead of going to college, we secretly married. He then began working to support his new family. A year later, James, Jr., was born. We were never really happy because by then, he was partying harder than ever."

"My father had started hearing the rumors of James' infidelity. It was said that he also had kids with several other women. Things had gotten so bad between us, James was partying all of his money away. I was so desperate, I had to track him down in the streets just to get money to feed our boys. I decided to move back in with my parents when he started staying out for days at a time. Since we were married for less than a year, I had no problem getting an annulment. My kids and I were literally starving, and the utilities were getting cut off. I had lost my opportunity for college, and he had thrown away his promising career to chase women, parties, blunts and booze."

"He made several attempts to reconcile, but it was rumored that one night, he came to my parent's home to see me. My father ran him off with a shotgun. Later, I met a good man, remarried, then moved to New Jersey. Two years later, I was blessed with Monica. My children banned together, saved my parents estate, then moved

us all back in. And there you have it. *Their father still lives in Pompano Beach. It took many years for them to forgive him for abandoning them, but they eventually did.* Nate actually paid for repairs recently on his father's home, and eventually paid it off.

However, James still holds a grudge, but he and Nate do manage to visit him from time to time."

"Mrs. Brande . . ."

"What did I **just** say?"

"I'm sorry, but I can't bring myself to call you that," apologized Ashley. "It just seems so disrespectful. May I please call you 'Mrs. S' instead?" Sheryl smiled as she thought about it. Ashley had been raised well, even though her parents passed away when she was young.

"Sure you can," she whispered.

"I'm confused. If Nate is the oldest, why wasn't **he** named after his father? I mean being his first born and all."

"I don't really know . . . Something told me that that particular name wouldn't be appropriate for him, so I gave it to his brother."

"What do you think, Melina?"

"I'm still trying to figure out how you knew not to give Nate his father's name. I find that to be so weird, yet fascinating!"

"Well, I credit that to divine intervention. I was all set to name him James, Jr., but when I held him in my arms for the very first time, a voice whispered 'Nathan' into my ear."

"From what I've heard about James, one thing's for sure . . . you most definitely got their names right!" smiled Ashley, while finishing off the last of the fresh fruit.

"Yeah, you're right. James **is** a lot like his father, bless his soul! He's a troubled young man, but with the love and support of a good woman, he'll be just fine," Sheryl promised, as she looked in

Ashley's direction. “Tell the boys I'll see them later. I could use a nap. And don't be discouraged by today's events, we're just getting started.”

“Honest Mrs. S, I'm fine . . . Enjoy your nap.”

The ladies yawned as they exited the elevator. Ashley waved her bracelet in front of the sensor to open the door. “Mya?! Where are you, you bad little girl?!” called Melina. Her new puppy had been busy! She had pulled one of the sheets off the bed, and left Melina's slippers in the middle of the floor. She got down on her knees and giggled, as Mya stuck her little beige and white face out from under the couch. “Come here! Come on!” coaxed Melina, but Mya wouldn't budge. “Here . . .” giggled Ashley, as she handed Melina the box of puppy biscuits. She placed one in front of her on the floor and watched as Mya slowly crept out.

“Got you!” she said, picking her puppy up to give her a hug. “E-w-w, puppy kisses!” she cried out. “I'll be back Ash, she needs to go out.” said Melina, as Mya finished her treat.

“Okay, I'm going to take a quick shower.”

“I don't think I've seen mom this happy in a long time,” noted James. “Everything seems to be going quite well.”

“Yeah I know. I keep waiting for the bottom to drop out at any moment,” remarked Nate. Oh, by the way, did you remember to double check to see that the order was ready?”

“Of course I did. Renaldo said everything’s available for pick-up.” “Well then, let’s do this!” The brothers got into their vehicle, then headed for Renaldo's Jewelry Shop.

“Damn, it's pretty crowded in here today,” said James. Nate raised his hand in an attempt to get Renaldo's attention. Renaldo nodded to acknowledge their presence. “Sandy, will you please escort the Brande brothers into the back room. I will be with you shortly,” he promised, as he finalized a sale. “Sandy, please assist the other patrons while I finish up things back here. I trust everything is as you instructed?" The jewelry was stunning. Everything sparkled brilliantly as Renaldo carefully laid out each piece.

"So that's what four-million-two-hundred-fifty-thousand dollars in diamonds looks like," said James.

"Not quite. The rest is over here," said Renaldo, as he directed James over to a separate table.

"What are you hiding over there?" asked Nate. "Nothing. I didn't want Ashley to feel left out, so I had something made special for her. Nothing extravagant, just a little something to show her that I care. Since you're getting engaged, I had better give Ashley something to keep her mind off of getting married!"

"Still afraid of commitment, huh?"

"I'm not afraid. I'm just not ready yet, that's all."

"Everything is perfect Renaldo. Here you are." Nate handed him his "Titanium Card" with unlimited spending.

"Nate, I'll take care of my own," said James, as he also handed Renaldo **his** card.

"Always a pleasure doing business with you gentleman." Sandy gift wrapped each piece and placed them in separate gift bags. "You ready?!"

"I'm set!"

"Then let's go!"

"I wonder if Richard still has his private cell? Well, I guess there's only one way to find out. After getting change from the Office, she headed out to the all-but-extinct payphone.

"Richard?"

"Valencia? Is that you?!"

"Yes, it's me. Who else would be calling this number, you bastard?! Why would you leave me here?! The police are all over the place! I expect them to be knocking at my door at any moment! Where the hell are you?!" whined Valencia.

"I can't tell you that. Let's just say I'm somewhere safe. Have you heard anything about my son?"

"How could I not. It's all over the news! He turned himself

in. They held his arraignment today. He'll be sentenced in about a week."

"Who's the judge presiding over the case?" "How the hell should I know, a Milton something."

Richard's face lit up like he had hit the lottery!

"Claybourne? Milton Claybourne?!"

"Yeah, that's him. So what's the big deal?"

"The 'big deal' is that he and I are old friends. I know he'll look out for my boy!"

"Well good for him! What the hell about me?! I need to get away from here Richard!" she pouted.

"Will you quite your whining and just listen up! Where are you?" "In a small town about five miles outside the city limits."

"I'm glad you called. Listen, I need you to keep your head together. I'll be coming back soon. Keep me updated on things, but don't call me unless it's extremely important."

"Why the hell would you want to come back here?!"

"Listen, don't ask questions, just do as I say, and I'll take you with me when I'm done. Deal?"

"You had better hurry up before that damn Sheriff tracks me down!"

"Just do as I say and we can live together like royalty. Bye."

"I'm glad she didn't get arrested yet. I could really use her info.

Maybe I **will** bring her here. I could really use some help with this damn Spanish," he thought as he groaned aloud.

"Will that be all sir?" whispered a young accented voice, as the maid got up from her knees on the side of the bed. She wiped her mouth then cleaned his deflating penis.

"Same time tomorrow my dear?"

"Yes sir." she mumbled as she accepted the inadequate payment for her services rendered. Richard watched as she got dressed. "It's not so bad here," he thought. "If I bring Valencia, I could be the only cock in my own little Latin Hen House!" He smiled as she walked out the door.

Meanwhile, Valencia was not coping as well as Richard was. She was really beginning to panic. It seemed as if every time she left her room, a trooper would drive by. "I don't know how long I can keep this up!" she thought. "I hope my little princess is doing okay. I really, really miss my baby girl. I pray that she forgives me for what I've done." Valencia sat on the edge of the bed crying. She was actually considering turning herself in. "Maybe I'll get the same judge as Junior and won't get that long of a sentence either," she thought.

"It's like I'm in jail already anyway. I've lost my home, my Daughter . . ." Valencia fell to her knees and began to pray for forgiveness. Suddenly, there was a knock at the door. Her heart pounded so hard, she could practically hear it! "Who . . . who is it?" she stuttered.

"It's me Ma'am." Valencia exhaled deeply after hearing the familiar voice of her landlord.

"Hello Mrs. Anderson, what can I do for you?" asked Valencia, as she opened the door with a smile on her face.

"You can put your hands behind your back!" answered the female State Trooper. Valencia just stood there in shock as the Trooper's partner rushed in to search the room. She reluctantly placed her hands behind her back while she was being read her rights.

"You here alone?"

"Y-y-yes Ma'am," she stammered.

"This is Johnson, we have one in custody. Requesting a Supervisor for transport." "Ten-four. I'm en route." "We received an anonymous tip that a suspect at large was staying in this room," stated Trooper Johnson. She held up the "BOLO" Alert, she had removed from her pocket, to confirm Valencia's identity. "Do you have any weapons or concealed sharps on your person that may result in my injury, before I search you?"

"No, ma'am, nothing." She just stood there quivering, as the officer thoroughly searched about her person.

"She's clean Rodriguez. You can put her in the car."

"Please wait. I have my life savings in the safe. I want to be here when you remove it. It's in the closet."

"Nice job you two," said Supervisor Ortiz, as he entered the room. "But why isn't she in the car?"

"The suspect claims to have money in the safe and wanted to witness the removal. She has been co-operative sir."

"Fine. Combination please." The troopers began a detailed inventory of Valencia's property while their Supervisor opened the safe.

"I can't believe that crippled bitch turned me in!"

"That's an awful lot of money to be carrying around little lady," stated Ortiz as he placed it on the table, in plain view of Valencia. "Twenty-three-thousand-one-hundred-fifty dollars."

He placed the money into a clear plastic evidence bag, then sealed it in front of her. "Anything else of extreme value in here?" "No sir. Just my money and some clothes."

"Okay then. I'll be taking Ms. Delgado and her money back to the station while you two finish up here." Valencia sobbed heavily. Ortiz struggled to keep her on her feet, as they walked to the car. "Two down and one to go!"

Chapter 26
A Leap of Faith: No Hesitations

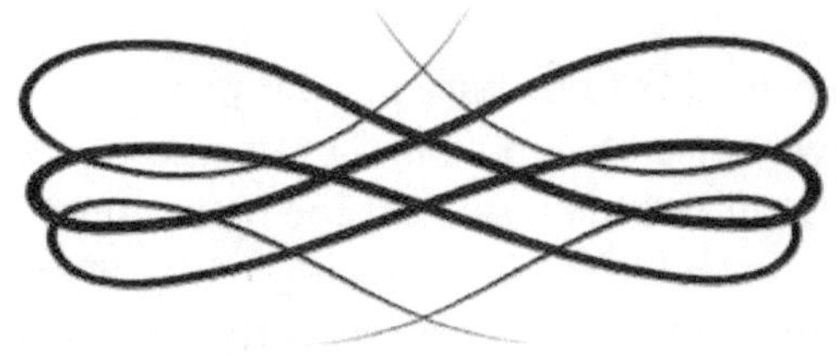

An intercom conversation between James and Nate:

"Will you move your ass! The limo will be here any minute!"

"Nate, will you please calm down! It's not like we have to be on time to keep our reservations. You own the place!"

"It's just that I want everything to go perfectly, that's all."

"Damn, I'll be down in five, okay? **Now** can I finish getting ready?!" **End of conversation.**

Nat stood nervously in the driveway, awaiting the car. He reached into his jacket pocket and removed the black velvet case containing the rings. He smiled as the diamonds twinkled like stars in the setting sun. The Engagement Ring was beautiful. The Oval Chocolate Diamond was about six karats on a raised setting, surrounded by two additional karats of Chocolate Baguettes. The matching gold band was also encrusted with four karats of Baguette; a total of twelve karats in rare jewels.

Nate took a deep breath, then exhaled slowly as he looked up at the stars. "Mom-mee, Pop-pop . . . I want to thank you for watching over me and sending Melina. She was the one thing missing from my otherwise perfect life. Mom-mee, I know it was you that sent this angel of a woman to me. She reminds me so much of you. She's loving, nurturing and tough. Melina has been through so much! I just want her to be as happy with me, as I am with her. I really hope and pray that I'm not moving too fast. Am I doing the right thing? I don't want to scare her away." Then suddenly, as if it had been written in a script, a shooting star zipped across the darkening sky. Nate nodded and smiled, as he watched it disappear across the horizon. "Thank you. And may GOD keep you both close!" he whispered.

Nate placed the box back into his pocket as the limo pulled into the driveway. He smiled as his Aunts approached, conversing happily, as they walked the path past the main house.

"Where is everyone?" asked Betty, as she and her sisters slowly approached the limo.

"They should be down shortly. You all look very lovely," said Nate, as he greeted each of his Aunts with a hug and kiss on the cheek. "Hi Mom. You all set?"

"I'm a little anxious. Just where **are** you taking us anyway?"

"It's a surprise, someplace none of you have ever been before." "Well it had better be nice!" interrupted Jean. "I don't get this dressed up for anyone very often, not even my dates!"

"I'm surprised you bother getting dressed at all!" joked Lorraine. "Yeah, you may as well cut through the chase!" added Betty. "We all know how it's going to end up anyway!"

"Oh ha-ha! You two are so hilarious!" remarked Jean.

"Will you all please play nice. Call a truce or something! These arraignments set me back a small fortune, so let's all have a good time, okay?" The sisters made their peace as the driver came around to open the door.

"Did you buy another limo?"

"No Mom, it's the VIP car used to pick up my special guests

for the club. I don't use it very often."

"Well, it's about time," stated Nate, as Monica and James exited the house.

"Just look at us," Sheryl remarked. "We have all been so blessed! What a beautiful family we have! Thank you, Jesus! *Glory be to GOD who watches from on high."*

"I think this is the first time, since you were little kids, that we have all gone anywhere together," recalled Jerri. "It seemed like only yesterday I was pushing you on the swings." The siblings smiled and listened as their relatives reminisced.

"You just made it," remarked Monica, as she watched Ken get out of his car.

"Hello everyone. Sorry I'm late." They all became silent, gazing as Ashley and Melina slowly walked down the steps. They looked exquisite from head to toe.

"I see someone's ready for the red carpet!" stated Betty.

"Damn, you boys hit the jackpot!" exclaimed Jean, as she walked over and stood between her nephews. "Don't let them get away!" she whispered, while patting them both on the shoulder.

Ashley and Melina were wearing matching dresses, Melina in dark green and Ashley in black. Both were form fitting, halter-style gowns with button back collars. Melina wore six-inch stiletto heels with lace style wraps. Her hair flowed with loose curls covering the left side of her face, draping down her back. Ashley wore the same style shoes with three-inch heels. Her hair flowed evenly over both shoulders and down her back. As beautiful as Ashley was, she still paled in comparison to Melina.

The driver did all he could to maintain his composure. He tugged at his collar and cleared his throat as they got closer.

"Just when I thought you couldn't get any more beautiful, you do," Nate whispered. Melina smiled as he took her by the hand and helped her into the car. He helped his mother in next. James assisted Ashley while Ken assisted Monica. They each assisted the rest of the family members, before getting in themselves. The conversation was light, as the ladies each gave one another compliments on their wardrobes.

It was a rather cool evening for this time of year. The temperature was around seventy degrees, but felt a bit chillier in the car while riding with the roof open. James closed the top when he noticed goose bumps forming on Ashley's arms. Loraine and Betty started handing out the glasses from the wet bar, while Jean removed the three bottles of Champagne, that were chilling in the ice, behind the bar. She passed them to Jerri, who in turn, handed one to each of the men. The ladies laughed, as they ducked and dodged the corks ricocheting around the compartment. The women held out their glasses, while the men poured.

"U-m-m-m, now this is delicious," whispered Melina as she snuggled back into the plush, sheep skin seating. "I feel more like a princess every day. I've been so spoiled by all of you over the past five months, you couldn't get rid of me now if you wanted to!" The group chuckled at her comment, which seemed to open the door for what happened next.

"Melina, do you have any plans for your future?" asked Jean. "Once all of the madness is behind you, what's next?"

"I really haven't given it much thought. The only life I have ever known was that of a housekeeper, cleaning the Sullivan's Mansion with my mother. However, I did always dream of owning my own business one day. My mother and I were saving our money to open our own little café' in a few years."

Until that very moment, Melina had forgotten all about the money she and her mother had been stashing over the past five years. "What's wrong dear?" asked Sheryl.

"Oh, it's nothing. I just remembered all of the money I left behind when I ran away. My mother probably took it and skipped town with Mr. Sullivan. Even though Nate has provided for my every need, it was nice knowing that I had my own little nest egg."

"Don't get me wrong. I'm very appreciative and thankful for all of this. I really am! I've been so blessed!" Nate smiled as she took him by the hand. Sheryl chose that moment to change the subject.

"So, just where are you boys taking us anyway?!"

"Yeah Nate, what's the big secret?!" asked Lorraine."

"No secret. I just wanted a nice evening out with my family, that's all.

"Destination in five minutes," announced the driver.

"Monica, you're awfully quiet over there. Where are we going?" "Mom, I have no idea. This is Nate and James's little excursion. I had nothing to do with it. I've been kept in the dark about this just as the rest of you have."

The driver slowly came to a halt as the gates began to open. "Where the heck are we?" asked Betty, as the limo eased forward past the gates. "This place looks deserted."

"Everyone, welcome to Dark Passions." They all sat forward quietly, in anticipation of seeing Nate's club for the very first time. The driver slowly advanced past the doors, then parked, as they began to close behind them. The family couldn't wait to get out. They were all standing in the lobby before the driver had a chance to get out and open the door for them!

"Good evening everyone. My name is Tony Clemons, the Maitre D'. I will personally be overseeing the events of the evening. If there is anything you require, please do not hesitate to ask." Nate proceeded with the introductions, as they walked towards the elevators.

"I must apologize. I had intended on giving each of you a tour of the suites, but they're all filled with guests," said Nate.

"That's the only problem with this place, it's always full," joked Tony. "There won't be an empty suite for the next five years!"

"Oh boo-hoo! It really must be tough counting all that

money!" teased Jean. "Here we are, the Rooftop Lounge." said Tony. "Welcome to the 'Divine Intervention Suite,'" announced Nathan, as the group slowly exited the elevator, while looking around in awe.

"Good evening, right this way," announced one of the waiters.

The room was beautifully decorated with palm trees and other tropical foliage. Water flowed down three of the perimeter walls of the lounge, giving the effect of being surrounded by waterfalls. Sheryl and her sisters stopped to gaze at the marble fountain. Smartly lit and exquisitely decorated, it was the center piece of the room. Sheryl placed the tips of her fingers over her mouth.

"Nate, is this . . ."

"Yes mom, it's your father's fountain." Seeing this brought tears to their eyes.

"I thought it was gone forever!" said Lorraine, as she wiped her eyes. "Why would you think that?!" asked Monica.

"Well, when daddy had his heart attack pulling into the driveway, he lost control of his truck, crashing into the fountain, destroying over half of it. We just assumed it was scrapped when the remodeling of the mansion began."

"To be honest, I wasn't sure **what** we were going to do with it at the time," stated Nate. "It was actually Monica's idea that we salvage it. We weren't sure it could be done until one of the contractors asked what we intended to do with it. Monica asked if it could be saved somehow and he told her about a guy he knew who might be able to do something with it. In the right light, you can see where some of the repairs were made, but overall, he did an outstanding job."

"Why didn't you have it placed back on the front lawn?" asked Jean.

"When I had this roof redesigned, it needed something special. James suggested we use the fountain. It was exactly what we needed to bring everything together. If I ever decide to sell this place, I'll bring the fountain home. I promise." Betty walked over and kissed Nate on the cheek.

"This is the perfect place for it," she whispered.

Three staff members waited patiently near the tables, as the aroma of fresh baked bread caught the group's attention. They finally made their way over and were greeted by the rest of the staff. As agreed upon weeks ago, Nate and Melina headed one table, while James and Ashley headed the other. The tables were draped in red, with white lace trimming, which was perfectly accented by white china and red and white roses.

"You are just full of surprises tonight, aren't you?!" Sheryl asked, as she took a close look at the china. "This was given to Mom and Dad as a wedding gift! Where on earth did you find it?!"

"It was packed away in the basement. I thought it would be a nice touch." Everyone settled in and chatted as the salads were being served and their orders were taken.

"This place is breathtaking," whispered Melina.

"Thanks. I really wish you could see the suites, but they're filled with celebrities. Maybe you'll get to meet some of them before we go." There was no way Nate was going to take Melina or any of his family into one of the private parties. He knew all too well what went on behind those closed doors. Strippers, orgies . . . anything goes. He and James had seen it all on camera, just prior to the video being deleted. Even though he had been invited to just about every party, Nate always declined. He knew to never mix business with pleasure. James, on the other hand, of course, happily participated from time to time.

Nate took Melina by the hand, then escorted her from the table. They slowly walked around the room as the soft music set the tone for the evening.

"The view is amazing," she said as she admired the distant

lights of downtown Miami. She placed her arms around the waist of her new-found love, then laid her head against his chest. She sighed as she exhaled deeply.

"What's wrong?"

"Oh, nothing. I was just wondering when the next bad thing was going to happen! You have changed my life completely and I'm so happy; but I keep expecting . . . I don't know; I guess it all seems too good to be true."

"Melina don't worry. My life is your life. You will never have to worry about anything for as long as you live. GOD brought us together and I will never, ever, take that for granted. What we have was preordained by the love of Jesus. We were meant to be together. Believe in that and you will always be safe. Together, we can get through anything! I love you!"

"And I love you, Nathan Brande!" The family watched, as the couple stared deeply into each other's eyes.

"Now that's **real** love." whispered Shirley.

"Tony, retract the roof please," whispered James.

Tony was standing near the service elevator, awaiting the arrival of the entrees from the kitchen. He flipped the switch on the wall, then watched, as the retractable dome opened overhead. The family was speechless. The stars were so big and beautiful, it was as if you could reach right up and pick one! Melina stood with her mouth ajar. It was as if she wanted to speak, but nothing came out, as she gazed up at all the stars.

"Now this is too much!" she whispered.

"No wonder this place stays booked, This is fantastic!" said Ken, as he and Monica slowly walked over. James and Ashley were on the other side of the room admiring the view. Sheryl and her sisters sat chatting about the children, and all they had accomplished.

The rattling of dishes broke the somber mood of the room.

The couples rejoined the rest of the family as the entrees were served. Nate asked his mother to say grace, while everyone bowed their heads and gave thanks. *Nate was always too shy to say grace for some reason, even though he was really good at it. When he spoke, people would comment that he could have been a preacher.* Wine was served to those who wanted it. Nate preferred water, while James had beer. As they finished dinner, Tony placed small covered dishes on the table for each of the women. The staff began collecting the dinner ware while moving the covered dishes into position.

The women thought they were about to have dessert, when James stood up, lightly tapping his glass with a fork.

"Nate and I have been thinking a lot about how much you all mean to us . . . Our family has never been closer, and we wanted to show you all how much we cared." Nate stood up, to join his brother.

"No matter how many times you say 'I love you,' it's never enough," he added. "So, we put our heads together and came up with this special dessert. We hope you like it." The ladies removed the silver lid from the black dish, now sitting in front of each of them.

"Oh my Lord!" gasped Betty. Loraine's hands shook nervously as she reached for the heart shaped, diamond encrusted necklace, neatly arraigned on the dish.

The women were speechless. Even Monica had tears in her eyes as she held it in her hands. They began to realize that each of them had a matching diamond necklace. They sparkled so much, you could almost light the entire room with them! As they began to get over the initial shock, James explained. "We wanted to give you all something special, a symbol binding each of you together forever. But we also wanted something that symbolized our love for one another."

"Nicely said," stated Nate. "What better way than to give you our heart!" he added. "We love you!" said the boys in unison. The men walked around and fastened the jewelry around each of their necks, then followed it with a kiss on the cheek.

Each woman was wearing fifteen karats of the most exquisite Chocolate Diamonds ever crafted. Even the necklace itself sparkled with gems. "Before you say anything, please don't complain about how much it must have cost us . . . **'Mother.'** We were honored to do it!" said Nate.

"The heart pendant was first given to our mother by our father," explained Sheryl. "He always told us that it was the love in his heart that gave him the strength and courage to persevere after he was disowned by his own family for marrying our bi-racial mother. No matter how strong you are, without true love in your heart, you will never be able to overcome the adversities of the devil, for true love conquers all. Dad gave her the necklace on their first wedding anniversary."

Melina and Ashley sat quietly, listening to Sheryl speak about her family's history. However, they were both a little confused as to why their dishes were empty. Nate and James slowly approached them.

"What happened to your gift?" asked Nate. James chuckled as if it were some kind of joke. Nate was a little confused as to why James did not give Ashley her gift, but he was more concerned with the task at hand. He felt about his person as if he was trying to find something. . . "Oh, wait, here it is," he said finally.

"Melina, for years, I have prayed for true love. After five long years, the Lord has seen fit to bless me. I never questioned why you were sent to me in the manner in which you were. I only gave thanks. From the first moment I set eyes upon you, I knew you were a gift from GOD, an angel sent by my grandmother to be by my side." Everyone gasped and slowly rose to their feet as Nate got down on one knee. Shocked, Melina slowly raised both hands, trembling, as she covered her mouth. "Baby, I could think of no better way to express my love for you than this . . ." Nate slowly opened the gift box. "Melina, you know my heart. It belongs to you . . . will you please, please be my wife?!"

The tension in the room was unbearable. It seemed like forever before Melina answered.

"I have given up on trying to understand why things happen the way that they do. All I know is that it happens for a reason. GOD watched over me that day. He gave me the strength to walk that long, dusty road. Just when I couldn't take another step, HE carried me the rest of the way. HE guided me to you. There could be no other explanation. I'm not shaking because I'm scared, I'm shaking because, tonight, you have made me the happiest woman in the world." Melina looked up to the heavens then whispered, "Thank You, Jesus!" She looked down at her man and quietly said, "I have also loved you from the first time I gazed into your eyes. Tonight, I am yours forever. Of course, I will marry you!" Nate steadied her hand as he placed the ring upon her finger.

Everyone began to clap as Nate slowly rose to his feet and took Melina by both hands. She could barely stand as Nate helped her to her feet. They kissed passionately. As they embraced, Melina whispered, "You have my heart, and my soul. I am now prepared to give you my body." Nate squeezed Melina so tightly, she could hardly breathe! The embrace was finally interrupted by James, as he again, rose to his feet.

"I was never good with words," mumbled James, as he got down on one knee."

"D-don't play with me James!" stuttered Ashley.

"Will you marry me?" he whispered, as he removed the ring from his breast pocket." Sheryl fell back in her chair! She never thought she would live to see the day when James would propose to anyone! Speechless, Ashley could only nod slowly, as she held out her hand.

James gently placed the ring upon her finger. "I love you," he said. Then they shared a kiss. Suddenly Ashley shouted, "Yes, yes, yes!"

"Well, I guess this is as good a time as any . . ." said Ken, as he stood up. "Mrs. Brande, I wanted to ask you this privately, but, may I please have your daughter's hand in marriage?" Sheryl nodded as she wept. All of her children in one night?! Her sisters helped her back to her feet as Kenneth proposed to Monica. Nate hugged, then congratulated his brother. "Damn, I just can't believe this . . . You Mister 'I'm-never-getting-married' James Brande, Jr?! I can't believe you just got engaged!"

"Beneath the heavens, in the presence of GOD, the love of Jesus has touched my children!" whispered Sheryl, weeping tears of joy, as the staff poured champagne. "To all of my children. Thank you for restoring our family name. You have been blessed by GOD for all you have done. Your reward is love. There is no greater gift, or blessing than that. Here's to all of you!" said Sheryl, as she raised her glass to toast the newly engaged couples.

Monica, Ashley and Melina gathered near the fountain to congratulate one another, and admire their Engagement Rings, while the staff served dessert. Ken joined James and Nate.

"This is too much!" he laughed. "I can't believe we all got engaged at the same time!"

"I knew you were up to **something** at the shop that day!" stated Nate. "I just never guessed it would be this!" he concluded.

"I told you I loved her."

"But you, married?!"

"Yeah, I still can't believe it myself!" chuckled James.

"And **you**, Dr. Kenneth Marshall, had better be good to our baby sister! Remember, we know where you live!" teased James, as he shook hands with Ken.

"That's right," added Nate. "You do want to live long enough to enjoy that Sky Box, don't you?!" They all laughed as they returned to the tables to have dessert and enjoy the rest of the evening.

"I'm sorry to interrupt Sir, but Mr. 'J.D.' and his entourage are calling it an evening," said Tony.

"Excuse me, but duty calls. I'll be back in about twenty minutes," announced Nate. "Melina, would you like to join me?" She smiled as she got up from the table to join her man. "The suite may be a little messy, but you can check it out, if you like." "Maybe some other time. I would rather enjoy the rest of the evening celebrating with your family."

"Soon to be **our** family," added Nate.

"Congratulations on your engagement, Miss Delgado," said Tony, as the elevator doors opened.

"Tony is my most trusted protégé'. He handles just about everything. I'm really going to miss him. He's considering moving back to New York to help his brother with his restaurant."

"As you have always said sir, family **always** comes first."

At that moment, Nate had an idea, but it would have to wait until he finished his business. "Calling it a night so soon?" he said, as he approached J.D. and his bodyguards.

"I have a show to do in a couple of hours," he said, as he stared at the tanned goddess.

"I would like you to meet my fiancé, Melina Delgado. Melina, meet music icon, 'J.D.'"

He took her by the hand then lightly kissed it. "Damn! No wonder you never came to one of my parties! She's the most beautiful woman I have ever seen, and you know I've seen a lot!" Melina blushed, said thank you, then looked in Nate's direction.

"Okay, let's do this." Nate, Melina and J.D. walked into the monitor room, while the bodyguards and Tony waited outside the closed door. Ten minutes later they walked out.

"You be sure to send me an invite."

"You got it."

"Melina, it was nice meeting you," said J.D., as he handed Nate his payment. The men shook hands then parted ways.

"Damn, and I thought 'B' was fine!" stated one of the bodyguards. "Watch it!" joked J.D. "You like your job, don't you?"

"Yes Sir! My apologies."

"You're right though!" they laughed.

As they headed for the elevator, Nate decided to tell Tony about his idea. "Do you think your brother would mind relocating?" Tony had a puzzled look on his face.

"What do you mean sir?"

"To be honest, I am really getting tired of coming here to handle the things **you** could be doing. I'm looking forward to spending more time with my fiancé, maybe even start a family." Melina's eyes widened at the thought, but she remained silent. She had never considered having children. She wasn't even sure if she could.

"My proposal is this. I'll make you the club manager. Your brother could run his restaurant here, with my chefs. We could combine menus. It would give the clientele a much broader selection. It's just a thought. Talk it over with your brother. You are the only person I would ever trust to do this. I could never replace you and I don't want to lose you. I will have James go over the surveillance system with you. It'll be prefect for the both of us."

"Sir, I really don't know what to say."

"Just think about it. The two of you could make a fortune!" Tony's face beamed as he pondered the possibilities. Nate and Melina exited the elevator to rejoin the rest of the family. Tony had a lot to think about.

Chapter 27
The Devil is Always Busy!

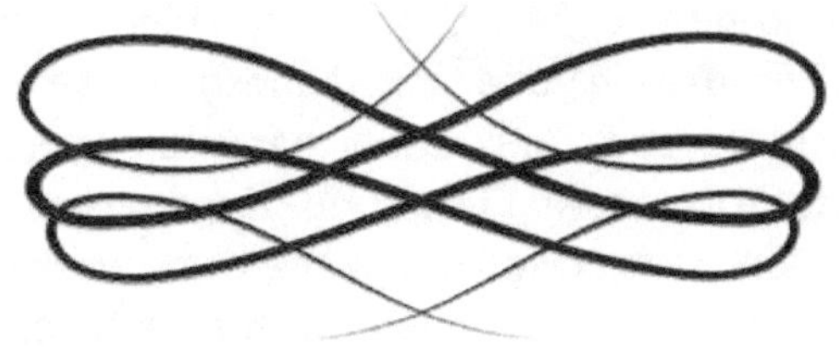

"I'm so happy for all of you," said Sheryl as she hugged the girls good night. Her sisters also gave their approval before the ladies parted ways. Ashley, Melina and Monica walked slowly up the steps and into the house. Still reeling from the events of the evening, all they could manage to say to one another was good night. The ladies admired their rings as the elevator stopped on the third floor. Monica smiled, then hugged the others, before exiting.

Ashley and Melina could hardly contain themselves as they opened the door. Once inside, they squealed, giggled and held hands, while jumping around like little kids. Melina followed Ashley as she entered her room, while taking off her shoes. "I still can't believe we just got engaged!" shouted Ashley, as she peeled off her dress.

"Yeah, I know!" replied Melina.

"I'm so numb all over, it feels like I'm dreaming!"

"Ow!" squeaked Melina, as Ashley crept up behind her, then playfully pinched her soft, voluptuous ass.

"I guess you're not dreaming after all!" laughed Ashley, as she ran into the bathroom, away from Melina, who was playfully, trying to pinch her back."

"Why don't you sleep with **me** tonight?" she called out, as she turned on the shower.

"Aren't you going to sleep with James tonight?!" "Just take a quick shower then come back, okay?!" Melina smiled, then walked out. Twenty minutes later, she returned, then jumped onto the bed with Ashley.

"Why aren't you going to spend the night with James?"

"Just because we got engaged doesn't mean he gets to taste any of this!" she teased, running her hands along her sexy frame. "Wait a minute. You're trying to get rid of me so you can see Nate, aren't you?!" Melina tried to lie, but the truth was written all over her face, as she struggled to come up with an excuse. Her face reddened from the embarrassing truth. Melina laid down on the bed, then tried to hide her horny shame, beneath the pillow.

"Don't be embarrassed," whispered Ashley, as she removed the pillow from her friend's face. "To be honest, my stuff is dripping wet! I want James so bad, I can practically taste him, but I'm willing to wait. Baby, you've come **this** far, can't you can wait just a little bit longer to sleep with Nathan? Don't give yourself to him just yet. Believe me, your honeymoon will be even that much more magical."

"O-o-o-h, my honeymoon . . ." cooed Melina. "Can you believe all of this is actually happening?!" she said. "I would never have believed that men with money could be so full of love and respect. I really thought all rich men were jerks; you know, like Mr. Sullivan."

"I never would have believed it either, but here we are," added Ashley. The ladies snuggled face to face, as they admired their rings. Sleep was just an illusion.

"I hope they don't stay at the club too long; I really would like to see James before I fall asleep."

"I think Nate is going to let that guy Tony, take over the club. He was talking about it as we went down to meet up with that Rapper, J.D."

"Wait! You met J.D.!"

"So? What's the big deal about him? You're kidding me, right?! He is only the biggest name in music, that's all! You really need to get out more!"

"I have everything I need **right here**, thank you very much." Ashley looked deeply into Melina's eyes. She could see that her friend was ready. She'd gotten past all of her hurt, fears, and inhibitions, and was now ready to make love, for the very first time.

"Are you sure you're ready to do this?" she asked.

"I've never been more sure of anything in my life," whispered Melina. "And I owe it all to you. If we had never met, I would never have gotten past my rape. I don't even tremble when I think about it anymore. You are my nurse; you are my friend; and you are my sister. I love you with all my heart. Thank you for helping to save my life." They held each other tightly. As they embraced, Melina's eyes widened as Ashley kissed her on the lips.

"I love you too," she whispered. Melina didn't shy away. She was very comfortable in her relationship with Ashley. So comfortable in fact, she fell asleep in her arms. Ashley smiled as she closed her eyes to join her friend in peaceful slumber.

As James and Nate finished erasing the last footage of the evening, Tony knocked on the door of the Surveillance Room. "I'm sorry to interrupt, but I thought you might want to see this . . ." Tony handed Nate his cellphone, as he brought up the local news. "Police have released the identity of a second suspect sought in the rape of Melina Delgado. (A photograph flashes across the screen.) The second suspect, Valencia Delgado, the mother of the victim, was recently apprehended by the State Police in a small motel just five miles outside of town. The third suspect, Richard Sullivan, Sr., is still at large."

"Thanks," said Nate, while handing the phone back to Tony.

"Are you going to tell Melina?"

"No, I don't think so."

"Listen. That woman obviously loves the hell out of you now. This is no way to build a trusting relationship. You're already keeping one secret and it's eating you up inside. I suggest you come clean about everything you know. She's a lot stronger now. I think she can handle the truth."

"Listen to you, giving **me** advice."

"Keep it up and I'll have to start charging you!" joked James. "Seriously though, she deserves to know the truth."

"I know she does, and I don't like keeping secrets. I just don't want to ruin her happiness, that's all.

"Did you see the look on her face when she saw her ring? She told me she was ready. She wants to make love. I want her so bad, I can taste it!" James chuckled, as the two men walked out towards the limo.

"So, what are you going to do?"

"I'm going to wait, that's what. I want our union to start out right."

"Then tell her the truth about her mother, father, and half-brother." Nate groaned loudly as he got into the limo. He knew that his brother was right, but how could he do that to the woman he loved so dearly. The brothers sat quietly as they reminisced about getting engaged. The silence made for a long ride home.

"Do you think they're still awake?"

"Are you kidding, it's four in the morning!" replied Nate, as he unlocked the door.

"I was really hoping to see her."

"You were really hoping to get some, you mean.

"Yeah right . . . Night bro."

"Back at you." James then exited the elevator. Even though

it was late, Nate still felt restless. After a quick shower, he poured himself a glass of Remy, then headed for the balcony. He knew his brother was right, but he just couldn't convince himself to tell Melina the truth. He looked to the stars and prayed for the strength he needed to do what he knew was right. He finished his drink, sighed, and then went to bed. He thought about the evening he spent with Melina and his family, then smiled as he drifted off to sleep.

The sound of rain awakened him. He stretched, then yawned loudly, before sitting up in the bed. "Man, what time is it?" he mumbled to himself. He struggled to focus his eyes on the clock hanging on the wall across the room. "Seven-forty?!" he groaned, as he fell backwards, stretching out across the bed. He looked over to see that he had, inadvertently, left the door to the balcony ajar. The downpour was brief, but heavy enough to force water into his room.

He jumped up and quickly dried the granite floor with a couple of large towels. He was always perplexed by Florida weather. It would often rain while the sun was shining. The balcony was already beginning to dry. He reached under his mattress and removed the Birth Certificate he had retrieved from the car a few days ago. He stared at it while he sat on the edge of the bed pondering his next move. "Maybe James was right. Maybe Melina **is** strong enough to handle the truth. But on the other hand, what if she isn't? News like this could cause her some serious pain! Shit!"

A light knock at the door broke him out of his trance. A second knock got his attention. He was puzzled. No one **ever** knocked at his door. Everyone used the intercom or just called his cell. He slipped on his robe, then opened the door.

"Good morning sleepy head, can I come in?" Nate was in shock. Melina was standing at his door! "Well, can I come in?!" she asked a second time. He stepped to the side and watched as she entered. She was wearing a tiny black silk robe which was just long enough to cover her magnificent and well sculpted, ass. He watched as it jiggled beneath the silk as she walked. He checked down the hall before quickly closing the door, then slowly walked in her direction.

"Nice place you have here," she whispered, as she wrapped her arms around his waist. Nate quickly tried to regain his composure. "Do you know how much trouble you could get into being in here?" Melina only smiled.

"What are you afraid of? I don't bite."

"Stop playing, you know what I mean!" She broke their embrace and backed away.

"What are you wearing under there?!" she asked, ignoring his comment, while attempting to open his robe.

"Stop it!" he laughed, as he backed away. Melina giggled, as she walked past him.

"Is that your bedroom?" she asked, as she walked towards the archway. As she slowly crawled across the bed, Nate could see she was wearing very skimpy, see-through lingerie. "So, is this where all the magic happens?" she asked coyly, as she laid on her side rubbing the over-sized mattress.

Nate walked slowly towards the bed. "There has never been any magic in **this** bed," he admitted sadly. "After Katrina left, I replaced the old bed with this one. This one's ready and waiting."

"Well, I'm here, so let's test it out." Nate chuckled and shook his head as he joined her on the bed. She smiled, as he lightly touched her face. "You are really making it difficult to wait," he whispered.

"What are you waiting for?" she asked, as she slowly opened her robe.

She was wearing a two-piece set that left very little to the imagination. Nathan couldn't answer. He was speechless as he surveyed every inch of her body. "How do you like my new haircut?" she whispered, as she ran her hand across her breasts, then down her stomach, pointing at her sheer panties. He could see that she had trimmed away most of the hair, leaving a small heart-shaped "M" design, just above her vaginal area. "What **is** that moving under there?" she asked, as Nate's erection began to rise beneath his robe. She looked deep into his eyes, as she slowly reached over and untied it.

"Melina, wait."

"No Nate. I don't want to wait anymore! It feels like someone just lit a fire between my legs!" She moaned and squirmed as she lightly touched between her thighs. Nate was so turned on, he kissed her so hard it hurt! She placed one leg across his waist, then rolled him onto his back, until she was sitting on top of him. It was so hot in that room, you could almost see steam rising from their bodies! Melina sat back and began to grind for all she was worth, moaning loudly. "I want to feel you inside me!" she panted.

"Baby, please stop!" whispered Nate, unconvincingly. He had very little fight left, and there was no way he was going to stop her. Nate had one chance to keep the relationship pure and stop Melina from going all the way. "I don't want to have sex before we're married," he said. But those noble words fell upon deaf ears.

He reached up and took a firm hold of Melina's breasts, pressing them together. This caused her to moan even more. He then reached down and took a firm hold of each of her ass cheeks as he glided her back and forth against his stiffened rod.

"Oh Nate, make love to me!" she begged. "Give it to me baby! I want all that dick!" groaned Melina, as she drenched Nathan's rock-hard erection.

It was time Nate made his move. He removed his right hand from her ass and reached down between her wet thighs. He began massaging her swollen clitoris with his fingers tips by using a fluttering type motion. This drove Melina absolutely wild!

Melina's arms slid backwards across the bed, from Nate's chest, down near his legs, as her body leaned back. Her knees slid wide across the bed. Suddenly, Melina let out the deepest, loudest, longest groan he had ever heard! Her body jerked uncontrollably. Nate could feel her warm juices squirt against his swollen rod, while running down his thighs. His silk sheets were thoroughly soaked with her juices!

Suddenly, his body began to tense up. Instinctively, Melina quickly sat forward, reached around with both hands and squeezed his swollen rod. She massaged it like a pro, using a sort of twisting motion, as she slowly stroked him. She moaned and climaxed repeatedly as she watched his thick white ooze spurt out onto his tightened stomach and chest. They climaxed together. This was the first time she had ever seen a man reach an orgasm, not counting Mr. Sullivan. She began to sensually rub the thick nectar about his stomach and chest as they each struggled to catch their breath.

Melina slowly collapsed down onto Nate's chest. She wanted to feel his warm sticky goo against her body, as she slowly rubbed her chest against his. He held her tightly as they both moaned. "It's hard to believe you've never done this before," panted Nate. "Where did you learn to do **that**?!"

"I don't know how I knew what to do. I just did."

"Well feel free to do it again anytime!" he joked. Now Melina had watched her mother use that twisting motion on Mr. Sullivan lots of times, but she would never disclose that to Nathan.

"I feel like we just made love," she whispered. "If I'm this drained after what we just did, I can't imagine what I'll feel like after we really do it." Nate squeezed her lightly. He had managed to keep their relationship pure while satisfying both their urges at the same time. They both smiled, exhaled deeply, then fell asleep.

"Nate, it's twelve-thirty, are you alright?" asked the voice over the intercom. "Was I dreaming?!" he groaned, as he slowly opened his eyes. But as he ran his hands along Melina's back, he realized it wasn't a dream after all. Melina looked up at Nate with a smile on her face.

"Did we do what I think we did?" she whispered.

"Did that put out the fire?" asked Nate.

"Yes, it did, and you didn't even have to use your hose. I'm impressed! I think I had better get up and back to my room before Ashley figures out where I am." Melina moaned as she slowly pushed herself up off of Nate's chest.

"I think you should get off of me **NOW!**" Nate decided. Melina's eyes widened as she felt him begin hardening again.

"I think you're right!" she whispered, as she leaned forward to kiss him.

Nate snickered as he watched Melina walk gingerly towards the shower, holding her sore and swollen coochie.

"And you didn't even put it in!" she complained. He watched as she entered the shower. "Aren't you going to join me?"

"There's no way I'm getting in there with you! We both know what will happen if I do." She could smell the odor of Nate's juices emanating from her body. Curious about the taste, she rubbed some from her belly button, then licked her fingers. She frowned as she turned on the water. "And my mother likes this stuff?!" she pondered, as she rinsed out her mouth.

After drying off, she put on her tiny robe, then picked up her wet lingerie. "There is no way I'm letting you walk out of her like **that**!" exclaimed Nate. "Here, put this on . . ." He handed her a pair of his silk boxer shorts and a "wife beater."

"What's this for?" she teased as she slipped her fingers into the slit of the boxers. She moaned as she felt around inside, then removed her moistened fingers. Nate took her hand and placed her two moist fingers into his mouth. Her eyes slowly began to close as his warm tongue caressed her fingers, tasting her sweet juices. She kissed him with such passion, she thoroughly soaked the shorts! As their lips parted, Melina whispered, "I think I need another pair of boxers!"

"Damn, marry me right now!" he begged, as he watched

her walk down the corridor towards the stairs. Melina looked back over her shoulder and whispered, "okay," as she quietly crept up the steps. Nate slowly closed the door smiling. He walked into the bedroom and stared at the huge wet spot in the center of his bed. He chuckled as he removed the linen. "U-m-m." he moaned, as he placed the sheets against his face and inhaled deeply. He gathered up her lingerie, then placed everything into the washer. As he showered, he couldn't stop thinking about Melina and the passion they shared.

No woman, not even Katrina, had ever made him feel so completely vulnerable. There was no doubt about it, he was definitely whipped! And he hadn't even had sex with her yet! *"Damn, I swore I would never let another woman into my heart ever again,"* he thought, as he dried off. Melina had not only gotten into his heart, she owned the f---ing keys to it!

"Oh, there you are... Do you know how worried I was about you!" said Monica. "I have never known you to sleep past eight." "I guess that was quite a night for all of us, huh?" she said, as she handed her brother a glass of juice.

"Yeah, it sure was," he smirked. "Have you seen Melina yet?" "No, and come to think of it, I haven't seen Ashley this morning either," she replied.

"They're probably still resting. What about James? You know how he is. Up and working, as usual."

"What are **you** smiling about?"

"Oh, nothing." answered Nate, who was sure he had gotten away with having Melina in his room. He was very private when it came to his personal life and didn't take being teased about it lightly.

"Monica, I need your opinion about something."

"Sure, what is it?"

"Last night, I found out Melina's mother was arrested, but I couldn't bring myself to tell her. But that's not all." He reached into the pocket of his robe, removed the Birth Certificate and handed it to his sister. After a few moments, Monica's eyes widened.

"Where on earth did you get **this**?!"

"Remember the day we all went to the beach?" Monica nodded. "Well, after we left, James and I went to Renaldo's. I stepped out to make a call and ran into Mrs. Sullivan. She handed it to me in an attempt to gain sympathy for her son."

"So, this is legit?!"

"It seems that way."

"You're telling me that Mr. Sullivan is her father and Junior is her brother?!"

Monica sat down at the kitchen nook, in an attempt to digest what she had learned. "Wait a minute. You're telling me you have known about this for over a month?!"

"I just didn't know what to do." admitted Nate. "I don't know what will hurt more, her mother being arrested or this."

"You may as well tell her about her mother. She's going to find out anyway. As for this . . ." Monica said as she handed him back the document. "You know what you have to do. It's just a matter of when to do it." Nate quickly placed the paper into his pocket when he heard voices coming down the corridor, which were heading towards the kitchen.

"It's about time you got up!" said James, as he entered the kitchen with Ashley and Melina. "I thought you were going to take the day off or something. Ashley had to help me change the DVD's this morning. I take it you and Melina had better things to do," hinted James.

"Well, I'm off to work. See you around eight. Keep my dinner warm!" said Ashley, as she quickly kissed James goodbye. "We have a lot to talk about when I get back young lady," she teased, as she looked over at Melina, who was avoiding eye contact with her. Her face was red as a beet, as she quickly turned and reached into the frig.

"Did I miss something?" asked Monica.

"Why don't you ask your brother," hinted Ashley, as she bit into an apple while waving as she left the kitchen. "Bye-bye!" she giggled.

Chapter 28
Your Weakness: The Devil's Strength!

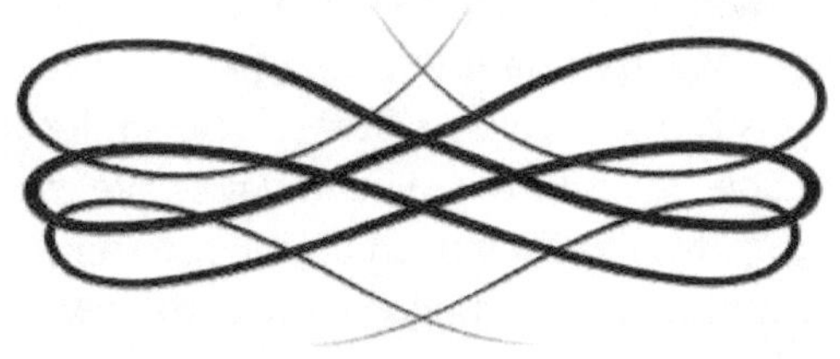

"Are you going to fill me in, or am I going to be kept in the dark?" "I'll tell you later. Right now, I need to speak with Melina, privately. Come on baby, let's take a walk," said Nate, as he took Melina by the hand. It was cloudy out today, but no rain was in the forecast. Nate slowly walked with Melina out back, past the pool.

"I'm sorry Nate. She was up when I got back to the room. I promise, I didn't tell her anything, but she could see I was wearing your underwear," admitted Melina.

"No, it's not about that. I really don't know how to tell you this. I have been struggling with it all night." Melina saw the look of concern on Nathan's face. She held both his hands and said, "Nate, baby, I love you. No matter how bad it is, we'll get through it together." Nate took a deep breath, then exhaled slowly.

"Your mother was arrested. I found out last night after dinner, but I couldn't bring myself to tell you. Baby, I'm so sorry." Melina said nothing, as she slowly lowered her head. The sound of birds chirping, in the nearby trees, helped to ease the awkward silence. She slowly raised her head, then spoke.

"Nate, it's okay. Don't feel bad. I knew this day was coming and I have been preparing myself for it. Don't let this spoil our engagement, or the celebration we shared this morning." She smiled then kissed him lightly on his lips. "Now that wasn't so bad, was it?"

"Baby, that's not the worst of it." Nate slowly reached into his pocket and removed the document.

"What's that?" she asked nervously. He explained all the details of how and when he obtained the document, as he reluctantly handed it to her. Melina's hands shook nervously, as she struggled to unfold it. "This is my Birth Certificate," she smiled. "Mother had always told me she had lost this. She always gave me excuses as to why she never . . ." Melina collapsed down into the chair. "This **can't** be right!" she mumbled. Tears began to stream down her face as she came to the realization of the document's meaning.

"**M-m-my FATHER?! HE'S MY FATHER!!!**" she stammered. Nate! My father raped me!" screamed Melina through the tears, as she leaped from the chair and into his arms. "Oh my God! My own father!" she sobbed. And then it dawned on her. "Oh my God! Junior's my brother?! I was raped by my own father and my own brother?!" James and Monica, who had been watching from afar, came running, as Melina collapsed in Nate's arms. The shock was too much for her. Overwhelmed, Melina fainted. Nate was so filled with guilt, he could hardly stand up himself, let alone support Melina.

James quickly caught her as she began to fall. He picked her up, carried her into the house, and then laid her on the couch. His eyes popped as her tiny robe flung open. He took a good long look at her in Nate's undergarments before closing it up. Monica assisted her brother, as they slowly made their way inside. James ran into the kitchen to get a cool cloth. Monica and Nate entered just as he was placing the cool compress across her forehead.

"I should never have told her!" he said, as he knelt down beside her.

"It had to be done," reassured Monica. "She just needs some time to process everything she has learned. Trust me, she'll be okay."

Melina slowly began to come around. Monica folded the document and placed it in her brother's pocket. As she tried to sit up, Monica helped her. "How could he?!!! How could my own father do that to me?!"

"Melina, try to stay calm," said Monica. Nate was now sitting in a chair across the room, listening. "And my own mother helped him?! Jr's my brother?! My mother, my father, and my brother, raped me?!"

"Melina, please forgive me. I never should have told you," interrupted Nate. She looked across the room at the man she loved, then held out her arms. Nate slowly got up, walked across the room, and then fell to his knees, welcoming her embrace. "Baby, I'm so sorry," he cried, while laying his head upon her lap.

"Baby, none of this was your fault. I know you were only trying to protect me." she whispered. "Please, don't beat yourself up about it." Monica tapped James lightly on the arm to get his attention. The two of them quietly left the room to give the couple some privacy. "Maybe she should go get checked out," whispered James. Monica agreed. It was clear to the both of them that Melina was not as strong as she appeared to be. She had come a long way since the attack, but this was going to be one major setback. Monica picked up the phone to make a call.

"Who are you calling?"

"Ashley," answered Monica. "**She's** the one Melina needs right now. She's a big part of the reason she has come this far anyway." "I know. Ashley's been like a sister to her," noted James.

Ashley pulled over, onto the shoulder of the highway, when she noticed the photo and number on the screen of her phone.

"Hey Monica. Miss me already?!" she chuckled. In an instant the look on her face went from blissful joy to that of concern. Monica explained what had transpired. Her mind raced as she took the off ramp to turn around. Her heart went out to her friend. "Melina must be an emotional wreck right now!" she mumbled, as she sped down the highway. "Damn, Mr. Sullivan's her father and Junior's her brother?! What the f--k?!!!"

Ashley was blinded by all of the confusing thoughts racing through her mind. "I need to get to her fast!" she mumbled. "How the hell did she find out?!" Ashley swerved through traffic as she raced to get home. She tried to fight back the conflicting tears of anger and sorrow, as she reached for her phone. She fumbled with the buttons as she drove. "Hello. This is Ashley Simmons. I know this is last minute, but I have a family emergency. I won't be in!" She hung up abruptly, not giving the person on the other end an opportunity to speak. Ashley struggled to hide her true feelings, she had a thing for Melina. (And not just in a close friend sort of way either!). She had never been with a woman before, yet there was something about Melina that touched her very essence. "Hang on baby, I'm coming!"

"Please Nate, I could use some time alone right now," whispered Melina, as she placed her hand against his chest. She then slowly walked past him. She stepped out of the elevator, then watched as the doors closed. It stood idle on the fifth floor, while Nate stood inside and stared blankly at the doors. Five minutes later, it automatically returned to the first floor, then the doors opened. However, Nate didn't move, not even an inch, as his brother and sister approached.

"Hey man, are you okay?" asked James.

"She wants to be left alone. She hates me," whispered Nate. "I knew I shouldn't have let her know."

"She told you it was alright, and she deserved to know the truth," added Monica. "Don't worry, Ashley's on her way back. She'll look after her. She just needs some alone time right now to digest everything she's learned, that's all."

"The devil is always busy, for he hates love and happiness. It is his weakness. For when we show love and compassion to one another, Jesus smiles and the devil cringes. He who is without love, wallows in sin. We are made to suffer the devil's wrath when we love one another. But stay strong and never falter, for he who loves, holds the keys to the gates of heaven and eternal joy!"

Too worn out from the stress, she just couldn't take the stairs. Ashley ran right past everyone, straight into the elevator. She paced back and forth until the doors opened. "Melina!" she shouted, as she opened the door. She ran into Melina's bedroom. "Baby, answer me! Where are you?!" However, there was no response. Ashley became nervous and her mind began to race wildly. "Please be okay," she whispered.

As she slowly walked about the bedroom, Ashley heard a faint whimper. Melina's puppy, Mya, was whining and licking Melina's face, as she lay motionless on the floor. Ashley rushed over to the opposite side of the bed. There she found her friend, curled up on the floor. Beside her was an empty prescription bottle that was once half filled with pain pills. Melina began to sob as she shook her head.

"I just took them all. I can't take it anymore!"

"Get up!" cried Ashley, as she struggled to pull her friend up off the floor. Monica, Nathan and James all arrived, just in time to see Ashley struggling with Melina.

"Help me!" she shouted. "She took a bottle of pills!" Nate ran over and quickly picked Melina up. "Take her over to the sink! If we hurry, we may be able to get her to throw them up! Monica got on the phone and dial '911'". Nate stood behind Melina and held her up, while Ashley put her finger down Melina's throat, causing her to regurgitate the half-dissolved pills. Ashley fumbled through the mucus . . . "Twenty-seven, twenty-eight, twenty-nine, thirty! They're all here!" she exclaimed. Nate was in tears as he struggled to keep Melina awake.

"Don't leave me. Please baby, don't leave me!" he sobbed. James, who was feeling guilty and helpless, ran out of the room towards the elevator. "I'll bring the paramedics up!" he shouted, while wondering if he had given his brother bad advice.

Monica grabbed some towels and soaked them with cold water. Ashley lightly slapped Melina's face to keep her conscious, while Monica applied cold compresses.

"I should have never told you!" shouted Nate, as he rocked Melina in his arms.

"Keep it together!" demanded Ashley. "She needs your strength right now." Melina coughed up some additional mucus, so Monica cleaned her face with one of the wet towels.

"I'm so sorry," whispered Melina.

"S-h-h-h. You just hang in there for me!" begged Ashley, as she opened Melina's eyes to check her pupils. "Her pulse is slowing."

It seemed like an eternity had passed, as they anxiously awaited the paramedics. "Keep fighting!" said Ashley, as she continued to check Melina's vitals. Ashley picked up the empty pill bottle and went over to the sink. She quickly placed what was left of the pain pills back into the bottle, then capped it. Nate prayed as he paced back and forth while carrying his fiancé. "Please lord, you just gave her to me. Don't let the devil take her away!" he repeated, time and time again. Melina partially opened her eyes and begged Nate for his forgiveness.

"It's okay baby, just keep fighting. I love you so much! You can't leave me. We have a wedding to go to, don't you remember?!"

Melina managed a slight smile, whispered "I Do" then suddenly, went limp in his arms.

"Ashley!" he shouted. She rushed to check her pulse.

"It's weak, but she does still have a pulse. Don't you dare quit on me!" she whispered, into Melina's ear. She couldn't hold back the tears any longer. Ashley fell to her knees and wept uncontrollably. Monica rushed to her side.

"Come on, you've got to get up! Ashley, we need you! We need Nurse Ashley Simmons!"

Her words fell upon deaf ears, as Ashley wept even harder.

James entered the room, followed by the paramedics. They tried to get Nate to place Melina on the stretcher so they could check her over, but he continued to pace while rocking her in his arms. He was in shock and didn't even realize they had arrived.

"Nathan Brande! You put her down this instant!" shouted a stern and familiar voice. Sheryl, his mother, had heard the sirens and seen the ambulance, then became alarmed. She walked up behind her son then whispered in his ear, "Nathan, if you don't put her down, they can't save her life." With that, he gently laid her down upon the stretcher.

The paramedics went to work quickly, hooking up monitoring equipment and IVs. Ashley explained what had transpired and handed them the bottle of pills she had recovered. "She regurgitated all of the pills, but as you can see, a lot dissolved into her system. They quickly rushed towards the elevator, where James was waiting.

He took them down and watched as they put her in the ambulance. "Nate, I'll ride with them," assured Ashley. "You get yourself together, then meet us there." Nate could only nod in agreement. He was overcome with sadness, but it was mostly guilt.

Sheryl tried to reassure her son, while he was getting himself together. Her words were of little comfort as he struggled to get dressed, fumbling about the room like a lost child. "When you're ready, I'll be out front. I'm driving." James returned to help his brother the best he could. One quick check and they were finally on their way out of the house. Sheryl sat nervously, as she awaited the arrival of her children. Ten minutes later, they were all in the car, speeding towards the hospital. The ride seemed to take forever, as the siblings sat quietly, anxiously anticipating their arrival. Monica prayed for her brother, and his bride-to-be, the entire way.

Nate could hardly stay on his feet. James put his arm around his waist and guided him most of the way in. After a brief stop at the Admissions Desk, they were given passes, but were told she was still in ICU. The group was given directions to the waiting room, then they rushed towards the elevators. Being a proud man, Nate fought desperately to hold back the tears around the other people in the elevator. He recalled something the pastor had said in church one day, when he was a little boy . . . *"Your weakness is the devil's strength."* That sentence played over and over in his head, giving him the motivation he needed to stay strong for Melina.

Dr. Marshall was standing by as they entered the Waiting Room. He was immediately bombarded with questions by all four members of the Brande family. "Listen, all I can tell you right now is that that they are still working on her. I'll let you know how things are progressing, as soon as I can. I'm sorry but that's all I can tell you right now. I must get back in there, so please excuse me." As he re-entered the ICU, one of the other doctors, who had assisted him in working on Melina, walked out with his head down.

"I'm so sorry," he said. "We really did all we could for her. She didn't make it." The words struck the family like a gun shot. They all huddled together and cried. "No!" shouted Nate, as he broke away from his family's embrace. He ran towards the door and tried to force his way in. "You let me in there right now!" he demanded. He snatched the doctor up by his smock and threw him against the door. "I said, let me in!" The doctor saw a look of rage and desperation in his eyes like nothing he had ever seen before. The doctor nervously held his card against the reader, giving Nate access to the operating room. During the brief scuffle, one of the nurses had called for Security.

The rest of the staff was slowly ushered out by Dr. Marshall to give Nate some time alone with Melina. His feet felt like they were full of lead as he struggled to approach the table. Melina's body was pale. Nate could see that she was gone. He fell to his knees and laid his head upon her cool chest. "I love you Melina," he wept. "I thank GOD for bringing you into my life. The short time we spent together will carry me throughout the rest of my days. There will never be another woman for me." The staff watched, from the other side of the glass, as the rest of the family was quietly allowed to enter. "You are my heart, my soul, my very essence. I would give my very life to have you back!"

Nate then raised up from the floor. He reached down and took Melina in his arms. "Please come back to me!" he shouted, as he held her cool limp body, in his arms. Nate looked up to heaven and begged, "Lord, please don't take her! Please GOD, sent her back to me!" Security arrived but was immediately dismissed by Dr. Marshall. Nathan squeezed her tightly, then gently kissed her lips.

"If you believe and trust in GOD, all things are possible. For in the blink of an eye, he created the Heavens and the Earth, and everything within. Blessed is he who believes!"

Nate glanced over and saw Melina's Engagement Ring in a tray on the other side of the table. He gently laid her down and walked over to retrieve it. He took her by the hand and said, "With this ring, I do thee wed." His family cried hysterically, as they listened to his words. As Nate placed the ring upon her finger, he leaned over and gently kissed her one final time. He took her hand in his, placed it over his heart, and then laid it over her own. *"Bless-ed is he who believes,"* he whispered, as he slowly, and calmly, bowed his head.

Suddenly, the monitors began to beep, as they picked up a faint pulse and heartbeat. Melina's pale body slowly began to regain its color, as she suddenly inhaled deeply. The staff rushed in! Nate backed away from the table smiling. "Thank you, Jesus!" he said. *"Glory to HE who watches from on high!"* The medical staff was dumbfounded! No one could believe what had just happened! It was medically impossible! The doctors asked the family to leave the room, but Nate refused. "I want to be here when she opens those beautiful green eyes of hers.

"How can this be? It's impossible! She was pronounced 'dead' nearly thirty minutes ago!" exclaimed one of the nurses.

"This is just another example of faith!" proclaimed Nate. *"God will always triumph over evil, so long as you believe! It was by the love of Jesus that He made it so!"* Nate was filled with joy and gave thanks, as all of Melina's vital signs returned to normal. Nate quickly returned to her side and took her hand as she moaned lightly. The doctor shook his head, alerting the staff to leave him be. She began to glow, as the breath of live restored her soul. She slowly opened her eyes and smiled. "I could hear you!" she moaned. "Your grandmother brought me back! Everything is going to be fine now," she whispered, as tears ran down the sides of her face.

Nate inhaled then exhaled deeply. He leaned over and kissed her lightly, then turned and left the room.

"GOD is good son," said his mother, as the family greeted him.

"She said Mom-mee brought her back!" Sheryl smiled. It was nice to know her mother was still by her family's side.

"God has big plans for the two of you." Nate nodded in agreement.

"Mom, I'm going to marry her as soon as she gets out of here!" They all hugged and gave thanks to GOD as they headed up to her room to await her arrival. Ashley was already in the room waiting, when they arrived. Dr. Marshall had texted her to give her the good news. Nate thought James would have a stroke, as Ashley leaped into Nate's arms, then kissed him repeatedly about the face when he entered the room.

"I heard about what you did. You saved her life! Nate, thank you so much!"

"It was the grace of GOD, not me," he whispered. She smiled, then walked over to James and hugged him tightly.

"Where were **you**? We just knew you would be in there with her," stated James, as he decided to overlook her excited episode with his brother.

"I was such a wreck when we arrived, the doctors wouldn't let me anywhere near the ICU! I tried to get myself together but couldn't. I ran into the nearest bathroom and just cried! The next thing I knew, Doctor Marshall was texting me. I couldn't believe what I was reading so I texted him back and asked that he repeat the message! I've been waiting here ever since!"

They all stood in shock as the orderly entered the room with Melina. They could not believe she was sitting in a wheelchair. Anticipating their questions, the orderly said, "She really is a ball of fire, isn't she?! After you all left, she fought with the doctors to get off the table! She actually wanted to walk! She refused to be transported by bed, so the doctor agreed to let her go in a wheelchair instead. Don't you know she complained about it all the way here!" As the orderly stopped and locked the wheels, Melina quickly got up and hurried over to her man. James smiled, and the orderly blushed as they both got a good look at her plumb bare behind.

"I'm so sorry for putting you all through this!" she said. She hugged Nate tightly and kissed him repeatedly about the face. "I'm so sorry baby! I swear I'll never do anything to leave you again! Can you ever forgive me?!"

"Of course," he said.

"I really need you to get into bed," complained the orderly. "If the doctor sees you up, he will have my head!"

"But I'm really alright!" complained Melina.

"Don't give him a hard time. Just get into bed. The doctor should be here shortly," said Ashley as she tied the back of Melina's gown. "You scared the hell out of us!" she stated as she fixed the sheets. Sheryl's cellphone rang, so she excused herself to answer it. While she filled her sisters in on everything that had transpired, Dr. Marshall entered the room. "I guess you liked it here so much the last time, you decided to come back!" he joked.

After exchanging pleasantries with the family, he got down to serious business. "First of all, that was a really stupid stunt you pulled young lady. What were you thinking? After everything you had previously survived . . ." Melina couldn't answer, as she lowered her head. "It was a good thing Ashley checked on you when she did, or we wouldn't even be having this conversation." After the brief scolding, the doctor went over her charts. "From what we can tell, everything is completely normal, but you will need to stay a few days for observation and further testing." Melina didn't complain. She understood the reason why he was being so stern.

An elderly woman entered the room and interrupted the doctor's conversation. "Hi, my name is Dr. Ashford. I will need some time alone with Ms. Delgado." As the group slowly began to exit the room, Dr. Marshall explained that, whenever there is an attempted suicide, the patient had to be evaluated. "You may as well grab something from the cafeteria. The questioning will be extensive and usually takes an hour or two."

"Nate, your Aunts send their prayers and said to call if you need anything."

"Thanks Mom."

"Hey bro, if you don't need me, I'll get back to the house to handle business," said James.

"Why don't you all go. I'll be home in a couple of hours.

Thanks for everything." They all hugged, kissed and said a brief prayer before leaving Nathan at the hospital.

Nate watched as his mother and siblings got into the car, then waved as they pulled away. He returned and waited patiently outside of Melina's room. Ashley walked over to keep him company. "What happened to cause all of this?" she asked, even though she had already spoken to Monica briefly about the incident. She listened quietly as he went over every last detail, from her mother being arrested, to receiving the birth records from Mrs. Sullivan, to Melina's reaction to the news that Mr. Sullivan was her father.

"It's no wonder she freaked out in the way that she did. After everything she had already gone through, this just pushed her over the edge." She noticed the depressed look on Nate's face. "Don't feel bad, it's not your fault," whispered Ashley, as she walked over and gave him a comforting hug. "She needed to know the truth and keeping it from her would have been the wrong thing to do. She has an Angel watching over her. I know she'll be just fine." Nathan smiled as they shared another brief hug.

Chapter 29
The Big Day Approaches

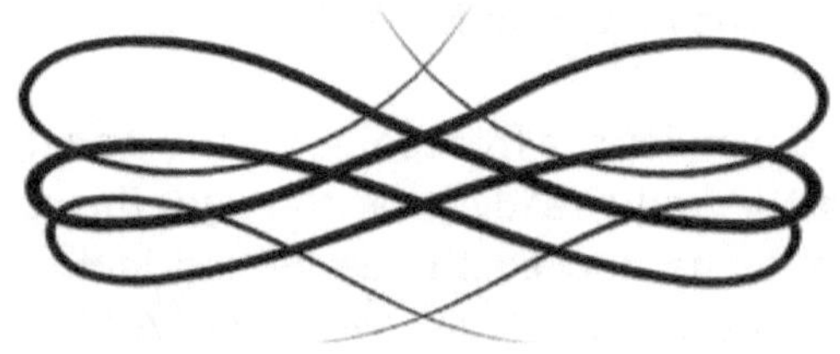

It's been two weeks since Melina's melt down. The house was quietly buzzing with excitement and anticipation. Wedding bells were in the near future. As far as weddings go, this was not going to be like anything anyone has ever experienced. Three siblings were getting married at the same time. The high-profile event was announced on just about every television and radio station and in every newspaper in the state. It was big news knowing that Nathan Brande was to be wed, but a triple Brande wedding was huge! The wedding was to be held in their grandparent's church on the first day of June, just a week away.

Shirley and her sisters took care of all the arraignments. Celebrities and friends of the family rushed to RSVP, this one of a kind event. This wedding had the potential of becoming a circus. Media would be swarming due to all the famous faces scheduled to attend.

“We are going to have to keep this guest list a secret. There are way too many singers and rappers attending. It's like they all took the day off to be here!"

"Look at this . . . movie stars, football players, basketball and baseball players . . . the church will never hold all these people!"

"Shirley, calm down!" said Betty. "We'll make it work. The main thing is keeping quiet about whose coming."

Meanwhile, Valencia was trying to cut a deal with the District Attorney's Office after hearing the broadcast about her daughter. "Look, I can get you Richard if you drop the charges against me.

I didn't really do anything!" she pleaded.

"No, you just held your daughter down while those bastards raped her. I don't even know why we're holding you," said the sheriff, sarcastically.

"Look, do you want Richard or not?" The legal group stepped out of the room momentarily to discuss an appropriate offer. They returned minutes later with a proposal.

"The best we can do for you is five to ten years with eligibility for parole in five," offered the D.A.

"What do you think I am, stupid? Catch him yourself. Send me back to my cell."

"Okay, listen. We'll make it three to five, with parole eligibility in three. That's my final offer; I suggest you take it." Valencia thought about it briefly. She was no fool; she knew this was the best offer she would get.

"I'll need to use a phone. He hasn't heard from me in a while and he's always on the move." The room came to a dead silence as the phone began to ring.

"Trace that call," ordered the Sheriff.

"It's about time you called. Where the hell have you been?"

"It's nice to hear your voice too, Richard."

"Forget the pleasantries. What's going on?"

"I had to move again. I told you the cops were always

hanging around. Listen, Melina's getting married on the first of June. I just thought you might want to know."

"The first of June huh? That doesn't give me a lot of time."

"Time for what?!"

"Don't worry about it! Let's just say it will be a day she'll never forget."

"Richard, please don't hurt my, our daughter. Haven't you done enough already?! She tried to kill herself!"

"Too bad she didn't get it right. I guess I'll have to show her how it's done!" he chuckled. "Call me back when you find out where the wedding's going to be. I have a lot of work to do and I'll need your help."

"With what?!"

"Don't worry about it! Just call me in an hour . . . bye."

"Please don't let Richard hurt my baby!" pleaded Valencia.

"Sorry Sheriff, the call wasn't long enough to be traced."

"Where is he?" asked the Sheriff. "Still somewhere in Mexico. I think he's going to come back for the wedding. He never calls me. I keep in touch with him and he never tells me where he is exactly."

"Let's be clear about this. If this doesn't work, you get the full sentence, with no breaks, understood?"

"Yes, I understand," Valencia answered.

"Okay, it's been an hour, call him back."

"Alright Richard, what do you need me to do now?"

"All I need is for you to get your hands on an invitation."

"Oh, is **that** all?!" said Valencia, sarcastically. "You may as well ask me to get you a front row seat! Do you know how high profile this thing is going to be?! The police will be all over the place!"

"You let **me** worry about that. Just get me one! I'll call you when I get into town on the day of the wedding to tell you where to leave it. Get this right and I'll bring you with me afterward, when the job is done. So, don't screw this up!" Richard then ended the call. "Still not long enough for the trace Sheriff."

"You did good. I'll handle the invitation," stated Sheriff Melbourne. "Play this thing right and you just may get off with time served."

"I just want to see his face when you cuff his ass!" Valencia explained. "It's because of him, I'm in this mess anyway. I'd gladly serve my entire sentence, if it meant that I could have my daughter's love back."

"Why on earth would you even be a part of something like that anyway?"

"I don't know. I just wanted to secure a home for my little girl. I had already saved some money if she had decided to attend college. I just wanted her to always have a place to call home." "So, you helped your daughter get brutally raped, in exchange for your house?! That's real nice," remarked the female officer sarcastically, who was assigned to watch over Valencia until she was returned to her cell.

"I really don't expect any of you to understand why I did what I did. Hell, sometimes, **I** don't even understand it, but don't judge me. None of you knows what it was like to grow up with nothing, to be passed around like a piece of meat because your family was struggling to survive. I'd been with the Sullivan's since I was a teenager. Mr. Sullivan started forcing me to have sex with him when I was eighteen. Hell, he was **my** first too!"

"He had me convinced that no one would believe me if I squealed, and I had nowhere else to go anyway. I thought to myself, 'It's not that bad,' and getting laid on the job was just another perk. After a while, it became just another part of the job. After Melina was born, I threatened to tell his wife, so he began paying me on the side for services rendered. A few years later, I convinced him to sign over the deed to the house in exchange for my secrecy. He would only agree to it if his son could have sex with Melina when she turned twenty-one. When she was old enough to start working, she and Junior became very friendly. It seemed like things would happen naturally, but Melina had no interest in men. She seemed to be waiting, as if she were saving herself for someone special. And the rest is history." The group just listened to Valencia in disgust.

"So how does it feel to narrowly escape a murder charge?" asked the female officer, Sheriff Lacey.

"Things weren't supposed to be like that. Richard was supposed to **watch** Junior. I really didn't think she would put up such a fight. Richard and I had sex in areas of the house where we knew she would catch us. We **wanted** her to watch. When the whole thing went down, Richard decided he wanted in. Then he ordered Junior to rape her again."

"So, you figured she would be an easy lay, just like you," said Lacey. "You didn't figure on her being a real woman with morals, huh? I don't want to hear any more of this bullshit. I think I'm going to puke! She was your child! How can you ever live with yourself?!"

"That's enough Lacey," said the District Attorney. "Let's just concentrate on catching the man that orchestrated the whole thing. Never let your personal feelings interfere with your work as an officer of the law."

"She doesn't deserve any breaks sir."

"Looking at the big picture, Lacey, I'm not sure she's getting one." "I don't understand sir."

"It's like this. She has lost everything: her daughter, her job, her home, everything. All she will have to show for her life is that little bit of cash we're holding. Her life is ruined, and it will never be the same again."

"I still think she's getting off way too easy."

"I'm glad you're on our side!" said the D.A. as he patted her on the back. "You can return her to her cell now."

"She must think I'm stupid!" said Richard Sullivan, as he

glared at the computer. He was checking the news when he came across the arrest footage of Valencia. "That bitch is trying to set me up! Well I've got a surprise for **all** their asses!" Richard began phoning in favors from every one of his old associates he had helped in the past. "If I play my cards right, I'll get Melina and still be back in time for my next 'massage.' But first of all, I'm going to get even with that double-crossing little cunt, Valencia." Richard sat at the computer for the next two days, formulating his plan.

The girls had spent the past few days looking for wedding dresses. They tried every shop in Miami, but just couldn't find what they were looking for. Sheryl recalled a small shop in Deerfield Beach, where she had bought her own dress years ago. After a brief discussion, the ladies got into the limo. "I haven't been here in years!" she exclaimed, as the driver slowed in front of the shop. It didn't take long for Ashley to spot her gown. She rushed into the shop and quickly removed it from the display, fearful one of the other ladies may want it. She then made a bee-line for the nearest dressing room to try it on.

Try as she may, Melina just couldn't find what she was looking for. Monica also had difficulty finding a dress that suited her. "Monica, if you don't mind, may I suggest trying on **my** old wedding dress? I really think it would look beautiful on you," suggested Sheryl.

"You still have it, after all these years?!"

"Of course, I do! Why would I get rid of something that reminds me so much of your father? I kept it in storage all these years, just in case you wanted it."

"But why didn't you tell me before now?!"

"Because I didn't want it to seem like I was forcing it on you. I wanted to see if you found something you liked first."

"But mom, I always loved that dress! I remember looking through your wedding album and dreaming of one day wearing it down the aisle." Shirley lit up like a Christmas tree. She had always envisioned her little girl, someday walking down the aisle in that very same dress.

Ashley exited the dressing room, then quickly headed for the register. "Hey!" shouted Melina, spotting Ashley, as she headed towards the front of the shop. "Aren't you going to let us see what it looks like?" The group of ladies hurried over to the register, a bit surprised at Ashley for acting the way that she was.

"I'm sorry," she whispered. "It's just that I never thought this day would ever come, me getting married?! I just didn't want to jinx it by letting anyone see my dress."

"It's alright," whispered Sheryl, as she placed her hand on the back of Ashley's shoulder. "Come on," she called, to Monica and Melina. "Sweetie, take your time. We'll just meet you back at the car."

"Half way to the limo, Melina stopped in her tracks. "Hey, what about **my** dress?!"

"Don't worry, I know where there's a huge boutique in Ft. Lauderdale. We can head there next. Now get in the car. It's way too hot to be standing outside." Each of the women grabbed a bottle of water from the fridge as they settled in. A couple of minutes later, Ashley emerged from the shop carrying her new dress inside a garment bag. The driver retrieved it, then carefully laid it in the storage compartment. "Thanks for being so understanding," she said, as she got in the car. "Fine, just don't expect to see mine," pouted Monica.

As they passed, admiring the view of the beach, the ladies began discussing the guest list. "I really wish my parents were alive to see me get married," stated Ashley.

"I just hope my parents get to watch it from a jail cell," added Melina. "Hey, what about your brother?"

"Let's just say that my brother would not approve of the family I'm marrying into. I'm ashamed to say it, but my brother is a bit of a racist. That's why I don't talk about him very often."

"Well, it's **his** loss," stated Monica. "But I'm sure your parents would wish you nothing but happiness." Ashley smiled, as she thought back to the brief, but wonderful, times she had had with her family.

"You know. I can still remember the fire just as if it happened yesterday . . . I was asleep in my bedroom when suddenly, there was this loud crash. A drunk driver lost control of his car and crashed into the side of our home. His car ended up in our kitchen, while the driver managed to stumble out onto the lawn. Unfortunately, the car ruptured the gas line connected to the stove. My parents instructed my brother and me to wait at the top of the steps. Just as they entered the kitchen, there was this huge explosion. They were both killed instantly. The drunk driver survived and is spending the rest of his life in prison." Melina hugged her friend tightly. "You know, I have never told anyone that story before. Until now, it was just too painful to talk about." "Even though we could never replace them, we're your family now," said Sheryl. Ashley smiled then said,

"And nothing could make me happier."

"I miss **my** father too," added Monica. "I wish he was here to walk me down the aisle." Melina and Ashley looked confused.

"Monica was born when I moved to New Jersey and remarried. James, Sr., is not her father." Not wanting to pry, Ashley changed the subject.

"Just how **are** we going to handle walking down the aisle anyway?"

"I have it all figured out," assured Sheryl. "I'll go over it with you during rehearsal. Don't worry about a thing. It'll all work out."

"If you say so," stated Monica. "I still think it's going to be a circus."

"Stay positive. Just remember, think happy thoughts!" smiled Sheryl.

The ladies paused, then looked over at Melina, who was

staring quietly out the window.

"A penny for your thoughts," whispered Ashley.

"Oh, I'm sorry," she said, snapping out of her trance. "I was just thinking about my mother. She always wanted to see her little princess find her prince charming and live happily ever after. We used to talk about it while we worked. She wanted nothing but the best for her little girl. In a twisted sort of a way, her dream came true. Nate **is** my prince charming and we are about to get married. A small part of me still wants her to be there."

"Even after everything she has done, I can't bring myself to hate her. Why?"

"Melina, that is called forgiveness. *Jesus is love . . . He wants us to love everyone, even those who wrong us* explained Sheryl. "It's good to see that you can forgive your mother, but what about your father and your brother."

"On one hand, I'm still filled with anger and hatred, but on the other, if it weren't for them, I probably would have never met Nathan, or any of you.

"Out of the darkness, the light will always shine. No matter how hard the devil tries, love will always prevail. Trust in Him!" "Amen!" shouted the ladies, as they took in every word Sheryl said. The limo slowed as it reached its next destination.

The women walked around the boutique for nearly two hours. Their feet were sore and they were all starving. "I'll never find a dress!" pouted Melina, as she became discouraged. She turned away dress after dress, as the sales persons brought them out, one after another. Just as she was about to give up hope, she noticed a dress, hanging in a glass case, in a remote corner of the shop. Melina slowly got up from the chair and walked over to get a better look. "I found it! I found it!" she shouted happily. The sales person unlocked the glass security display case.

"This gown is quite expensive," noted the clerk. Melina frowned at her remark.

"Why would you say that?!" she asked annoyingly.

"I really didn't mean anything by it. I was just saying . . ." stated the sales person, nervously. Melina snatched the gown, then headed towards the dressing room.

She smiled. Though it was a bit loose and too long, the dress fit almost perfectly. A knock at the door startled her as she made different poses, while admiring how beautiful she looked.

"I'll be out in a minute!"

"Melina, we'll be across the street at the Boston Market getting lunch."

"Okay, I'll be right over." Melina quickly got dressed and headed to the counter. The store manager was at the register when she arrived. Melina reached into her diamond studded clutch purse and removed her credit card Nate had added to his account. The clerk's eyes widened slightly, as she noticed the Visa "Unlimited" Titanium Card. Melina caught the surprised expression on the clerk's face.

"Just because I'm Latina doesn't mean I don't have money," she said annoyingly.

The manager looked over at her employee, whose face was beet red from embarrassment.

"You should really teach your staff to have better manners. If I didn't love this dress so much, I would leave it right here at the counter. The commission on a thirty-thousand-dollar sale is a lot of money to lose out on, just for being ignorant."

"I must apologize for any inappropriate actions or comments my employee may have made. I assure you, we operate our business with nothing less than the utmost professionalism."

"I can't tell," smirked Melina.

"I'm so sorry Ms. Delgado," whimpered the clerk.

Melina placed the card back into her purse, took the garment bag off the holding station, then walked out without further comment. "Linda don't say another word! If you were paying attention, you would have noticed the ladies as they got out of that limousine! Did you even look at the designer purse she was carrying?! It's real! Just go to lunch. . .and **don't** come back. . . you are so-o-o fired!" whispered the manager, as she watched Melina walk over to the limo, which was parked just across the street. The driver placed the dress into the storage compartment with the other one, while Melina walked over to Boston Market. She was so happy about the dress, she had already forgotten the incident involving the clerk.

"Wow, what a day!" sighed Sheryl, as she and the women got out of the limo. "Do you hear that?" asked Monica, as they approached the front door. "Are they having a party or something?" stated Ashley, as they walked into the house. They stood in the doorway, staring in amazement, as they watched the men dance around.

Nate, James and Ken looked like total idiots as they danced around shouting, "We're getting married. We're getting married!" Still unaware that the women were home, James shouted, "And we're finally, gonna get laid!"

"Not if they keep **that** up!" whispered Monica, as she and the other ladies slowly crept over to join in the celebratory dance.

Startled, Nate said, "Oh, we didn't here you come in," as he stopped dancing and tried to catch his breath. The ladies laughed at the embarrassed look on their men's faces.

"I've seen all I need to see!" said Sheryl, laughing. "I think I need a nap. I'll see you all later. Monica, come with me if you want your gown. I want to see how it fits."

"We had a great time with you Mrs. S. Thanks for everything!" said Melina, as she and Ashley gave her a hug. Monica and her mother walked happily out the door.

"So, how did you make out?" asked James. "I found my dress at the first stop," bragged Ashley. "Your sister is wearing her mother's gown. But as usual, Melina had to be difficult. We drove around all day trying to find something she liked. Just when we were about to give up hope, she found her dress."

"You leave my baby alone," said Nate as he hugged Melina. "My Princess deserves nothing but the best."

"Thank you, baby," whispered Melina, as she kissed him on the cheek.

"Aw-w-w barf!" added Ashley. They all chuckled, as Ashley gave a demonstration, by acting like she was putting her finger down her throat. After about thirty minutes, Monica returned with her gown. Kenneth's eyes teared up a little, as she stood before him with the garment bag. "I love you so much!" he whispered.

"Well, I know one thing," stated James. "You get no more nookie from my sister until you're married!"

"Just because **your** lady is holding out doesn't mean I have to!" added Monica. "But that's not a bad idea." Ken raised his eyebrows at the comment. "You have a problem waiting a few more days?"

"Well, it **has** been nearly a week already. I was hoping to celebrate a little tonight."

"Well you will just have to wait. I promise, it will be worth it!" whispered Monica as she kissed him on the cheek.

"I don't want to hear about it!" Nate demanded.

"Oh, grow up!" countered James. The ladies boarded the elevator to take their dresses up to their rooms.

"I don't know about you guys, but I could use a swim," suggested James. The men quickly ran up the steps to change. "You can have a pair of **my** shorts Ken," stated Nate. While the men played around in the pool, the ladies each tried on their dresses. Each thought of their parents, as they stood in front of the mirrors wishing that they could be there to share in their happiness.

Chapter 30
Don't Let It End This Way!

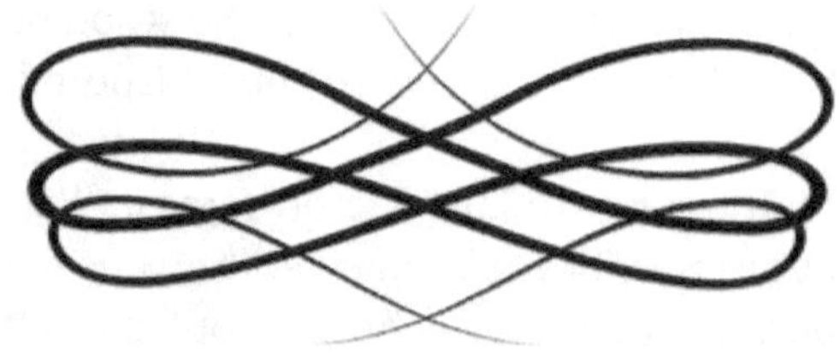

Sheriff Lacey ran as fast as she could. She arrived back at Valencia's cell as the phone rang a seventh time.

"What the hell took you so long?!" barked Ray.

"I was in the shower."

"Meet me at the old shack. Hurry your pretty little ass up! I don't want to be hanging around here longer than I have to!"

"Where's the Sheriff?!" shouted Valencia. "I need to get out of here right now! Richard's on his way to the shack, back on his farm! Did you hear what I said?!"

"You just sit tight. Did you really believe we were going to let you meet up with him?!" Sheriff Lacey snatched the radio from her hip and made the call.

"That's a ten-four, Lacey," answered the Sheriff, as he and several patrol cars, accompanied by State Troopers, sped towards the location. The entire department raced to cover the back roads and any possible getaway routes Richard may have.

Valencia sat in her cell dumbfounded, as Lacey walked away

laughing. Tears began to stream down her face as she began to realize that the D.A. was going back on his word. She would not be getting out early after all. She threw the phone against the wall, smashing it to pieces.

"Stop laughing at me, you bitch!" she shouted, as she fell onto the bed.

"That phone is coming out of your holdings," said Lacey.

After being awake all night, anticipating her release, Valencia was exhausted. She eventually cried herself to sleep. Sheriff Lacey returned to her desk to drink her coffee.

"Where the heck is Johnson?" she thought, as she took the final few sips.

"The coffee tastes a little off today," she noted. "Johnson, where the hell are you?! He's probably out catching a smoke," she concluded. As she headed towards the entrance, she became dizzy, and began to stagger as she neared the door. Then suddenly, she fell to the floor . . .

The chime sounded, alerting James and Nathan of a visitor at the front gate. "I'll get it," stated Nate. He quickly got out of the pool and headed for the intercom.

"Who is it?"

"It's Mrs. Sullivan."

"Give me a minute." Nathan buzzed the gate, giving her access.

He dried, then slipped on his t-shirt, as he headed for the front door.

"Come in, Mrs. Sullivan." She had never been inside the mansion before today.

"Your place is breath-taking," she stated, as she looked around. "What can I do for you? And please, no more surprises. I don't think Melina would live through another one. That last one nearly killed her."

"I promise, this time I have nothing but good news. Is it

possible that I may speak with her?" After a brief hesitation, Nate walked over to the intercom and called her room.

"Melina, could you please come down. You have a visitor."

"Please, have a seat." Mrs. Sullivan tried to relax as she awaited the arrival of Melina. She began to admire the art work displayed about the room. She got up and walked around to get a closer look. James met up with Nate just outside the lounge.

"What is **she** doing here?"

"She wants to speak with Melina."

"Are you out of your mind?!"

"She assured me this would be a pleasant visit."

"I hope you know what you're doing."

"Yeah, so do I."

The boys entered the lounge to find Mrs. Sullivan admiring one of the golden statues dug up in Egypt. Monica had somehow managed to acquire several pieces while on vacation a couple of years ago.

"This is quite a remarkable collection you have here. These pieces are exquisite . . . and priceless."

"Thank you, our sister designed this lounge. As you can see, she is fascinated with Egyptian Culture. She's always in search of new pieces."

The conversation was cut short by the arrival of Ashley and Melina. Melina was caught off guard. She did not expect to see Mrs. Sullivan.

"First of all, I want to apologize for the Birth Certificate."

"I'm over it. What do you want?" snapped Melina.

"Please Melina. I have always thought of you as my daughter. I never wanted anything bad to happen to you. Please don't be angry with me. I'm just trying to help. You know how much I have always loved you." Melina sighed.

"I apologize and you're right. I have no reason to be angry

with you. Everyone, it's okay. Could you give us some time alone?

"If you need anything, I'll be in the kitchen," said Nate, as he kissed her on the cheek. Seeing Melina calm and content with the situation, they left the lounge to give the women some privacy.

"Melina, I'm so sorry about what happened. I just don't have the words to express my shame and humiliation. I hope my husband gets everything he has coming, and more. That bastard hid the fact that you were his daughter from Junior and me. It doesn't make what my son did to you right, but I'm sure he would never have done it if he had known you were his sister." Melina could feel her heart pounding as her pressure rose. She tried to suppress her anger, but she had heard enough.

"If you're here looking for sympathy for your son, you will get none from me!"

"Oh, my dear, you have come to the wrong conclusion; that's not why I'm here at all!" "Then why don't you just stop stalling and get to the point."

"Fine, I will . . . While Junior and I were going through Richard's study, he found your Birth Certificate hidden in back of the wall safe. He also found the original deed to your house."

"What do you mean **my** house? **That** property belongs to my mother."

"Well, what your mother didn't know was that Richard gave her a fake deed." Patricia opened up her briefcase, removed the original deed to the house Melina grew up in, and handed it to her. Her mouth fell open as she read the document. "Wait. This can't be right . . ."

The document not only gave Melina the house, but it also gave her possession of twenty acres of farm land.

"Yes, Melina, it's official. I could have had the deed destroyed, but you deserve that and so much more."

"I don't know what to say," whispered Melina.

"You don't have to say anything. The land is yours to do with as you please. There was also a substantial amount of stocks, bonds, gold bars, coin and stamp collections stored inside which were left to Junior. He asked me to sell off everything I could and leave the money in a Safe Deposit Box so he could start a new life when he got out of prison."

Melina began to feel like such a heel. She had completely overlooked everything Mrs. Sullivan was going through.

"I must apologize for being such a bitch. I'm sure this has not been easy for you either."

"You're right, it hasn't. Anyway, before he turned himself in, Junior made me promise that I would give you half of everything I was able to liquidate." She reached back into her briefcase and removed a cashier's check for seven-hundred- and fifty-thousand dollars. Stunned, Melina finally managed to say, "I'm sorry, but I can't accept this!" She attempted to hand the deed and check back to Mrs. Sullivan.

"Melina, listen to me. For what Richard did to you, you deserve this deed. My son tells me every day how much he regrets doing what he did to you. It haunts him even in his dreams. He said that he could never expect you to forgive him, but maybe you can do some good things with the money his father left. He wanted me to give it all to you, but I explained to him that I was selling our home and moving out of state. He was going to need some money to start over. I suppose knowing that you accepted this check would give him a sense of closure, like he was being forgiven somehow.

"When are you planning on leaving?" asked Melina, as she placed the items onto the coffee table.

"I have just about gotten all of my affairs in order. The only thing I have left to do is sell the property."

"Please Mrs. Sullivan, I would consider it an honor if you would attend my wedding." Patricia smiled, with tears running down her cheeks, as Melina handed her an invitation. "I want you to go in place of my mother. I wish you to sit in her place." Patricia's hand began to shake as she reached for the invite. The ladies then embraced with a mutual understanding for one another.

Melina stood quietly in the corridor as Mrs. Sullivan slowly walked out the door. She stopped momentarily, took a deep breath, and then exhaled. She had kept her word to her son, and now it was time for her to move on. She would take the best offer for the land, then get as far away as possible. Melina returned to the lounge and just stared at the documents left behind by Mrs. Sullivan, while attempting to grasp the full meaning of what had just transpired. It felt as if all the hurt had been taken away, but the anger would linger on, as long as Richard, Sr., was free.

"Everything alright?" asked Nate, as he looked into the room.
"Yes, everything is just fine," she whispered.

"Why are you crying? Did she say something to hurt your feelings?"

"No baby. In fact, it was just the opposite. I even invited her to sit in my mother's place at the wedding. At first, I was really pissed, but then I realized that I should not be directing my anger towards her. Mrs. Sullivan was the closest thing I had to my real mother and she always treated me like one of her very own. But unfortunately, she did have to remind me of that fact. I guess when I looked at her, I saw Richard and Junior. She helped me to feel, and understand her pain, as well as my own."

"Before she left, she gave me this." Melina slowly handed Nate the documents left behind by Mrs. Sullivan.

"Baby, do you know what this means?! If you sell all the property, you'll be a rich woman! Melina, the land alone is worth well over a couple of a million dollars!" Melina just couldn't feel happy about what she had just heard. It was as if she was still in shock over her meeting with Mrs. Sullivan. "Melina, what is it. Why do you look so sad?"

"She lost everything because of me: her family, her home . .

. everything."

"No Melina, none of that was your fault!" whispered Nate, as he got down on his knees in front of her, while she sat upon the couch.

He gently took her by the hands in an attempt to comfort her. "The money came from Junior. She said it was the only way he could show how sorry he was for what he did to me. The land was left to me by his my father. I can't believe that bastard actually left it to me! Mrs. Sullivan said they found the deed in a safe along with my Birth Certificate." Melina was an emotional wreck. Her feelings went from hatred to sorrow, then from joy to pain. Nate could see the look of confusion on the face of his bride-to-be. He knew there was nothing he could say or do to make things better. This was something she had to work out, and get past, on her own.

I'll tell you what. Why don't we take these documents into town? "You can open an account and place the deed in a safety deposit box until you figure out what you want to do with it."

"Baby, I really don't feel like going anywhere else today. Can you hold onto them for a little while? I just want to lie down."

"Okay, I'll put them in the safe until you're ready." Melina smiled, then stood up.

"Could you lay with me for a while?" she whispered, as she hugged him tightly.

"Sure Melina, anything you need," smiled Nathan, as they slowly headed for the elevator.

As the couple walked towards the elevator, Ashley and James came out of the kitchen.

"Is everything okay?" asked Ashley. Melina could only nod as she placed her head against Nathan's chest. As the elevator doors opened, Nate stated that he would explain everything later in the evening and that Melina just needed to lie down for a while. "James, could you let mom know. She wanted to go over some of the wedding plans with us, but Melina's just not up for it right now. Tell her we'll be over in a couple of hours or so."

"No problem. I'll take care of it."

"Thanks bro, I'll talk to you later."

"Nothing like a little horse tranquilizer to keep things quiet," whispered Richard, as he searched the Sheriff's pockets for the access card. "Damn, you're kinda fine beneath this uniform." Richard took the opportunity to feel up the unconscious woman while she lay there defenseless. As he squeezed her breasts, he found what he was looking for. "Oh, there you are," he said, getting in a few extra feels. He reached for her side arm, then headed for the door. With a quick swipe of the card, Richard had access to the holding cell area.

"I thought I told you to meet me back at the shack?!" Valencia looked up in terror.

"You bitch! How dare you try to set me up!"

"Richard, I'm sorry!" pleaded Valencia. "Please Richard, just let me explain! I just wanted to save my daughter!" sobbed Valencia.

"Well she's as dead as you are!" Three shots thundered throughout the empty corridors of the station. When the echoes of gun fire subsided, an eerie silence blanketed the building. Richard watched eagerly, as Valencia's body twitched. He could see her pupils begin to dilate, as Valencia became motionless in her bunk. Her life sustaining blood dripped onto the floor of her cell, painting it a crimson shade of red as she exhaled one last time. **Fade to black** . . .

I hope that you have enjoyed Volume One of
"A Taste of Forbidden Fruit."

This novel is the product of my life-long
search for fulfillment . . .

The reason, I feel, GOD placed me on this Earth.

Though most of the book is fictitious,
it is filled with facts about my life,
which is illustrated by the use of *Italic Print.*

Some of my family's oldest and darkest secrets
have been revealed.
{Along with a few of my own!}

The history of the Baker Generation
means so much to me.

Even though I may never meet my Grandfather's
side of the family, my heart goes out to them;
for they have lost out on so much!
May God Bless You All!

(Author's Signature)

Coming Soon:

"A Taste of Forbidden Fruit"

Volume Two
"Bitter Juices"

Meet the Author
Mini Biography

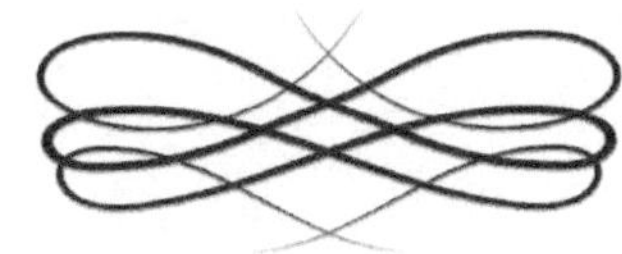

Nikita C. Hughes I
was born January 10th, 1960 in Fort Lauderdale, Florida. He lived with his Grandparents, John and Fannie Mae Baker in Deerfield Beach where he completed his first for years of grade school. Shortly thereafter, he, his sister Bethenia, and his brother Rufus Jr. were relocated to live with his mother and stepfather in New Jersey. After a short term in the Air Force, Nikita returned to New Jersey were he rekindled his relationship with his childhood sweetheart, Lisa Spence. Thirty-eight years and five children later, they are still happily married and currently living in New Jersey.

www.ingramcontent.com/pod-product-compliance
Lightning Source LLC
Chambersburg PA
CBHW020419260626
47156CB00007B/2467